A CLOCK OF STARS

THE SHADOW MOTH

A CLOCK OF STARS

THE SHADOW MOTH

FRANCESCA GIBBONS

Illustrated by
CHRIS RIDDELL

HarperCollins *Children's Books*

First published in Great Britain by
HarperCollins *Children's Books* in 2020
HarperCollins *Children's Books* is a division of HarperCollins*Publishers* Ltd,
HarperCollins Publishers
1 London Bridge Street
London SE1 9GF

The HarperCollins website address is
www.harpercollins.co.uk
1

HB ISBN: 978–0–00–835503–6
TPB ISBN: 978–0–00–835504–3
B-FORMAT ISBN: 978–0–00–835505–0

Typeset in Adobe Caslon Pro 12/18
Printed and bound in England by CPI Group (UK) Ltd, Croydon CR0 4YY
A CIP catalogue record for this title is available from the British Library.

MIX
Paper from
responsible sources
FSC™ C007454

This book is produced from independently certified FSC™ paper
to ensure responsible forest management.

For more information visit: www.harpercollins.co.uk/green

For Mini and Bonnie, who will always be little to me

A Cast of Characters

IMOGEN AND MARIE

ZUBY

KING DRAKOMOR

MIRO

ANNESHKA MAZANAR

LOFKINYE LOLO

YEEDARSH LOKAI

BLAZE'N BILBETZ

ANDEL

OCHI

PROLOGUE

The monster stood alone on the side of the mountain. He held out his hands.

'Fly with courage and speed and the will of the stars. If you just do one thing, help return what is ours.'

He parted his claws so there was enough space for the moth to escape. It crawled over the back of his hand and circled his wrist. It had a silver-grey, fluffy body.

'Fly with courage and speed and the will of the stars. If you just do one thing, help return what is ours.'

The moth opened and closed its wings to show it was thinking. Then it travelled up the monster's arm. 'I'd forgotten how strange you creatures are,' said the monster, scratching his bald head. 'All the other moths just flew away.'

The moth's tiny legs tickled the monster's collarbone. He closed his eyes and repeated the words for a third time.

'Fly with courage and speed and the will of the stars. If you just do one thing, help return what is ours.'

The monster opened his eyes. The moth was crawling across his face, past his teeth, which stuck out like tusks, over his squished-in nose and on to the top of his head.

'That's it,' he said. 'You've reached the end of Zuby. There's no more of me.'

There was a faint flutter and he looked up. The moth was flying away, but it wasn't travelling across the forests, like the moths he'd released before. It was heading up the face of the mountain.

Zuby soon lost track of its shape in the darkness, even with his sensitive eyes.

'Where are you going?' he called. 'You won't find it among the stars!'

PART 1

CHAPTER 1

'Now, you slithering monster of the deep, prepare to die!'

The knight charged. The giant sea slug bared its teeth and growled, moving to protect the treasure. But the knight was quick. Her sword plunged into the soft, slimy flesh of the monster.

'This is the bit where you die,' said the knight.

'I don't want to die,' said the sea slug.

'But you have to. You're the baddy.'

'Why do I always play the baddy?'

'Marie! You said you would.'

'How about – this time – the knight dies and gets dragged away by the sea slug to—'

'No. That's not the story. That's not how I wrote it. The knight kills the monster and reclaims the treasure and they all live happily ever after.'

'All except the sea slug . . .'

'It's just a bit part.'

The sea slug began to peel off her costume.

'What are you doing?' said the knight. 'We haven't finished yet.'

'I have.'

'But what about the dress rehearsal?'

The monster opened the treasure chest and ran her feelers over the gems. 'Well, if I'm just a bit part, then you'll be fine without me.'

'Hands off – that's my rock collection,' said the knight. She dropped her sword and reached for the treasure chest. The lid moved more easily than she'd expected and it came down hard, squashing a few of the sea slug's tentacles. The monster yowled.

This time they really fought. Underneath her outfit, the sea slug was a little girl with pinkish skin and wild red hair. Her name was Marie.

Marie stuffed the stolen rocks into her pockets. 'You said I could keep one stone!' she yelled.

The knight had short brown hair that she'd cut herself and smudges of freckles that ran across her pale cheeks like warpaint. Her armour was constructed from tinfoil and cereal boxes, and her name was Imogen. She was older than Marie, so she knew better – about pretty much everything.

'I said you could keep one stone if you acted in my play,' said Imogen, 'and you haven't.' She grabbed Marie and emptied the stones from her pockets.

'Mum!' cried Marie. 'Imogen's picking on me again!'

'No, I'm not!' yelled Imogen, releasing Marie's arm.

Marie ran into the house with one hand in her pocket. Imogen wondered if she still had a stone. She'd extract it later.

Imogen picked up her rock collection as rain began to fall. If only she could act every character in the play herself, then she wouldn't need Marie. It was hard work making her sister a star.

She followed Marie inside and dumped her cargo by the back door. Mum was standing in the hallway, wearing a long red dress that Imogen hadn't seen before. Marie was hiding behind her, with just one eye and a few curls visible.

Imogen knew how this would go. She was about to get told off. Imogen hated being told off. After all, she hadn't meant to squish Marie's fingers in the treasure chest.

Imogen eyeballed her mum. 'Why are you so dressed up?' she said.

'Never mind that,' snapped Mum. '*You* are in trouble. I'm not putting up with this behaviour any more – the fighting with your sister, the mess you've made in the garden—'

'It's a sea-slug cave!'

'Imogen! You're too old for this nonsense! And you're certainly too old to be making Marie cry.'

'She started it.'

'Well, I'm finishing it,' said Mum. 'Grandma's looking after you for the rest of the day and she'll take you to the tea rooms if you're good. Are you going to be good?'

'Where are you going?' asked Imogen.

'It doesn't matter where I'm going. I've left you home-made pizza for tonight. You'll have a great time. Now promise me you'll be nice to your sister.'

Marie's face had turned blotchy from fake crying. She looked like a half-ripened raspberry. Imogen did *not* want to be nice to her sister.

'Come on, Imogen,' said Mum in a softer voice. 'I'm counting on you.'

The doorbell rang and Mum turned in a circle. 'He's early!' she cried.

'Who's early?' asked Marie.

'You'll see,' said Mum.

CHAPTER 2

Mum opened the door and a man strode into the house. He was wearing a smart shirt and shiny black shoes. Imogen noticed the shoes because they squeaked with every step, as if he was walking on mice.

'Cathy! You look gorgeous,' said the man in his man voice. He gave Imogen's mum a kiss on the cheek, then he turned to the girls. 'And these must be the two little princesses I've heard so much about.'

'I'm not a princess,' said Imogen, looking down at her armour. 'I'm a knight and she's a giant sea slug. Who are you?'

'Imogen!' gasped Mum.

'It's all right,' said the man. He looked down at Imogen and moved his lips into a smile. 'My name's Mark. I'm friends with your mother.'

'She never had any friends called Mark before,' said Imogen.

The man rocked forward in his squeaky shoes. 'Is that so? Well, things change quickly in the grown-up world.'

Imogen opened her mouth, but Mum cut across her: 'Girls, help me shut all the windows before Grandma arrives. It's turned nasty out there.'

Mum reached up to the little window facing the garden, but she must have seen something because she jumped back in horror.

'What is it?' said Imogen, running to Mum's side.

'Something moved! Something moved behind the curtain!'

Mark was there in an instant. 'Let me see,' he commanded, and he whipped back the curtain.

A moth crawled down the fabric towards Mark's hand. From one angle, its wings were grey; from another they were silver. Imogen wanted a closer look.

'Don't worry, Cathy,' said Mark, 'I've got this.' He moved as if to squash the moth and Imogen didn't have time to think. She darted in front of him and cupped her hands round the insect. Mark tried to nudge her aside, but she stamped down hard – right on the toe of his squeaky shoe.

Mark swore. Marie squealed. Mum was already telling her off, but Imogen ran away from them all. She opened the back door with her elbow and dashed out into the rain. She could hardly feel the moth inside her hands – it was so light. Only the gentle brush of its wings against her fingers gave it away.

Mum was shouting, but Imogen sprinted to the bottom of the garden and knelt by a low bush. She didn't care that she'd lost some of her armour on the way. Here, beneath all the greenery, the moth would be safe.

Imogen parted her hands and the moth crawled on to a leaf. Its silver-grey wings blended into the shadows. 'I shall call you the *shadow moth*,' said Imogen, wiping rain off her forehead.

The moth opened and closed its wings three times as if to say *thank you*.

'You're welcome,' said Imogen.

When the moth's wings were open, it was about the same size as the palm of her hand. When the wings were closed, they folded across its body so that it was hardly wider than a fingernail. Its back was covered in velvety fur.

'I didn't think moths came out in the day,' said Imogen.

The moth moved its antennae to the left and the right. They were shaped like feathers.

'I suppose you must be different from the others.'

Imogen looked at the house. Her mum was standing at the back door with her hands on her hips. Imogen narrowed her eyes. No one could make her say sorry.

She walked back to the house as slowly as she could.

'Apologise to Mark,' said Mum. 'You can't go around stamping on people's feet.'

'You can't go around murdering things either,' said Imogen. 'Why don't you tell Mark *that*?'

CHAPTER 3

Five minutes later, Grandma arrived and Mum left. Imogen changed out of her tinfoil armour and put her rock collection under her bed.

'Your mother tells me you've been badly behaved,' said Grandma. 'But we're going to the tea rooms anyway. It's not fair to punish Marie for your behaviour and I can't leave a seven-year-old home alone.'

'I'm eleven,' said Imogen. 'I can look after myself.'

'Seven. Eleven. It's all the same,' said Grandma. 'Just get in the car.'

Marie started humming as soon as they pulled out of the drive. It was one of her worst habits: humming tunes that she'd just made up. 'Will you stop that?' said Imogen.

Marie continued to hum, but very quietly.

'Stop it!' yelled Imogen.

'That's enough,' snapped Grandma, 'or neither of you will have any cake.'

That shut them up. Grandma didn't mess about and it was best not to distract her when she was driving. Last time they'd argued, Grandma had run over a squirrel. She'd made the girls get out and say the funeral rites.

'Where has Mum gone?' said Imogen, locating Grandma's eyes in the car mirror. Grandma kept her eyes fixed on the road.

'Your mother has gone to the theatre.'

'Why?'

'She likes the theatre.'

'Does she like Mark too?'

For a brief moment, Grandma's eyes met Imogen's. 'Of course she likes Mark. They're good friends.'

'Friends,' said Imogen, turning the word over in her mouth as if it was a new one. 'Are you sure he's not another boyfriend?'

They stopped at traffic lights and Imogen pushed her face up against the car window, letting out a long breath in the shape of an O. Something caught her eye through the foggy glass and she wiped away the condensation to make a gap she could see through.

There, flying towards the car, was the shadow moth. It was struggling through the rain. *What an incredible insect,* thought Imogen. It looked like a messenger from ancient times, determined to deliver its message even at the cost of its life.

The traffic lights changed and the car jerked into motion.

Imogen turned to look through the back window, but the moth was nowhere to be seen. *The poor thing's probably been squished by the rain,* she thought. *When you're that small, every droplet is a meteor.*

CHAPTER 4

The tea rooms were part of a grand estate. Or rather they were part of what used to be a grand estate. These days the Haberdash Mansion was all shut up, apart from one room where Mrs Haberdash lived with her dogs.

Mrs Haberdash ran the tea rooms from a mobility scooter behind a counter. She would sit there in a faded lace dress, with antique earrings gleaming against her copper-brown skin and grey corkscrew hair piled up on her head.

Imogen and Marie sat in the corner of the tea rooms. They ate cake and drew in their sketchpads. Imogen was working on a portrait of Mrs Haberdash's dogs.

Grandma was talking at Mrs Haberdash. 'Winifred was a fool to trust a male hairdresser,' she said, leaning across the counter. 'I told her it was a ridiculous idea. You might as well ask your dogs to serve high tea.'

Mrs H nodded, making her earrings rattle.

Imogen tried to imagine the old lady's dogs balancing cups and saucers on their heads. Perhaps next time she'd draw that, but she'd had enough of sketching for today. She tried to get Grandma's attention, but Grandma was in full swing.

'I've finished,' said Marie, holding up her drawing. Imogen narrowed her eyes. It was nearly identical to her own dog portrait.

'Grandma! Marie's copying me!' cried Imogen.

Grandma pretended not to hear. She carried on talking to Mrs Haberdash: 'I told my GP that I'd already spoken to Bernie and Bernie said that if I took six paracetamol the problem would be gone in no time.'

Imogen directed a death stare at her sister and stomped out of the tea rooms. She marched across the car park, but Grandma's car was locked. Fine. She'd sulk outside instead. She'd sulk for the whole summer holidays if she had to. At least it had stopped raining. She looked around for a place to sit.

There was a gate in the corner of the car park that Imogen hadn't noticed before. Friendly letters hung above it, saying *Welcome to the Haberdash Gardens*. Less friendly letters were painted across the gate: *NO TRESPASSING!*

Imogen wasn't sure what 'trespassing' meant, but it sounded like fun. She glanced at the tea rooms. No one was watching. When she turned back to the gate, her moth was sitting on it. Or, at least, she *thought* it was her moth.

She bent down to get a closer look and the moth stared right back.

'It *is* you,' said Imogen, smiling. 'I thought the rain got you.' The moth flew off the gate and into the Haberdash Gardens.

Imogen tried the gate's lock. It had rusted and came off in her hand. *Well*, she thought, *Mrs Haberdash really should have had that fixed*. She dropped the lock and stepped into the gardens. 'Wait for me!' she called.

The gate swung shut behind her.

CHAPTER 5

The Haberdash Gardens were at war. Trees battled under the weight of creepers and ivy strangled the roses. The weeds had almost succeeded in reclaiming what was rightfully theirs.

Imogen had to walk quickly to keep up with the moth. She wanted it to stop on something so she could get another close look. A twig snapped. Imogen turned on her heel, but there was no one behind her.

The moth flew on and Imogen followed. Tendrils threw themselves, kamikaze-style, across her path. She turned right and there was a river. Fat frogs lurked among the bulrushes.

In her haste, Imogen tottered too close to the water. A frog belched, hopping aside just before her heel plunged into the spongy earth. Cold water seeped in through her shoe, but there was no time to stop. The moth was getting away.

Imogen hurried along the riverbank, and the moth flew across the water. 'I can't follow you there,' she said, looking around for a bridge. But in this place where everything was falling apart, things also fell into place. A dead tree lay across the river.

Imogen climbed up the roots and spread her arms out wide, placing her left foot on the trunk, then her right foot. Woodlice ran for cover as she disturbed their rotten paradise. She made her way across the dead tree slowly, hardly daring to breathe in case it affected her balance.

The last part of the tree was slippery so Imogen lowered herself on to her belly. She wriggled forward, rubbing dirt into her top. When the trunk was above earth instead of water, Imogen rolled off and landed on her feet. She smiled, pleased with herself, and continued on her way.

The plants on this side of the river had won the war against the gardeners. They had no interest in looking how people wanted them to look. Oversized shrubs had thorny throats. Wayward flowers bobbed their heads as Imogen swept by and the further she went into the Haberdash Gardens, the more she got the feeling that she wasn't welcome.

She heard a noise from somewhere behind, like the patter of feet. She turned. There was no one there.

Imogen did think about going back to the tea rooms,

but she was sure that the moth was trying to show her something and she wanted to see what it was. A large drop of water landed on her forehead and she glanced up at the sky. Another drop splashed on her cheek and then the rain poured down. The moth flew faster. Imogen ran to keep up. Again, there was a sound behind her, but she couldn't turn back. She wouldn't turn back. She sprinted as fast as she could. Mud splattered up her legs.

The shadow moth led Imogen to an enormous tree. The highest branches seemed to touch the clouds and, under the jabbering of the rain, Imogen was sure she could hear roots drawing up water from the depths of the earth.

She stepped under the tree's canopy and put her hand on the rough trunk. The moth landed next to her fingers and moved its antennae in circles. In this light, it looked more grey than silver, camouflaged against the bark.

Imogen couldn't wait to tell Marie what she'd found: the biggest tree in the world. Marie would be amazed (and perhaps a little bit jealous).

The moth crawled away from Imogen's hand and she followed its progress. Soon it wasn't walking on gnarled bark, but smooth wood. Imogen ran her finger over this new texture. She knew what it was. She stepped back a few paces. Yes, it was as she'd thought.

There was a door in the tree.

CHAPTER 6

The door was smaller than most. A grown-up would have to stoop to fit through, but for Imogen it was just the right height.

She wondered what was on the other side. Perhaps the tree was a hiding place for treasure; the kind of treasure Mrs H might forget she'd got hidden.

The moth crawled down the door and stopped at the keyhole. Imogen knelt next to it, grinding more soil into her jeans, and peeped through. All she could see on the other side was darkness. She pulled back.

'Is this what you wanted to show me?' she asked.

The moth folded back its wings and wriggled through the keyhole.

'I think that's a yes,' said Imogen. She stood up, pulled open the door and stepped through.

At first, it was very dark. Then, as Imogen's eyes adjusted, towering shapes swam out of the gloom. A few seconds later, she realised that they were trees. She was standing alone in a forest just before sunset. Branches shredded the low-lit sky into ribbons.

Imogen's head filled with questions. How could a forest fit inside a tree? Why wasn't it raining here? How come it was so dark and quiet? It was as though the forest had been smothered by a giant duvet.

Imogen looked back at the door and realised that she hadn't imagined the noises behind her. She really had been followed. There, just stepping over the threshold, was her sister.

The light from the gardens shone round Marie. Her hair had turned dark in the rain, her clothes were covered in mud and her eyes were wide. She pushed the door closed behind her. The hinges must have been well oiled because it moved easily, clicking as it shut. The sisters' eyes met.

'Marie!' cried Imogen. 'What are you doing here?'

For a split second, Marie looked afraid – caught off guard – but she quickly regained self-control.

'What am *I* doing here?' she said. 'I could ask you the same thing.'

'So it was *you* following me,' said Imogen, folding her arms.

'You're not allowed in the Haberdash Gardens.'

'Neither are you,' said Imogen. 'Can't you let me do anything on my own?'

'I'm going to tell Grandma. You're doing trespassing.'

Imogen scowled. It was her moth, her garden and her secret door. Marie hadn't even been invited; she'd hijacked Imogen's adventure and now she was threatening to destroy it. Imogen wanted to throw something at her sister. She wanted to pull her ponytail. No, she wanted to make her disappear.

'Go on, then. Go and cry to Grandma.'

'Fine! I will!' Marie turned and grabbed the door handle. Then she glanced over her shoulder.

'Well, what are you waiting for?' demanded Imogen.

'It won't open,' said Marie.

'Move out of the way.'

Imogen tried the handle, but the door wouldn't budge. 'Oh, well done!' she shouted.

'I didn't know it locked itself!' squealed Marie.

'You stupid baby. If you're not sure what something does, leave it alone!'

'You shouldn't have opened it in the first place,' said Marie.

'You should have stayed at home where you can't spoil everything!'

Imogen felt panic rising in her chest. She kicked the door and hammered with her fists, but it wouldn't open.

The shadow moth she'd followed was nowhere to be seen.

CHAPTER 7

M arie looked like she might cry and Imogen knew it was up to her to get them out of this mess. She also knew that they couldn't stay put. It was much colder here than it had been in the Haberdash Gardens and she was already shivering in her damp clothes.

'We need to get moving,' she said, turning on her heel like a general.

'Do you think we'll be back in time for tea?' asked Marie, with a wobble in her voice.

Imogen thought that was unlikely. It didn't feel like they were in the gardens any more. It was as if they were in a different place altogether, but she couldn't stand it when Marie cried so she murmured something reassuring about how Grandma would be out looking for them.

Above, the first stars began to stir. They winked at each other and looked down at the girls walking through the forest, tiny among the trees. A person who knew how to read the stars might have said they were smiling.

Imogen didn't tell Marie, but she was secretly relieved

that she wasn't alone in this strange place. It was hard to see and she kept tripping over roots and snagging her jeans on brambles. She strained her eyes, hoping to catch the flutter of wings in the darkness, but her moth had gone.

Every so often, Imogen heard the whisper of her worry creatures. *Lost in the forest*, they hissed. *Lost in the forest and so far from home.*

Imogen walked faster.

'Hey, I can't keep up,' moaned Marie.

Imogen looked over her shoulder. The worry creatures were scurrying from tree to tree, but they fed off her fears, not her sister's, and Marie couldn't see them.

'Come on,' said Imogen. 'I want to get out of this wood.'

As the girls walked, the trees grew further apart, and something caught Imogen's attention. Something that wasn't a worry creature. 'Hey, Marie, can you see that?'

'It's one of those bugs with a light in its bum,' said Marie.

'A glow-worm? No. It's bigger than that. And further away.'

'Maybe it's Grandma! Out with a torch!'

Imogen steered Marie towards the light. It was too low to be a star – it was too still to be Grandma – and yet it lured her on. There was something reassuring about the soft glow. Imogen wanted to be there, among other people. That was what light meant: life, warmth, a flicker of hope, a toasted teacake and a short drive home.

The girls came to the edge of the forest and Imogen's heart sank. They were standing in a valley surrounded by huge looming shapes that looked like mountains. Imogen couldn't see what was at the bottom of the valley, but the light she'd been following was there. She guessed it was two miles away. Maybe three. All of Imogen's teacake-shaped dreams vanished. This place was vast and foreign and full of shadows. There would be no easy way home.

This was the part where a grown-up was supposed to turn on the lights, fold away the forest and send the girls off to bed. But there were no grown-ups and the forest was real. Imogen wanted to cry.

'That doesn't look like the tea rooms,' said Marie.

Imogen bit her lip. Blubbing wouldn't help.

'What are we going to do?' said Marie. 'I'm cold. I want to go home.'

Imogen's pent-up tears turned to rage. 'I don't know the way,' she snapped. '*Someone* slammed the door, remember?'

'It was a mistake!' shouted Marie. Her words echoed round the valley and she jumped behind her sister, spooked by the ghosts of her own voice. 'Anyway, I didn't slam it. I gave it a gentle push.'

'Oh good, well, that's fine, then,' said Imogen.

For a moment, neither of them spoke. Then Imogen took a deep breath. 'Look,' she said. 'Look at that light.

There must be people there who can help us get home.'

'Do you think so?' said Marie.

'I'm sure of it,' said Imogen.

Together they walked towards the light at the bottom of the valley.

Marie held Imogen's hand. Imogen didn't stop her.

PART 2

CHAPTER 8

The two sisters walked through meadows and hopped across brooks.

The moon was a sliver, but it seemed to be larger than usual and, with no branches overhead, there was just enough light for Imogen to see where she was putting her feet. In some places, the grass was cropped close to the ground; in others, it grew long and wild. Field mushrooms gathered in circles, as though assembled for a night-time dance.

'Do you think Mum's having a good time with Mark?' asked Marie.

'I hope not. I didn't like him,' said Imogen, making an extra effort to trample the grass. 'I don't know why she bothers with boyfriends. She's got us, hasn't she?'

'Yes . . . but he might be nice.'

'I doubt it,' said Imogen. 'He was wearing stupid shoes. He was saying stupid things. I bet it'll go wrong, just like it did with the other boyfriends.'

'Grandma says you can tell a lot about someone from their shoes.'

'Grandma's right,' said Imogen, 'and Mark's shoes were stupid.'

'I wish Grandma was here right now,' said Marie.

Imogen led the way through the meadows until they stood at the foot of an enormous wall. Behind the wall she could see the shadowy outlines of tall buildings. 'Wow!' whispered Marie. The wall was three times higher than a house and each stone was as large as a car.

'There must have been some big battles in the olden days,' said Imogen, 'to need a wall like that.'

'How do we get past it?' asked Marie. 'The light's on the other side.'

'I think there's a gate. It's hard to make out, but look over—' Imogen was interrupted by a bell. The sound was deafening. More bells joined the din. She clapped her hands over her ears.

Marie was hopping up and down and yelling, but Imogen couldn't hear what she was saying. Marie pointed at the gate. It had started to lower.

Imogen ran and Marie followed. The bells continued to toll. The stars flickered with excitement and even the crescent moon was unable to tear his gaze from the two silhouettes dashing towards the gap between the ground and the lowering gate.

As the bells struck their final note, Imogen threw herself

on to all fours and crawled through. 'That was close!' she gasped, getting to her feet, but when she turned round Marie wasn't there. Her hoodie was caught on the spikes that ran along the bottom of the gate. She was centimetres away from being skewered.

'Help!' she shrieked, trying to claw her way forward. 'Imogen, I'm stuck!'

CHAPTER 9

Imogen ripped Marie's hoodie free and grabbed her by the wrists, dragging her through on her belly. The gate hit the ground. Imogen collapsed. They'd made it.

'I – I almost got squished to death,' said Marie, breathing hard. 'Imagine what Mum would have said if I'd got squished to death.'

'Bet I'd have been the one in trouble,' muttered Imogen.

'Maybe,' said Marie in a small voice. 'But . . . um . . . thanks for saving me.'

When Imogen had recovered, she helped Marie to her feet and looked around. On this side of the wall, there was a city with painted houses and tiled roofs and pointy towers. Some of the buildings were decorated so delicately that they reminded Imogen of the birthday cakes Mum made – all frosted flowers and piped icing.

The girls walked through the city streets towards the light. There were no people. Instead, the place had been given over to the dead – or what was left of them. Thigh bones dangled from windows like crooked wind chimes.

Strings of vertebrae decorated doors. Strangely shaped skulls poked out between stones.

Imogen felt vaguely sick. She wasn't sure what was more alarming: the not-quite-human dead things or the thought of what might have killed them.

'Whose skulls do you think they are?' asked Marie.

'How do you expect me to know?' said Imogen, who didn't want to have this conversation.

'They're very small. Do you think they belonged to children?'

'No.'

'And look what a lot of teeth they have ...'

'Come on, Marie. We have to keep walking.'

Imogen took a deep breath and relocated the light. It looked like it was coming from the heart of the city. That was the way to go.

Every building the girls walked by was shut up. There was no light seeping between the shutters. No smoke from the chimneys. Instead of welcoming words, they were greeted by skeleton smiles.

The only things that seemed to be alive were the moths that were flying in every direction. They were small and shimmering. They were large with speckled wings. They were blue like midnight or pink like the dawn. Imogen kept looking for *her* moth – the one that had shown her the door

– but it was nowhere to be seen. These were just normal insects. They weren't going to show her the way home.

Imogen and Marie crossed a bridge that was guarded by thirty black statues. Imogen counted them as she went. Counting things usually made her feel better, but this time it didn't work.

The statues were all stern-looking men. Someone hadn't agreed with the sculptor about how many limbs they ought to have. Arms had been amputated. Legs were sliced off at the knee. A few heads were missing and the stonework was covered in scratches.

The deeper the girls walked into the city, the taller the houses grew, rising from hunched cottages to proud, five-storey mansions. A grand house had skulls embedded in its walls. Marie paused to examine one. 'Hey, Imogen, come and see this.'

Imogen didn't like the look of the skull. Not only did it have a lot of teeth, but they were pointed, almost triangular. 'We've fallen into a nightmare,' she muttered. 'I think we should keep moving.'

'Just one second,' said Marie, and she moved closer to the skull so that the eye sockets stared down at her upturned face. She stretched out her hand, reaching into the gaping jaw. Her fingertip hovered above a fang, nearly touching

the point. Then she jumped, startled by a terrible scream. Imogen jumped too.

'What was that?' cried Marie, whipping back her hand.

'I don't think we want to find out,' said Imogen. 'Time to go!'

The girls rushed through the streets. Fear gave them energy. That scream had sounded wild and furious and it had come from somewhere near the city walls.

Imogen tried to focus on the light, to navigate towards it, but with every wrong turn her heart beat faster. Suddenly even the buildings seemed hostile, with their slanting window-eyes.

Another screech. Louder, closer.

Imogen banged on the door of a house. Moths flew out from between the shutters, but no one came to help.

Imogen kicked the door and cursed the shadow moth. She cursed her rotten luck too. She promised God, the moon, whoever was listening, that she wouldn't run away again. She'd eat liver and broccoli. She'd share her stuff with Marie. Just let them be back home, tucked up in their beds.

More screams. 'They're coming this way!' cried Marie.

'Follow me,' said Imogen.

She swung round the corner, half expecting a dead end, but instead the girls found themselves in a large square. There was a dark castle at the far side, crowned with towers and turrets. Light shone from the top of a tall tower. 'That's it,' said Imogen. 'That's where the people must live.'

Imogen and Marie sprinted across the square and pounded on the castle door.

'*Let us in! Let us in!*'

There was no response so they hammered harder. The shrieks were closing in – the monsters would be in the square any second – but the castle door remained locked.

There was nowhere to go.

CHAPTER 10

'Oi! You two – over here!' A boy's face poked out from a little door that was cut into the larger entrance.

Imogen and Marie didn't hesitate. They ran over, the boy opened the door wider and the girls fell inside. He pulled the door closed, shutting out the starlight and monsters. Keys jangled in the dark.

'They won't get through that,' he said, and a candle illuminated his face. He had far-apart eyes, dark olive skin and a mop of curly brown hair that couldn't quite hide his sticky-out ears.

He pressed an ear to the door and the girls did the same. Claws scratched on cobbles. The boy put his finger to his lips. The shrieking creatures, whatever they were, were very close. Imogen held her breath. The door rattled. The children jumped back and Marie let out a whimper.

Outside, the monsters were screaming to be let in. 'They won't get past the door,' whispered the boy. 'They never do.'

Sure enough, after a few minutes, the noise receded.

The children stood still for one minute more, not daring to move until the shrieks had faded away.

'Right,' said the boy, putting down his candle. 'First things first.'

Imogen wiped her hand on her jeans in preparation for a handshake.

'Face the wall and put your hands on your head.'

'What?'

'You heard me,' said the boy. 'Turn round and put your hands up.'

Reluctantly, Imogen did as she was told. The boy searched inside the top of her socks. Then he turned her pockets inside out.

'What are you doing?' said Imogen.

'Checking for weapons,' said the boy.

'Why don't you just ask?'

'Peasants can't be trusted. Besides, if you'd come to kill me, you'd never hand over your knives willingly.'

Imogen had never been called a peasant before. She looked down at her mud-streaked clothing. Perhaps he had a point, but still it was hardly polite.

'You're all clear,' said the boy. 'Stand aside.' Next he searched Marie. He lifted up her ponytail with great suspicion, and gave it a shake as if expecting a dagger to fall out.

Imogen watched him. She guessed he was about her age, perhaps a little older. He was dressed very strangely, in an embroidered jacket that looked like it was made out of fancy curtains. He wore rings on almost every finger.

'We're not peasants,' she said, but the boy wasn't listening. He was going through Marie's pockets and he'd found something. He held it between his thumb and index finger, inspecting it in the candlelight.

Imogen saw the shiny surface and she knew what it was. 'That's my stone,' she said. Marie must have had it in her pocket since their fight.

Marie lowered her hands and turned round, guilt written all over her face.

The boy continued to study the fool's gold so Imogen said it again. 'That's mine. That's from my rock collection.'

'What's a peasant doing with a precious stone?'

Imogen could feel that familiar quickening of her pulse, but she spoke each word slowly. 'Give. It. Back. I am not a peasant.'

Marie looked from her big sister to the boy and back to her big sister. 'Sorry, Imogen . . . I was going to give the treasure back eventually, I promise. I just wanted to borrow it . . .'

Imogen advanced on the boy. 'Give me my gold, you thief.'

'Who are you to call *me* a thief?' he sneered. 'This is my

kingdom and so is everything in it – including you, your friend and your so-called treasure.'

That was the last straw. Imogen pounced. She knocked the fool's gold out of the boy's hand and pushed him to the floor. Marie caught the stone. Imogen and the boy were a tumbling mess of arms and legs. His elbow clipped her chin, making her jaw bang shut. She retaliated with a knee to his stomach.

'Ow! You filthy urchin! Get off me!'

'Marie,' cried Imogen, 'grab his arms!'

Marie shoved the stone back into her pocket and went for the boy's wrists. She caught one. Imogen trapped the other hand with her foot, making the boy cry out. The rest of him thrashed wildly. 'Help me!' he shouted. 'Somebody help! They're trying to kill me!'

Imogen kicked the shoe from her other foot, whipped off her sock and stuffed it into his mouth. She pulled the scrunchie from Marie's hair and wrapped it round the boy's wrists, handing control to Marie. That freed up Imogen to grab his ankles. The boy stopped wriggling.

'Hah! So you know when you're beaten, then?' crowed Imogen.

'He looks kind of angry,' said Marie. 'His face is going red.'

'Well, that's tough, isn't it? He shouldn't take other people's things.'

'Is someone squeezing your head?' cooed Marie to the boy, enjoying her position of power a little too much.

Imogen paused. 'Wait. What do you mean his face is going red?' She couldn't see him properly from her position at his feet.

'He looks like a beetroot . . .' said Marie.

'The sock!' cried Imogen.

'Ooh, look how his eyes are bulging! He's really very cross.'

'Marie, the sock! Take the sock out his mouth!'

Marie obeyed. The boy inhaled and Imogen let go of his ankles. The sisters were silent for a moment while the boy rolled on to all fours, spluttering and gasping.

'Why, I ought – I ought to set the Royal Guards on you!' He struggled to his feet. 'I ought to have you both beheaded! I ought to have you chopped up and fed to my fish. I—'

'That's enough,' interrupted Imogen in as kind a voice as she could manage. 'We didn't mean to choke you.' She pulled the scrunchie off his wrists and handed it back to Marie.

'You must forgive my sister,' said Imogen.

'Hey! It wasn't just me that tied him up!'

Imogen shot Marie a meaningful look. 'She was dropped on her head as a baby.'

The boy looked at Marie with his far-apart eyes. 'Is that what turned her hair orange?'

'It's not orange,' said Marie. 'It's red.'

'Looks orange to me,' said the boy.

Imogen stepped between them. 'Look, I think we got off on the wrong foot.'

The boy let out a long sigh. 'You're right,' he said. 'I don't normally do that to guests. To be honest, I don't normally have guests at all.'

'What a surprise,' muttered Imogen.

The boy didn't seem to hear. 'When my uncle has people to visit, the Royal Guards confiscate their weapons.'

'Oh right,' said Imogen, thinking that was probably the correct response.

'So, when Petr's not about, I have to take precautions.'

'I see,' said Imogen, who didn't see at all.

'How about we just start this whole thing again?' said the boy.

'A rematch?' cried Marie.

'No! Let's say you just came through the door. Pretend you did. Yes, that's it. And I've just locked it and you say, *Hello, Your Majesty, what a pleasure to meet you.*'

Imogen wasn't sure about the script. She didn't think the boy should cast himself as royalty. However, she was in a tricky situation. She needed his help.

'Good evening, Your Majesty,' she said, giving a wobbly curtsey. Marie did the same.

'What a pleasure it is to meet you,' said Marie.

The boy bowed low. 'The pleasure is all mine,' he said. 'Welcome to Castle Yaroslav.'

CHAPTER 11

'I am the prince of this castle,' said the boy, 'and you are my most honoured guests.' He straightened his jacket, checking that the stiff collar was still pointing up.

Throughout this performance, he kept a very serious face. *Either he's a good actor*, thought Imogen, *or he's completely off his rocker*.

'Now!' The boy picked up the candle. 'Tell me ... what were you doing out there? I thought the peasants rounded up their children at dusk. Not runaways, are you?'

'To start with, we're not peasants,' said Imogen, puffing herself up to her full height. 'As I said.'

'What are you, then? Pickpockets?'

'Of course not!'

'Assassins?' He took a step back.

'We're lost!' said Imogen. 'We're not supposed to be here at all.'

'Where are you supposed to be? Are you from the forests?'

'I suppose you could say that ...'

The boy moved the candle closer to Imogen. 'You don't look like you're from the forests,' he said, inspecting her T-shirt and jeans. 'You're not wearing enough green to be a lesni. In fact, what *are* you wearing? Are those nightclothes?'

Imogen clenched her fists and then released them, reminding herself that she needed all the help she could get.

'You'll have to stay here for the night,' said the boy. 'You'd be eaten alive out there.' He seemed to take great delight in saying that last sentence. He glanced at the girls to see if his words had had any effect. Marie looked horrified.

'That would be lovely,' said Imogen. 'Thank you.'

'Excellent. Follow me.' The boy walked away, taking the small circle of candlelight with him.

'Do you think we should go with him?' whispered Marie.

'I don't see what choice we've got,' said Imogen.

'It's just that Mum always says not to go with strangers. Do you think he's a stranger?'

'He's strange all right, but I'm pretty sure Mum wouldn't want us eaten by monsters either.'

'No,' said Marie. 'Although she never talked about it pacifically.'

'It's *specifically*. Anyway, if someone loves you, they don't have to say *don't get eaten by monsters*. It's obvious.'

Imogen thought of Mum getting back from the theatre

to find that the home-made pizzas were untouched. Mum always left them something special to eat if she was going to be late, and pizza was one of Imogen's favourites.

Then she thought of Grandma, with her walking stick, searching the gardens. It made Imogen feel sad so she brushed the thought aside. 'Come on,' she said to Marie. 'His Royal Highness is getting away.'

CHAPTER 12

The girls followed the boy through tapestry-lined corridors and across rooms that were as big as the sports hall at school.

He stopped at the foot of a spiral staircase. 'This is the entrance to my quarters,' he said. 'No commoners have ever set foot beyond this point. Apart from the servants, that is. You'll be the first.'

Bonkers, thought Imogen as she nodded along.

The further up the stairs they climbed, the narrower the staircase became. 'Keep up!' shouted the boy, who had disappeared ahead.

The steps took them to a circular room. 'I've never seen so many candles,' said Imogen. 'Is all this stuff yours?'

'Yes,' said the boy.

'Where did you get this from?' Marie's enormous eye peered through a magnifying glass.

'It was my father's.'

'And this?' Marie lay down on a fur rug.

'I don't remember.'

'What about this?' asked Imogen, and she blew dust from from the sleeping face of an old clock.

'Don't touch that,' snapped the boy. 'It's the only one of its kind.'

Imogen leaned in. She wanted a better look at the thing she mustn't touch.

The clock was made of wood. In front of its face, there were five motionless hands and an array of jewelled stars. Imogen couldn't work out what was holding the stars in place. They seemed to hover, but she couldn't see any wires. A silver moon peeped out from behind the biggest hand, as if too shy to reveal itself fully.

'What's inside that hatch?' asked Imogen, stepping back and pointing to a tiny door at the top of the clock. It was about the right size for a hamster.

'I don't remember,' said the boy. 'It stopped working years ago.'

'Why?' said Marie.

The boy fiddled with the rings on his fingers. 'I think you've asked enough questions for one night.'

Marie cast a longing glance at the room's four-poster bed, with its plumptious pillows and downy quilt. She looked at Imogen, who nodded. The next second, Marie was kicking off her shoes and wriggling under the sheets.

Imogen turned to the boy. 'Just one more question . . .'

'Yes?'

'Why are you helping us?'

'I told you,' he said. 'You'd be eaten alive if you stayed outside.'

'But where are all the other people?'

'They're here. In their houses. Around the castle. I'm just the only one who keeps candles burning.'

Imogen walked to a window and looked out at the city shrouded in darkness. They had made it to the light that she'd seen from the forest. 'We must be in the castle's tallest tower,' she said, half to herself.

'Not quite,' said the boy. 'This is the *second* tallest tower.'

Imogen removed her shoes and slipped into bed next to Marie. 'We should blow out the candles,' she said, yawning.

'Why would I do that?' asked the boy.

'It's a fire hazard.' She was parroting her mum. Mum was always banging on about fire hazards.

'A fire what?'

But Imogen didn't reply. She was already fast asleep.

As Imogen slept, monsters flitted in and out of the darkness below. Like grotesque shadow puppets, their forms danced across shuttered windows. They reclaimed the streets, calling to each other across the empty squares.

In the big houses near the cathedral, if you were to peep out at just the right moment, you'd see a silhouette squatting on top of the bell tower. It might look like a child. Or perhaps a very old man. But, if you dared to look closer, you'd see that its shoulders were too muscular, its arms were too long and its teeth were too sharp.

The monsters travelled from roof to roof. They tiptoed along gutters. They hid in eaves. They hung down from bedroom windows by their claws.

All night, the city belonged to them.

CHAPTER 13

There was sunlight behind Imogen's eyelids. Bells tolled. That was odd. There were no churches near her house. A cockerel crowed. *Definitely* odd.

And she couldn't hear the familiar noises of home: her mum's radio, the cat demanding breakfast. Where was the smell of fried eggs? She opened one eye. Where was her orange juice? She opened the other. Where was any of it?

And then Imogen remembered. Propped up on her elbows, she looked around, detangling her dreams from last night's reality. The forest was real. The city full of bones was real. The boy who rescued them was real. In fact, he was awake and observing her from a chair by the fire.

Hmm, thought Imogen. What was the appropriate thing to say? Perhaps *Good morning* or *How did you sleep?* Those were the things Mum normally said to guests. But Imogen was the guest so she cut straight to the chase: 'You have to take us back to the tea rooms. We're not supposed to be here.'

The boy slouched in his chair. 'Aren't you supposed to say something like, *Thanks for saving my life?*'

Imogen hopped out of bed. 'What time is it?' she asked. 'Morning,' he said.

'I can see that, but what's the time?' She pulled on her shoes and went to wake Marie.

'What does it matter?' said the boy. 'There's no rush.'

'Of course there is. Our mum will be worried. Or angry. Or both.'

The boy's feet didn't quite touch the floor and he swung his legs as he spoke.

'Don't you remember?' he said. 'My clock's broken. I don't know the time. There are bells at dawn and bells at dusk. Everything in between is day. Why rush back to see a bunch of angry grown-ups anyway?'

'I don't want to go to school,' murmured Marie, still half asleep.

The boy slid down from his chair and added, a little petulantly, 'I thought you'd at least stay for an evening meal.'

'What planet are you living on?' said Imogen. 'We've been gone all night. Mum must have got home ages ago and I bet Grandma's called the police. They'll be out there in the gardens, searching for us with dogs.'

'Oh, come now. Peasants go missing all the time. Nobody goes looking for them. Especially not dogs.'

'This is the last time I'm going to tell you: *we – are – not – peasants.*'

Marie was awake now and peering round the room with bleary eyes.

'Come on, Marie,' said Imogen. 'We're leaving.'

The boy ran to the door. 'No, you're not!' he cried, blocking the exit. 'I won't allow it!'

Marie rubbed sleep from her eyes. 'Imogen, I want to go home.'

'I command you to stay!' cried the boy.

'Don't worry,' said Imogen, helping Marie out of bed. 'We're going. Put your shoes on.'

'Is this how you repay your rescuer? Is this the way to treat a prince?'

'I don't care who you are,' said Imogen. 'Move!'

'Shan't.' The boy glowered at the sisters.

Imogen considered her options. There was a pair of axes hanging above the fireplace. They looked heavy. There was a crossbow by the door. She had no idea how to work that. And then she saw a sword mounted on the wall by the bed.

She climbed on to the headboard.

'What are you doing?' said the boy.

Imogen held on to the four-poster bed with one hand and reached for the sword with the other.

'Leave that alone!' cried the boy. Imogen grabbed the sword's hilt. She tugged at it until it swung free. The boy let out a little squeak. The sword was heavier than Imogen had expected and it fell to the floor with a thud. Marie ran over, suddenly wide awake and eager to help. She picked up the sword with two hands.

'Now,' said Imogen, jumping down from the bed, 'stand aside.'

The boy's face fell. 'Shan't,' he said, sounding a little less certain than before.

The sisters advanced. Marie was slashing at the air in a way that made Imogen nervous. 'All right, Marie, rein it in,' she hissed.

'I'm not doing it on purpose,' said her sister. 'It's really heavy.'

The boy's eyes followed the blade. 'You can't go!' he said, standing his ground. 'Not until after dinner! It isn't fair!' At the last moment, he lost his nerve and dived to the right, leaving the door exposed.

Marie dropped the sword. Imogen opened the door and hurtled down the spiral staircase. 'Come on!' she called to her sister. 'Follow me!' But she didn't get very far. She collided with a figure who was coming up the stairs. She stumbled back into the boy's room, tripping and landing on top of Marie.

'What's this?' said the figure. 'A pair of peasants come to steal from His Royal Highness?'

'We didn't steal nothing!' said Marie passionately.

'*Anything*,' corrected her sister.

'Is that so?' said the figure, stepping into the light.

An ancient man in a black robe stood wheezing in the doorway. His face was shrivelled and deathly white. He looked like a creature that had lived under a rock for too long. When he'd caught his breath, he pointed at Imogen and Marie.

'We'll let the king decide what to do with you two,' he said.

Chapter 14

'Oh, Yeedarsh, it's you!' said the boy.

'At your service,' said the old man, giving a shaky bow. 'I caught these thieves escaping down the staircase. I'll get them taken to the dungeons, Your Majesty. Don't you worry. We'll find out how they broke in.'

Marie hid behind Imogen and Imogen turned to the boy. 'We're not thieves,' she said. 'Go on – tell him.'

The boy folded his arms and looked out of the window so Imogen couldn't see his face.

'Oh, we've got plenty like you down in the Hladomorna Pits,' said Yeedarsh, and his mouth curled into a nasty smile. 'Plenty who say they didn't do it. But they always come clean in the end.' He wet his lips, eyes darting between the boy and the two girls. 'Don't they, Your Highness?'

'Um . . . yes. They do.'

'I'll get the Royal Guards,' said Yeedarsh. 'They'll be no more trouble for you. Or perhaps we could just throw them out the window? Save ourselves the bother?'

The boy glanced around as if unsure what to say.

'That's what we used to do when we were short of room in the Pits,' continued the servant. 'Your grandfather never regretted tossing his enemies out of the window. Apart from that one who landed in a pile of manure. Hopped off with nothing but a sprained ankle—'

'Yeedarsh, you're getting carried away,' said the boy.

'Well, what *do* you want to do with them?'

There was a long pause.

'What time's tea?' asked Imogen.

'What's that got to do with anything?' snapped Yeedarsh, scrunching up his face so it looked like an old tissue.

'We were going to stay for tea,' she said quietly. The boy didn't turn round. Imogen held her breath.

'Pah! Thieving peasants for dinner?' croaked Yeedarsh. 'Our prince would rather dine alone than with the likes of you. Isn't that right, Your Highness?'

'Dine ... alone?' said the boy.

'Yes. As you always do, Your Majesty.'

'Why would I do that when I have guests?' He nodded at Imogen and Marie.

'Guests? You mean to say you invited these ... people into the castle?'

'Yes.'

'But why? Does the king know? He ought to know.'

'Just leave it with me, Yeedarsh,' said the boy.

Yeedarsh was visibly perplexed. He kept making as if to leave and then coming back, opening his mouth and then closing it again.

'We'll be wanting breakfast for three,' said the boy. 'Tell the kitchens.'

'Er ... very good,' said the old servant. 'But, if any of the silver cutlery goes missing, your uncle will have their heads. I'll be counting the spoons ...'

CHAPTER 15

After breakfast, Imogen and Marie were given clear instructions on how to spend the hours before dinner. The boy said they were to play around the castle, but they mustn't venture outside. They should return to the room at the top of the second tallest tower when the bells sounded at dusk.

The castle was so big and sprawling that the girls had no problem avoiding grown-ups. There hardly seemed to be anyone around. Instead of people, the castle was populated by strange and beautiful objects. Some rooms housed a few decorative items; others were so full that you could hardly open the door.

In one room, there was a large group of ferocious-looking warriors. At first, Imogen was terrified, but she soon realised that they were just suits of armour.

Marie tried on a helmet. 'We'd better not be asked to eat anything with its face left on,' she said. The helmet covered her eyes and nose, but her mouth continued to talk: 'If he serves fish, I'm out of here.'

Another room was entirely dedicated to paperweights. There were paperweights of blown glass and paperweights of metal. There was even a wooden one carved into the shape of a bear. The room had a large window that overlooked the square that the girls had run across the night before.

'There are the city walls,' said Marie, 'and the meadows we walked through to get here.' Imogen joined her at the window.

Beyond the meadows there were forests and mountains. They seemed to enclose the valley, leaving no way out. The forests were dark and deep and the mountaintops were as sharp as arrowheads. Some of the trees were already turning gold, which was strange because at home it had been the start of the summer holidays.

'Imogen, how are we going to find the door among all those trees?'

'It's not going to be easy,' conceded Imogen. 'We could go now, try to retrace our steps.'

'What . . . not stay for tea?'

'That boy isn't going to stop us. He wouldn't even know we'd gone until it was too late. He said he has *his own affairs to attend to.*'

'But we promised we'd stay for tea,' said Marie.

'I don't remember promising anything.'

Marie pressed her lips together in the way that she did

when she was thinking. 'What if the monsters are still out there?' she asked.

Imogen looked down at the square where some kind of market was taking place. It didn't seem as if there were any monsters, but she could still remember that terrible screeching and the fear of being chased. A shiver ran down her spine.

'Perhaps it *is* worth staying for tea,' she said. 'Perhaps, if we play the boy's little game, he'll help us get home. He might even know how to make the door in the tree open.'

'Yes, that's a good idea,' said Marie, brightening. 'With a bit of help from someone who lives here, we'll be back with Mum in no time.'

Imogen nodded. There was a thought buried so deep in her mind that she was barely aware of it, but it was there all the same: the castle was interesting, and so was the city, especially now there were no monsters. Maybe it wouldn't be such a bad thing if Mum had to wait for them to come home. Maybe it was only fair.

After all, if Mum could go off with her 'friends', leaving Imogen behind, then Imogen could do just the same.

CHAPTER 16

Prince Miroslav – whom Imogen thought of as *the boy* – never told his guests exactly how he spent that day.

He didn't tell them that he'd been frantically making arrangements for the evening: instructing cooks, sending servants on errands. He wanted it to appear normal. He wanted the girls to think he had guests for dinner every week.

He certainly never told them how his belly squirmed as he approached his uncle's study. Two guards stood to attention on either side of the entrance. 'Is King Drakomor in?' Miroslav asked.

'Yes, Your Majesty.'

He struggled with the heavy door, prising it open just wide enough to squeeze through.

The king had shut the sun out of the room, but it wasn't to protect delicate parchment. There were very few books in this study. Instead, the shelves held golden trinkets, rare ornaments and precious stones.

The study was becoming increasingly crowded. Prince

Miroslav had to suck in his tummy so he could fit past an enormous painted vase. That was a new one.

The king magpie, collector of it all, sat at his desk in the centre of the room.

One jewel, mounted on a marble base, stood taller than Miroslav. As he walked behind it, his figure turned orange.

'Miroslav, is that you?'

Miroslav froze like an insect in amber. 'Yes, Uncle.'

'Don't skulk. I can't bear skulkers. Especially not among my collection.'

Miroslav peeped out from behind the jewel. 'Sorry, Uncle,' he said.

'You didn't touch that vase, did you?'

'No.'

'Good. It's five hundred years old, from the Nerozbitny Dynasty. The only one of its kind.'

Miroslav didn't know how to respond to that information.

King Drakomor was busy at his desk, cleaning a necklace with a tiny brush. He was wearing a single glass lens, so that, when he turned to Miroslav, it was with a blinking, oversized eye.

He didn't look like his nephew. His nose was smaller, straighter. He was fair-skinned with grey, close-set eyes, and he wore his hair parted to the side, as was the fashion.

Miroslav sometimes wondered if his uncle would love him more if they looked alike.

'Why are you here?' said the king, putting down the necklace. Miroslav's heart beat fast in his chest. What if the old servant, Yeedarsh, had got here first? What if he'd told Miroslav's uncle to send the girls to the dungeons?

'Out with it,' said the king, and he drummed his fingers on the table so his rings tapped against each other.

'You know how I don't have a tutor at the moment,' said Miroslav.

'How could I forget? Yeedarsh never shuts up about it.'

'Well, I was wondering if, in the meantime, perhaps I might have some other children to play with?'

The king raised an eyebrow, sending the glass lens tumbling to the desk. 'What other children?' he said.

'Oh, just a few friends.'

'You don't have any friends.' The king didn't say this unkindly, but in a matter-of-fact way. Still, Miroslav flinched.

'They're just a couple of peasants I met when I was visiting the market,' he said. 'No one important.'

'Peasants? I don't want them stealing my collection,' said the king. 'And I don't want you picking up their dirty habits.'

'I won't.'

'And I certainly don't want you getting in my way. I'm expecting some guests of my own. I can't have a load of children running around.'

'You won't see us, I promise. You won't even know we're here.'

'Hm.' The king stroked his moustache.

'Please, Uncle,' said Miroslav.

King Drakomor put the glass lens back in his eye and continued to polish the necklace. He didn't look up as he spoke: 'All right, boy. You can keep them. But, if I so much as *smell* a child over the next few days, your little friends will be thrown out after dark, to be killed by the skret. Do we understand each other?'

Before Miroslav could answer, the king jumped up. 'Damn it!' he shouted, climbing on to the desk. 'It's one of those moths – the ones that eat cloth.' The king swatted the air above his head. 'If that thing has got at my silk, there'll be hell to pay!'

A pale purple moth fluttered above him, just out of reach. 'Quick, boy, go and fetch a servant!' cried the king. 'Tell them to bring a net!' The moth flapped away, circled the giant orange stone and settled on the five-hundred-year-old vase. Miroslav followed it.

'Kill that moth!' shouted the king. Miroslav could hear his uncle scrambling down from the table.

He approached the vase cautiously. The moth was beautiful, with wings like faded peacock feathers. His uncle was advancing at speed. 'Move out of the way!' cried the king.

Miroslav pounced. He caught the insect in his cupped hands and hopped aside. His uncle came careering towards him, tripped over a stuffed lynx and – for a moment – was suspended in mid-air, before he flew towards the vase.

There was a terrible crash followed by a howl. The guards dashed in and Miroslav dashed out. He ran to the nearest window and released his prisoner. The moth fluttered away, leaving spots of silvery dust on his palms.

CHAPTER 17

The evening began like clockwork. The sun slipped down and, as if connected to it by invisible pulleys, the crescent moon swung into position. It was the kind of dusk where even a passing moth sounds mechanical – with the soft whirring of wind-up wings.

The stars turned on, the city lights turned out and, at the top of the second tallest tower, the stage was set. A long table had been erected. It was piled high with tempting delicacies: candied orange peel, airy pastries filled with lemon curd and pistachio truffles. The boy had lit the candles again and the room was ablaze with light.

Servants, balancing a dish in either hand, careered past each other, with all the pace and poise of prima ballerinas. There were too many of them for the space, but somehow they managed their movements without touching each other. Conducting the performance, standing on a chair so his gestures could be seen, was the boy.

Imogen entered the room and looked about in amazement. Marie stared too, her eyes like saucers. The boy clapped his hands and the dance came to an abrupt end. 'Please,' he said, hopping down from his chair. 'Have a seat.' Chairs were pulled back. Napkins were placed on laps.

The only diners seemed to be Imogen, Marie and the boy. He'd changed his outfit for the occasion, and was now sporting a blue tunic covered in gold stars. His boots had pointy toes and flared out at the top, where they almost touched his knees.

'Sparkling wine, madam?' asked a servant with a curled moustache.

'Er, no thank you,' said Imogen, wrinkling her nose.

'Perhaps some Parlavar?' The servant brandished a bottle of pink liquid. Imogen shook her head.

'Red Ramposhka?'

'I'm eleven,' said Imogen. 'I normally drink lemonade.'

The servant straightened up. 'Hmm, *limon-eeeed*. I'm afraid we don't have that vintage.'

There was a lot of cutlery. Five knives, six forks and three spoons. Imogen caught sight of her warped face in a dessertspoon. What on earth, she wondered, was she supposed to do with all this?

A chain of servants passed dishes up and down the spiral staircase – taking away the empty plates and bringing up more food. During one course, a violinist played and Marie clapped along, even though it wasn't the right kind of music for that.

At the end of the third course, Imogen turned to the boy. 'Isn't it strange?' she said. 'We're all here, eating together, but we haven't even been properly introduced.'

'What do you want to know?'

'Your name would be a good start.'

The boy cleared his throat. 'I'm Prince Miroslav Yaromeer Drahomeer Krishnov, Lord of the City of Yaroslav, Overseer of the Mountain Realms and Guardian of the Kolsaney Forests.'

'And what do people call you?' said Imogen.

'Your Highness.'

'No, I mean what do your friends call you?'

The boy looked uncomfortable. 'Your Royal Highness?'

'I don't believe you,' said Imogen.

'You can call me Prince Miroslav, son of Vadik the Valiant . . . or Miro. That's the name my mother used.'

'Miro,' said Marie. 'That's a nice name.'

They tucked into the fourth course: honey-roast pig and steaming, buttered veg. Imogen attacked it with a soup spoon. Marie tried the fish knife.

'Don't you want to know our names?' asked Imogen. Then, not bothering to wait for an answer, she said, 'I'm Imogen Clarke and she's Marie Clarke. We're sisters.'

'Sisters. I se—'

Suddenly the conversation was interrupted by a terrible scream. The girls dashed to the nearest window. 'It's the monsters again!' said Marie. 'It sounded like it came from over there.' She pointed to the city outskirts.

Miro helped himself to mint tea and waited for his guests to return to their seats.

Imogen peered at him. 'You don't seem very concerned.'

He shrugged. 'It's normal.'

'What *are* they?' asked Marie.

'The skret,' said the boy.

'Skretch?'

'Well, you certainly can't be from the forests if you've never heard of skret.'

'We're not really from the forests,' said Marie. 'Please ... tell us about the monsters.'

'The skret are nocturnal mountain creatures,' said Miro. 'They're not much bigger than you or me, but they have bald heads like old men and they can see in the dark. Their teeth are sharp and their hands are clawed. Sometimes they walk like humans and sometimes they crawl like spiders. They come down from the mountains at dusk, running through the city and killing anything they find. If you don't have skret where you're from, you're lucky.' He took a sip of his tea. He was clearly enjoying having an audience.

'Was it skret that were chasing us last night?' asked Imogen.

Miro nodded.

'And they would have eaten us if they'd caught us?'

'No, no,' said the boy.

'That's a relief!' said Imogen, remembering how afraid she'd been. 'They'd kill you all right – make a nice mess of your body.'

'Oh.'

'But I was joking when I said they ate people.'

Hilarious, thought Imogen.

'Can't you stop them from getting into the city?' asked Marie.

'My uncle tries. He's the king, you see. He has the guards shut the city gates at nightfall. And he told everyone to put skret bones out, to show the monsters what happens if they keep coming here . . . but none of it seems to work. That's why we ring the bells: to warn everyone that the skret are on their way. Of course, none of this happened when my parents were about. The skret weren't a problem back then . . .'

Imogen didn't speak. She was thinking about the little skulls, with the triangular teeth, that decorated the houses.

'But we're safe up here,' said the prince, signalling to the servants to clear away the plates.

'Shouldn't we have the lights out? Like other people do?'

asked Marie, looking around at the candles.

'Oh no. The skret can't get into the castle, let alone all the way up my tower. They aren't smart or big enough. Their brains are only a third the size of a human brain.'

'Sometimes,' said Marie, 'even little things can be quite fierce.'

'Besides,' said the boy, 'I've got weapons. I'd have no problem fighting off a few monsters.'

Imogen blinked at him. She thought that highly unlikely.

'Where are your parents?' she asked. 'You said things were different when they were about.'

'Oh. Yes. They're with the stars now . . . I don't think we need to . . .' Miro ran his fingers through his thick curly hair.

There was a pause.

'Would you like some tea?' He filled up their cups. 'I tried to organise a dancing bear for tonight – one of the small ones – but apparently they can't catch them any more. There's a dancing bear shortage.' He snorted with laughter. Imogen didn't get the joke.

'So how did you come to be running from skret through my city?' he asked. 'If you're not peasants, and you're not from the forests, where *are* you from?'

'Ah,' said Imogen. 'Well, that's kind of complicated.'

CHAPTER 18

As they drank mint tea, Imogen told the prince about her journey through the Haberdash Gardens. She didn't mention the shadow moth. She didn't feel like sharing *all* of her story with Miro and her sister. Not just yet.

Marie kept interrupting, but she got things mixed up so Imogen had to tell her to be quiet. When Imogen got to the part about the door in the tree, Marie piped up again. She made it sound as though she had helped find it. Imogen lost no time putting things straight: 'Marie just followed me. She's always copying my ideas.'

'Am not.'

'Are too.'

'I want to hear the rest of the story,' said Miro, so Imogen kept going.

She finished at the moment when she and Marie entered the city. The prince asked, 'What about the bit where I rescued you? You haven't told that part.'

'Well, you know what happened then. I don't need to tell you,' said Imogen.

'I should like to hear it all the same.'

'Don't be ridiculous. I'm not telling you a story about yourself.'

'I am the prince and I want to hear it.'

Imogen rolled her eyes. 'Fine. Marie, you can tell this bit.'

Marie finished the story, telling it with too many frilly words and too favourable a portrayal of the prince.

'Anyway,' cut in Imogen, 'the point is we need to get home.'

Two pairs of eyes turned to Miro. 'I have to admit,' he said, 'I've never heard of this garden kingdom or the queen who rules it.'

'She's not a queen,' said Imogen. 'She's just Mrs Haberdash.'

'I've certainly never heard of anyone putting a door in a tree. The people where you come from must be very odd.'

'Are you going to help us get home?' said Imogen. 'Because, if you're not, we might as well leave now.' She pushed back her chair to show she meant business.

'Right after we've finished pudding,' added Marie.

Miro started fiddling with his rings. Tonight he had several stacked on his index fingers and a big one on each thumb. 'I thought I was doing you a favour,' he muttered. 'I rescued you from the skret and I let you stay for dinner, even though you're peasants.'

'Stop turning your rings,' said Imogen. 'It's driving me mad. We're not peasants and I'm sure we can find the door on our own if we have to. I just thought, what with you being a prince and all, you'd be able to do *something*. I thought you'd at least have a servant who could make the door open. It's not as if we're asking you to slay a dragon.'

That hit the mark. The prince's face flushed. 'My ancestors killed this kingdom's last dragon.'

'That's a shame,' said Imogen.

Silence.

'Okay,' said the boy. 'I'll help you. In fact, I'll make a pact.' He rummaged through an old chest and pulled out a dagger. Marie gave a squeak.

'Don't worry,' said Miro. 'I only need one drop.'

'One drop of what?' said Marie.

'Your blood, of course.'

'My *blood*?'

'Not just yours – everyone has to give a bit. That's how we seal the pact.'

'Can't we just shake hands?' said Imogen.

'Or cross our hearts?' said Marie.

'I'll go first,' said Miro.

The three children stood together underneath the old clock with the sleeping face. Miro held up his left thumb for the girls to see, like a magician about to do a trick. In his right hand, the blade glinted. He touched the soft pad of his thumb with the tip. 'I promise to do everything

within my powers to help these two peasa—'

'—Imogen and Marie.'

'—To help *Imogen and Marie* get home.' He looked at them, seeking approval. Imogen nodded.

The blade was sharp. A little pressure and it pierced his skin, bringing up a ruby-red drop of blood. He turned to hide his face, but it was too late; Imogen had seen him wince. He held out the dagger. 'Now you.'

'What am I supposed to be promising?' she asked.

'To be my loyal subjects,' said Miro.

Imogen didn't take the dagger. 'Loyal subjects? What does that even mean?'

'You know . . . you go where I go. Have dinner with me and things.'

'What things?' she demanded.

'Go fishing. Play in the gardens. Whatever I fancy,' said the prince.

Imogen snorted. 'You mean be your friends? You want us to promise to be your friends?'

'Call it what you will.'

'You must be joking,' she said, but the prince's expression was deadly serious. He offered her the dagger again.

'Just until we go home?' she said. 'You know we're not staying long?'

'Oh yes,' said the prince. 'Just until you go home.'

Imogen took the dagger. 'This is absurd.' She placed the blade on her thumb. 'Okay, I promise to hang around with Miro, to be his loyal . . . friend. Just until we go home.'

'Great, now do the—'

'I know, I know.' Imogen pricked her skin and passed the dagger to Marie.

'I won't do it,' said Marie.

'You will too,' said Imogen.

'Why? Why should I have to?'

'Because, Marie, if you don't do it, you haven't earned your ticket home.'

'It doesn't need two of us, does it?' said Marie and she turned to Miro with a pleading expression.

'One of you is probably enough,' said the prince.

'Oh, stop being such a baby,' said Imogen and she grabbed Marie's wrist. 'Repeat after me: I promise . . .'

'Imogen!' cried Marie.

'Don't wriggle. I'm only drawing a bit of blood, not cutting off your hand.'

'You're hurting me!'

'Come on,' said Miro. 'I think two of us is enough.'

'Oh, fine. Be a baby.' Imogen released Marie's wrist.

Imogen and Miro pressed their thumbs together. 'That's it,' said Miro. 'The pact is sealed.'

As they stepped apart, the clock behind them sprang

into motion. The hands spun, cogs whizzed and mechanical stars flew about. It was going too fast: chiming for midnight, then midday, skipping through days in seconds.

Suddenly it all stopped, or rather it started behaving like a normal clock. The hands ticked along as if they had never been doing anything different.

This time, as the clock reached midnight, the little hatch opened and a carving of two girls trundled out. The smaller one had long wavy hair in a ponytail. The taller one had short straight hair.

The miniature girls curtseyed, turned a full circle and went back into the clock. The hatch closed behind them.

CHAPTER 19

Imogen lay in the big bed at the top of the second tallest tower. Her thumb had stopped bleeding and, with her belly full of food, she fell asleep in no time. But, as so often happens when you're not sleeping in your own bed, Imogen slept fitfully, and her dreams were strange and frightening.

She was back at home. She could hear her mum in the bathroom, making crying sounds. Imogen opened the door and Mum was sitting in the bath, fully dressed. She hadn't run the water yet. She was just staring at the taps, as if stuck on the question of whether to turn them on.

This was what Mum had done in real life when Ross, an old boyfriend, dumped her, but that was years ago. Imogen knelt by the bath and peeped over the side. Mum's make-up was smeared down her cheeks.

'Is it Mark?' said Imogen. 'Did you have a fight?'

Mum looked confused.

'You know, your friend that you went to the theatre with?'

The bathroom started filling with water. It lapped against Imogen's legs, but she didn't move.

'I know Mark,' said Mum, 'but who are you?'

'It's me . . . it's Imogen.' The water in the bathroom crept up to her waist.

'How did you get into the house?'

'Come on, Mum. We've only been gone one night—'

'Where's Mark?' said Mum in a shrill voice.

Imogen stood up as the water flowed into the bath, making Mum's clothes balloon. 'You have to get up,' said Imogen, holding out her hand. 'The room's going under.'

But Mum just closed her eyes as the water sloshed across her face. She was gripping on to the bath with both hands.

The water lifted Imogen off the floor and she began to panic. She swam back to Mum and shook her by the shoulder. Mum opened her eyes and smiled. 'It's okay,' she mouthed.

'No, it's not!' cried Imogen in a voice full of bubbles.

She came up for air. The water had nearly reached the ceiling. Why wouldn't Mum listen? How could she have forgotten them already?

Then she heard a strange sound . . . bells. There were bells in the bathroom.

Imogen opened her eyes, coming to the surface for a second time. She was lying in a four-poster bed. Her mum was nowhere to be seen. The bells of Yaroslav were ringing for dawn and it was raining.

Imogen lay still until the last bell tolled. It was just a dream. Of course Mum knew who she was. She was probably looking for them right this minute. She'd never forget her girls. *Would she?*

Imogen turned over to see Marie asleep next to her. Miro was curled up at the foot of the bed like an overindulged poodle. He opened his eyes as his clock began to chime. A new figure came out of the hatch. It was a hunter. He shot an imaginary arrow from his tiny bow before disappearing back inside the clock.

Miro yawned and said:

'You cannot trust a hunter,
for you never really know
if it's just the deer he's after,
with his arrows and his bow.'

'What's that?' asked Imogen.

'Just an old rhyme,' said Miro. Suddenly, he sat bolt upright. 'Huntsman. Now there's a thought! We could get Blazen Bilbetz to help find the door in the forests.'

'Who's Blar-zen?'

Miro glanced at Imogen with disbelief. 'You don't know Blazen Bilbetz? He's only the best hunter in Yaroslav. I bet he'd be able to find your door in no time, and I bet he'd kick it open. After all, the forests are his hunting grounds. Let's go and ask him. Wake Marie.'

Imogen glanced at her sister. She looked so peaceful, like a sleeping baby. 'Let's go without Marie. She'll only slow us down.'

'Won't she be sorry to be left behind?'

'Probably, but she's no good on adventures. We'll come back for her in a few hours – when it's all sorted.'

If only it had been that easy. It would be many hours before Imogen and Miro returned.

CHAPTER 20

That same day, in a big house by the river, a young woman called Anneshka Mazanar received a very important invitation. She opened the front door to a pot-bellied man. He was wearing the crimson uniform of the Royal Guards and he'd been drenched by the rain.

He stared at Anneshka with his mouth slightly open, as if he'd slipped into a trance. Anneshka was used to people gawping at her and she didn't really mind. In fact, she liked it. Her beauty was the talk of Yaroslav. They said that she'd been drawn, not born. They said that her heart-shaped face was perfect, with her violet eyes, pouty mouth and cascade of golden hair.

'Can I help you?' she asked.

The Royal Guard snapped back to life, brushing water from the tip of his nose. 'Yes, miss, sorry, miss. I've got a letter for your father. Will you see that he gets it?'

'Of course,' said Anneshka, giving the guard one of her best smiles before snatching the letter and running to her room at the top of the house.

Her fingers trembled as she broke the royal seal. It was as she had hoped – it was an invitation from the king. The letter said that her parents were to visit the castle, along with their 'charming' daughter. Anneshka's heart fluttered.

She looked out of her bedroom window, towards Castle Yaroslav. There was no way her parents were coming with her. No way in hell. It was *her* that the king wanted to see and her parents had only been invited for the sake of decency.

She read the letter again. The king said that it had been a 'delight' to meet her at the royal ball. Anneshka remembered it well. During her first dance with King Drakomor, she'd seen how handsome he was, with grey eyes and an elegant moustache.

During their second dance, she'd seen something else; something that other people missed. She'd seen that he wanted to be rescued. After that, winning his heart had been easy.

Although the ball had been Anneshka's first encounter with the king, she'd had her mind's eye on him for years. She'd known that she would be the queen of Yaroslav ever since she was seven. Anneshka's mother had been plaiting her hair when she first told her the story.

'The stars have great things in store for you,' said her mother.

'How do you know?' said little Anneshka. Her mother had done her hair too tight and it hurt.

'Hold still and I'll tell you. The night that you were born, I was visited by the forest witch – the one they call Ochi. She was cast out of the city long ago and your father didn't want her in the house, but I knew why she'd come. I told him to let her enter. The witch swaddled you and gave me something for the pain. Then she offered to read the stars.'

'For me?' said Anneshka. She wanted to turn round and look at her mother to see if she was telling the truth, but her mother pulled on her plait. Anneshka cried out.

'I said hold still!'

'Sorry, Mother . . . But what did the stars say?'

'Ochi read your stars and I paid her well. Too well, some might say. When she was done with her stargazing, the witch came back to my bed and whispered in my ear. She said you would be a great queen.'

'A great queen of where?' said Anneshka.

'Of Yaroslav, of course.'

'But how will it happen? I'm not a princess . . .'

'No,' agreed her mother. 'Your father's not even the wealthiest man on this street, but I've spoken to him and it's agreed. You will want for nothing. When fate comes calling, you'll be ready.'

Anneshka's mother gave her hair another twist. 'There. You can move now. Your hair is done.'

It wasn't until King Drakomor was crowned, and Anneshka came of age, that she saw her route to the throne. It was so obvious, as if that too had been written in the stars. King Drakomor did not have a wife.

Anneshka sat down at her writing desk to pen her reply to the king. She stroked her chin with the tip of the quill.

'Now,' she whispered, 'how does Father normally begin his letters . . .?'

CHAPTER 21

Imogen and Miro set out to find Blazen Bilbetz. Miro said they'd know the hunter when they saw him. He was built like a bear, the tallest man in Yaroslav, and clothed in the furs of the beasts that he'd killed.

Imogen borrowed a cloak to wear over her clothes and keep out the rain. Water washed off roofs and splashed down cobbled streets, forming little streams at the side of the road. Some people had shoved skret skulls on the ends of their gutters, like home-made gargoyles. Water rushed out through their jaws.

Despite the cloak, Imogen's fingers were soon numb and her shoes wet through. As the afternoon faded, she began to wonder if Blazen was a figment of the prince's imagination. She'd lost count of how many inns they'd visited, but there was no sign of the man.

Miro seemed to have an endless supply of stories. Blazen was up against some impossible task, Blazen almost died, Blazen triumphed and was called a hero. It was the same plot. Every single time.

'It's going to get dark soon,' said the prince. 'This will have to be the last inn for today.' Imogen peeped through the grubby window of the Hounyarch. Candlelight was just about visible on the other side.

'Fine by me,' she said.

Inside the inn it smelled of warm bodies and beer. Imogen ducked under elbows and squeezed between bellies. The top of the bar was level with her eyeballs. To her left, frothy ale sloshed and glasses clinked. To her right, money changed hands between quick-fingered card players. Above, the heads of badly stuffed animals looked on: a fox with one glass eye bigger than the other, a pigeon with a very long neck and a bear with a strangely human expression.

'Excuse me,' said Miro, standing on tiptoes. The barmaid didn't respond. She was shouting at an old man who was face down on the bar.

What an odd place to sleep, thought Imogen.

'This is useless,' said Miro. 'They're all drunk.'

'You did say he might be out hunting . . .' said Imogen.

'But it's getting late. Even the bravest hunter returns from the Kolsaney Forests before dark.'

'And is he? The bravest hunter, I mean? Are you sure it's not just stories?'

'Oh yes. They've made statues of him. And he's in all

the songs: Blazen Bilbetz knows no fear, Blazen makes the ladies swoon, Blazen Bilbetz saves the day, Blazen brings the monster's ruin.'

Miro was interrupted by the barmaid. She was shouting at him. No – at something behind him. Imogen turned to see a gigantic, bearded man climb on to a table. In one hand, he carried a sack with pipes hanging off it. In the other, he brandished a beer. He roared as he mounted his stage. The men round the table cheered. The barmaid screamed, 'Get down!'

The man took a gulp of his drink and put his lips to the instrument's mouthpiece. The sack inflated. The sound that followed was like nothing Imogen had ever heard. A low, loud honk. A cow with a megaphone. There was no sensible way to describe it.

Every head turned and, after that first blast, the man was off: fingers running up and down the pipes, elbow squeezing the sack, filling the room with a wild melody and uneven rhythm. He alternated between singing, blowing into the instrument and drinking. Sometimes he got the three mixed up and beer got into the mouthpiece. But his audience didn't mind – they loved it and they loved him. They were stamping their feet and singing along.

Imogen turned to Miro. He was grinning. 'What are you so happy about?' she demanded.

'That,' he shouted over the noise, 'is our man!'

'Him?'

Miro nodded.

'With the bagpipes?' asked Imogen.

'Zpevnakrava,' corrected Miro.

'Huh?'

The city bells tolled, hardly audible over the music. 'Did you hear that?' said Imogen. 'We need to leave!'

But Miro wasn't listening. He was working his way closer to Blazen.

Imogen looked at the door. There were a lot of bodies between her and the exit. Even worse, instead of leaving, people were battening down the hatches. Shutters closed. Fire out. Door bolted.

One song swung into the next. The piper's cheeks puffed in and out, turning his face a ferocious shade of red. Why wasn't Miro doing something to get the man's attention?

The bells stopped tolling. The skret were in Yaroslav.

Imogen groaned. She was stuck in the Hounyarch for the night.

CHAPTER 22

Someone splashed beer on the back of Imogen's neck. Cold foam ran down her spine and suddenly she'd had enough. Enough trawling round the city in the rain. Enough waiting while grown-ups did stupid grown-up things. She wasn't here for the music. She wasn't here to have a good time. She was *here* because Miro had promised that Blazen Bilbetz would help her get home.

She walked up to Miro and gave him a jab in the ribs. 'Aren't you supposed to be asking that man to help us?'

'Yes, yes,' said Miro. 'After the next song.'

But, as one song ended and another began, Miro just clapped along.

Imogen decided to take matters into her own hands. She reached up to the table and prodded the giant man's leg. He didn't react. She grabbed his calf and gave it a shake. He looked down and flicked his foot, as though he'd stepped in something nasty, sending her tripping backwards.

Things were going to have to step up a notch. There was a knife on the side of the bar. It didn't look razor-sharp, but it would probably do the job. Imogen forced her way through the crowd, grabbed the knife and went back to the hunter.

She climbed on to the table, reached up to the instrument's sack and pierced the skin. It deflated at speed, making a terrible wheezing sound. Beer trickled out of the hole. The people closest covered their ears and howled.

Blazen Bilbetz stopped blowing into the mouthpiece and looked down a pipe. 'That's funny,' he boomed. 'It's never done that before.' Then he saw Imogen crouched by his feet. 'What do you think you're doing?'

'I . . . I wanted to get your attention,' said Imogen, suddenly feeling very small.

'Well, you've got it all right. I'll skin you alive, you little hovinko!'

Enormous hands lifted Imogen up by her arms. She wriggled and kicked, but the giant's grip only tightened. 'Put me down!' she shouted.

'What do you think?' said the man, giving her a shake that made her ribcage rattle. 'Shall we have her stuffed and mounted on the wall?' The crowd laughed. 'Do you know who I am, peasant? Do you know whose zpevnakrava you've vandalised?' His eyes, wide and bloodshot, didn't look to Imogen for the answer, but to his fans below.

'I am the man that killed one hundred bears, seduced the

Queen of Mikuluka, rode across the Nameless Mountains wearing nothing but a squirrel skin. Yes, it's all true.' He paused for dramatic effect.

'It was *I* who slayed Zlo the Wolf with my bare hands. *I* who single-handedly protected the Pochybovaci Cathedral and its nuns from the excesses of five hundred marauding Yezdetz. Why . . . I've even delivered a baby behind that bar. I cut the cord with my teeth and wrapped the child in a hanky.'

'Get on with it!' – a heckler.

'*I* am Blazen Bilbetz,' said the giant as he drew himself up to his full height. 'Who are *you* to come here and interrupt my merrymaking?' He breathed beer into Imogen's face, but didn't wait for her to answer. 'Whoever you are, you're going to have to pay for what you've broken.'

'Then you owe me for all the tankards you've thrown!' – the barmaid.

Blazen rolled his eyes. 'Cough up, girlie,' he said to Imogen. 'My zpevnakrava is worth a fair bit.'

Imogen felt like all the air was being squeezed out of her. 'I haven't got any money,' she gasped.

'That's a shame, isn't it!' cried the giant. 'Perhaps you think someone else should pay for your mistakes?'

'I'll pay!' – Miro this time.

'Who said that?' Blazen looked around.

'Down here. I'll give you your money, but first put her down.'

'Oh, look, a knight in shining armour.' Blazen chuckled.

'Me? I thought you were supposed to be the hero,' said Miro. 'That's what everyone says. Blazen the Brave. Blazen the beast-killer. But look at you! You're nothing but a big bully.'

The room fell silent.

'You can't pay,' said Blazen, sounding a little less sure of himself. 'You haven't got twenty crowns. You haven't even got two crowns!'

But the crowd had turned. 'That's enough, Blazen!' someone yelled from the back of the room.

'You've had your fun,' said another. Faces turned back to the bar and the normal hum of talk resumed.

'All right,' said Blazen to Miro. 'Twenty-five crowns and you've got yourself a deal.'

'Done,' said Miro.

Blazen released Imogen, tossed his punctured zpevnakrava aside and climbed down from the table. He turned to Miro with greedy eyes. 'Right, hand it over.'

'I've got another idea,' said Miro. 'How do you fancy earning *one hundred* crowns?'

'You haven't got that kind of money,' said the hunter, suspicious.

Miro placed a small bag on the table. Blazen seemed to

recognise the sound. The soft tinkle of gold on gold.

'You have my attention,' he said slowly.

Imogen sat at the edge of the table, rubbing her sore arms. 'We want you to take us into the forest,' she said.

'Is that so?' Blazen's eyes were still fixed on the bag.

'We're looking for a door in a tree.'

'A door to where?' said the giant.

Imogen took a deep breath. 'A door to another world.'

'There's no such thing,' said Blazen.

'One hundred crowns says you're wrong,' said Miro, pushing the bag across the table.

Blazen's head stayed still, but his eyes followed the money. 'That's a lot of ground to cover, searching for something that doesn't exist. I'd need my men with me.'

'One hundred crowns now and one hundred crowns when it's done,' said the prince.

Blazen held out his shovel-sized hand. Miro shook it.

'We'll start at first light,' said the hunter. 'After the bells have tolled.'

'What are we supposed to do until then?' asked Miro. Blazen grinned, displaying yellow, gold and missing teeth.

'Why, drink, of course!'

And he did. He drank beer, he drank liquor, he drank some cloudy green stuff that smelled like aniseed sweets. He drank with the card players, the barmaid, the inn's cat.

He drank until every surface was strewn with bodies, like the scene after a battle. And then, realising he was the last warrior standing, he allowed himself to sink to the ground. Cradling a half-empty bottle of grog, he closed his eyes.

'How do we wake him?' said Miro.

'I don't know. Give him a pinch,' said Imogen.

The prince did as instructed. 'Well, that didn't work.'

'Harder,' said Imogen.

'You do it,' said Miro.

'Water. Fetch some water. That's how they do it in films.'

'In what?'

'Just try it,' said Imogen.

Splash!

For a few seconds, Blazen fought wildly, thrashing about on the floor, waving his legs and arms like an upturned beetle. 'I'm drowning!' he cried. He smashed his grog bottle and held up the sharp end. 'What do you want, you little hovinko?' It wasn't really a question.

Miro looked down at the giant. 'We want you to do as you promised.' Blazen belched. 'We want you to take us to the Kolsaney Forests.'

'Fine,' said the hunter. 'But first I need my morning beer.'

Imogen had a bad feeling about this.

CHAPTER 23

As the sun began to set that evening, Imogen and Miro returned to the second tallest tower. They were not in good spirits. Miro was two hundred crowns poorer and they were both completely exhausted.

Their search through the forests had been unsuccessful. They'd travelled in the direction that Imogen thought was correct and they'd seen thousands of trees, but not a single door.

Marie was curled up in one of the big seats by the fire. Imogen could see that she'd been crying.

'I thought you'd be back last night,' said Marie. 'I was worried.'

'So did we,' said Imogen, collapsing on the bed. 'We spent the night stuck in an inn, and the day searching the forests. Did you get my note?'

Imogen looked round for the scrap of paper she'd left by the bed. It had been a hastily scribbled message telling Marie not to leave the tower and that they'd be back soon. Marie glared at the fire and Imogen understood. She'd burned it. What a baby.

'Marie, you know I had to leave you behind. You would have been afraid in the forests.'

'I would not!' said Marie, her voice shrill.

'You would too,' said Imogen. She removed her cloak and let it fall off the edge of the bed. 'Anyway, we didn't find the door. It was a wasted journey.'

'But it must be there *somewhere*,' said Marie. 'Perhaps we should go back and look for it tomorrow.'

'There's no point,' said Miro. 'If Blazen Bilbetz can't hunt it down, there's no way we'd spot it on our own. It's like the door doesn't want to be found.'

Over the next few days, Imogen tried everything she could think of to get home. She asked Miro if she could send her mum a letter, but there was no postal service and Imogen didn't know how a postman would find the door in the tree.

She asked about sending a text, but there were no phones. She'd have had her own if Mum had got her one for her birthday, but Mum was always going on about phones not being good for you.

Miro hadn't even heard of the internet. He said he didn't believe in magic. The grown-ups Imogen spoke to had never heard of a door in a tree. They didn't believe in magic either.

At night, when Imogen was lying in the four-poster bed, her worry creatures began to reappear. They waited until

Miro and Marie had drifted off, then they'd crawl across the covers and hold Imogen's eyes open. They hissed bad thoughts in her ears. *You'll never make it home. Your mum doesn't even want you back.*

'What do you expect me to do?' Imogen whispered. 'I've tried everything I can!'

She shook the quilt, throwing the worry creatures to the floor. If she was lucky, they'd creep away after that, slinking off into the darkness. If she was unlucky, it could be hours before they'd let her sleep.

In the morning, Imogen would check under the quilt. No worry creatures there. She'd peep behind the curtains. No worry creatures there either.

Looking out of the window at the bright blue sky and the cheerful red roofs of Yaroslav, Imogen felt sure that everything would be okay. The worry creatures were wrong. She'd find her way home eventually.

In the meantime, why shouldn't she have a little fun? After all, this was a place with no school, no chores and no bossy grown-ups.

CHAPTER 24

Anneshka's visit to Castle Yaroslav was going well. King Drakomor expressed his sadness that her parents weren't able to join them, but Anneshka could see that he was secretly glad to have her all to himself.

The king gave her a tour of the castle, pointing out the favourite bits of his collection. Yeedarsh, the old servant, followed them from room to room. He poured them mead and fetched them apricot-filled doughnuts, but Anneshka didn't like his presence. She could feel his eyes on her, even when he was supposed to be stoking the fire. He was too sharp, too observant.

On the third day of her visit, the king sent Yeedarsh away and showed Anneshka into his study. He helped her squeeze past an enormous orange jewel and held her hand as she stepped daintily over a row of exotic lizard eggs. When she got her skirts caught on the teeth of a stuffed wildcat, King Drakomor bent down to set her free.

In the middle of the study there was a desk. Behind the desk there were bookshelves filled with precious stones.

They glinted and glimmered in the low light.

'What do you think?' said the king.

'It's magnificent,' said Anneshka. 'Really, I've never seen anything like it.'

'I brought you here because I want to speak in private.'

Anneshka kept her face still. This was it. Just as the stars had promised.

'Since we first met . . .' King Drakomor groped for the right words. 'From the very first moment . . .' He held on to the corner of the desk to steady himself.

'Go on,' said Anneshka.

'I intend to make you my wife,' he blurted.

Anneshka moved a hand to her mouth. 'Your Majesty!' She hoped she sounded sufficiently surprised. 'Your Majesty, I had no idea . . .'

'Of course, I had intended to firm things up with your father first—'

'He'll be delighted,' she said, rushing forward and taking the king's hand. 'And so am I.'

The king smiled and Anneshka could see her outline reflected in his eyes.

He took a black box out of a drawer in the desk. 'This used to belong to my brother,' he said, removing a gold ring from the box. 'And this one belonged to his wife.' He showed her a smaller ring. 'I would like them to become ours – from one king and queen to the next.'

'They're lovely,' said Anneshka.

'I'll send them off to be polished, get them looking as good as new. We'll need to think carefully about how we make the announcement. Once we've told the people, they'll expect the wedding within a matter of days and I would prefer it if we could take our time ... We'll need to speak to the prince when we're ready.'

'The prince?' She couldn't quite keep the surprise out of her voice.

'Miroslav, my brother's son.'

'Oh ... I assumed that you'd sent him away.'

'No. He's somewhere in the castle with his friends ... Peasants, I gather. The boy's running quite wild.'

Anneshka would have to choose her words carefully. 'And what does he mean for our future,' she asked, 'if we *are* to get married?'

'What do you mean?' The king looked confused. 'You don't have to mother him, not if you don't want to ... although it might do him some good.'

'Never mind, láska. That's not what I meant, but there's no rush to deal with the boy. Especially if we're not announcing the wedding yet. I just wanted to get you thinking ... to set the cogs in motion as it were.'

CHAPTER 25

Time flew by. At least that was what the girls would have said if someone had asked. The truth was Imogen and Marie had stopped thinking about time altogether. They no longer knew how many days had passed since they'd walked into the Haberdash Gardens. They didn't even know what day of the week it was.

When they were out of sight of Miro's clock, time was measured by hunger and rounds of hide-and-seek. Evening bells meant go inside. The first star meant dinner. Bedtime was a surprise every night. One minute they'd be jumping on the bed; the next someone had curled up in it.

There was only one rule: if you heard the king coming, you had to hide.

The girls started dressing like they lived in Yaroslav. They wore Miro's clothes: midnight-blue tunics with gold stars, shirts with billowing sleeves, embroidered jackets lined with fur and boots with fluffy tops. Most of it was too big for Marie so Imogen helped her to roll up the sleeves and legs.

Sometimes the girls talked about home. They talked about it as if it was a place where they used to go on holiday and hoped to return to next summer. They talked about how Grandma cheated at cards and how Mum's cheesy pasta parcels would melt in your mouth. But there was one thing they didn't talk about. There was a gap among all of those words.

'Why don't you ever talk about your father?' said Miro. The girls were warming their toes by the fire. Miro sat nearby, folding bits of scrap paper into stars.

'Because there's nothing to say,' replied Imogen. 'We don't have a father.'

'Do you mean he's dead?'

Imogen kept her eyes on the flames. 'No,' she said. 'I don't think so.'

'We don't know who he is,' said Marie. 'Sometimes Mum has boyfriends, but we never like them.'

'Boyfriends?' Miro stopped folding the paper. 'Like me?'

'No, nothing like you,' said Imogen.

Miro looked sad and she couldn't think why.

'A boyfriend is a man you might marry,' said Marie. 'Not a boy who is your friend.'

'Of course,' said Miro, brightening. 'I knew that.'

He picked up one of his paper stars and threw it into the fire. The flames hissed and the star was gone.

'Perhaps your father is the master of a big house,' he said. 'Perhaps your mother has been sworn to secrecy.'

'What are you on about?' said Imogen, looking at the prince through narrowed eyes.

'Yeedarsh told me about that kind of thing. Sometimes the serving girl is sent beyond the mountains to have the baby.'

'Our mother is not a serving girl!' cried Imogen. 'She just didn't like Dad enough to keep him. Or perhaps he didn't like us ... I don't know. We don't need a dad.'

Miro picked up the rest of the paper stars. 'Me neither,' he said, releasing the stars into the fire. 'I don't need anyone.'

The fire crackled louder. There must have been some ink on the paper because the flames licked blue and green.

'You know ... Miro ... you never told us what happened to your parents,' said Marie.

'I did,' said the prince, sounding a little defensive. 'I told you they're with the stars.'

'Does that mean ...' Marie hesitated.

'Does that mean they're dead?' said Imogen, cutting to the chase.

Miro picked up another handful of scrap paper. He folded the first piece into a star before he spoke. 'My father was the best king Yaroslav has ever known,' he said. 'Everyone says so and the Krishnov dynasty has ruled in this valley since the dawn of time. I got my eyes from him.

'My mother was from far away – a princess beyond the mountains. She came here to marry my father and she was beautiful. Everyone says that too. I got my colouring from her.

'Anyway . . . they both died five years ago . . . It was a hunting accident.'

'I'm sorry,' said Marie. 'That must have been horrible.'

'It was. But Uncle looks after me now – not that I need looking after. He's looking after the throne too – until I'm sixteen.'

'That's nice of him,' said Marie.

'Yes,' agreed the prince. 'Yes, it is.'

CHAPTER 26

In the castle garden, the prince introduced his visitors to the velecours. The biggest of these colourful birds was as tall as a horse. The smallest was no larger than a Shetland pony. After they'd been tamed, the velecours were so docile that you could climb on to their backs and race them. And that was just what the children did.

The only problem was the birds were too stupid to be trained, making them impossible to steer. Riders had to hold on to their velecour's neck and hope for the best. This was tricky because they moved as though they'd been fired from a faulty cannon – fast and in an unexpected direction. Imogen had so far been thrown into a well, a bush and a wall. Surprisingly, the bush had been the most painful (thorns).

'They don't look like they can fly,' said Imogen, sliding off the back of her favourite bird.

'Yes, look, their wings are a funny shape,' said Marie, lifting one up. The velecour it belonged to squawked.

'That's because the feathers have been clipped,' said Miro.

'Why?'

'Because they're ours. We don't want them to fly away.'

'But where do you get them from?' asked Marie.

'The forests. My uncle pays people to catch them. It's no easy job. You should hear them screeching when they first arrive – especially the ones with babies. They make quite a fuss when they're being separated.'

'Why do you separate them?'

'It's easier to tame them individually. And, when they've forgotten about the forest, they get released into different parts of the garden where they make new groups ... just like the old ones, but with different birds.'

'Then are they happy?' asked Marie.

The prince looked puzzled. 'Happy? Who cares! They're only velecours.'

One afternoon, the children were playing outside when Imogen noticed that the giant birds had gathered by the garden wall. They were staring at the gates without blinking.

'What are they doing?' she asked.

'They look like they're waiting for something,' said Marie.

'They are,' said Miro. 'Let's watch.' He darted behind the topiary and beckoned for the girls to follow. There was a hole clipped into the hedge at just the right height for the prince to peep through. Imogen could see when she stood very straight. Marie could see when she stood on a plant pot.

'It's best to be hidden,' whispered Miro. 'The velecours go loopy at feeding time.'

The children watched as two women entered through the garden gates. They were pushing a high-sided wheelbarrow. Imogen couldn't see what it contained, but the velecours started clucking so she guessed it was something they liked.

The taller woman had a tawny-brown face and her hair was tied up in two knots. The shorter woman was actually a girl. She seemed to look to her companion for instructions – or perhaps approval – Imogen wasn't sure which.

'Well, that was a successful hunt,' said the girl.

'That wasn't hunting,' replied the woman. 'It was more like gathering mushrooms.'

'Don't the Royal Guards know you're a huntress?'

The woman scowled. 'They know, but they'd rather see us starve than let us catch our own supper.'

That doesn't make sense, thought Imogen. *Blazen Bilbetz is allowed to hunt . . . He's worshipped for it . . .*

The velecours stamped their feet with impatience.

'At least the birds won't go hungry,' said the woman as she stuck her hand into the wheelbarrow and removed an enormous worm. It looked like it was made from silk – soft and shiny and squirming to be free. The woman threw the worm high and the velecours sprang up to catch it, squawking with excitement. A flash of beaks, a blizzard of claws – and the worm was no more.

The girl and the woman threw grub after grub. Some were as big as marrows. Some were no larger than slugs. The birds swallowed them whole. One worm tried to burrow to safety, but a velecour plucked it from the earth at the last moment. Imogen could have sworn she saw the worm wriggling as it travelled down the bird's throat. Miro smothered a laugh. Marie looked horrified.

Eventually, the feeding frenzy came to an end and the velecours lumbered off, calm as cows. Only a young bird remained. It still had its first winter plumage and it squawked with its beak open wide.

'I think he's still hungry,' said the girl.

'We can't have that, can we?' The woman leaned over the wheelbarrow and removed one last juicy grub. She grinned as she tossed it to the young velecour. The bird trotted off and the girl and the woman slipped out through the gate. The garden was quiet once more.

'Who were those people?' asked Imogen.

Miro shrugged. 'No one important . . .'

But Imogen had a feeling he was wrong. *Important to who?* she wondered.

CHAPTER 27

And so one day slipped into the next. Imogen, Marie and Miro chased each other through the castle, dodging round the king's collection. Some rooms were crammed full of collectables: coral, fossils, scales from the last dragon. These places could only be entered with ninja-like care. The smallest slip, even a sneeze, could end in thousands of crowns' worth of damage.

It wasn't until the children played chess that things started to unravel. There were three chessboards in the library and Miro had them all in use. He was playing against himself.

'So you're the whites and the blacks,' said Imogen, 'all at the same time?'

'No. I'm the whites when I'm standing on this side . . .' He moved round the board. 'And the blacks when I'm standing here.'

'But you always know what your opponent is thinking?'

'Yes.'

'And you always win?'

'I suppose so . . . It takes a while to finish. That game on the end has been going for years, since before my parents—'

'Doesn't sound like much fun,' said Imogen.

'Okay, how about you be the whites? Pick up where I left off,' suggested the prince.

'No, I want to start from the beginning.' Imogen began resetting the board.

'Stop!' shouted Miro, rushing over and grabbing a knight from her hand. 'You're cheating!'

'Cheating? This whole thing is a cheat. I'm not playing if we can't start from scratch.' And, to show she meant it, Imogen continued moving the pawns back to the second row.

'Put that pawn down,' said Miro.

'I thought you wanted to play.'

'This isn't how the game's supposed to go.'

Miro was getting flustered, rushing round the table, trying to move the pieces back to where he had them before. Imogen watched him. His eyes really were too far apart.

'Well, that's the thing about playing with other people,' she said. 'You don't get to control exactly how the game goes.'

Miro glared. Imogen smiled. She'd touched a nerve.

'You promised!' he cried.

'Promised what?'

'To be my friend!'

'Yes, that's right – friend! Not servant.' She flicked over the white king. 'Or don't you know the difference?'

'Put that back – put it back now – before I call the Royal Guards.'

'You don't get to tell me what to do.'

'I think you'll find I do. Put – back – my – king.'

But Imogen did no such thing. She swept her arm across the board, sending all the chess pieces tumbling to the floor. Miro let out a wail. 'Get out!' he screamed.

'Come on, Marie,' said Imogen.

Marie didn't move.

'Marie, we're off. I've had enough.'

Marie shook her head.

'Are you serious?' said Imogen.

'I don't want to go,' said Marie.

'This is ridiculous.'

Imogen went to grab Marie's hand, but Miro stepped between them. 'Don't you get it?' he snarled. 'You don't get to tell her what to do.' His face was centimetres away from Imogen's. She wanted to hit him. She wanted to stamp on his toes. She wanted to do something to make him be sorry and get Marie to behave.

But she couldn't fight them both so instead she turned and left. She marched out of the library, through the castle's main door and across the square. Before long, she was walking through the city's bustling streets.

CHAPTER 28

Imogen stood at a crossroads, not far from the castle. She knocked a row of skret skulls off a wall, enjoying the dry way they cracked on the cobbles. They looked like oversized, smashed eggshells. 'Not so scary now, are you?' she muttered, grinding a bit of bone under her heel.

She hoped the skret were noisy tonight. She hoped Marie was afraid. The way she'd hidden behind Miro . . . it was like they'd been planning it.

But Imogen could make her own plans. She didn't need Marie. She was going to find that door in the tree and she was going to walk back through it. She would feel no guilt when she returned without her sister. Of course, Mum would be upset to begin with, but perhaps after a few days she'd let her have Marie's bedroom.

Imogen didn't pay much attention to where she was going. She didn't notice the way the houses changed; the way, in this part of the city, they seemed to fold in on themselves. She didn't notice the stray dogs or the old man who watched her pass with eyes that were yellow where they should have been white.

It wasn't until a girl ran by, shrieking, barefoot, and about the same height as Marie, that Imogen began to look around. She watched the girl disappear into the crowd.

The smell of sausages wafted from an open window. It reminded her of Saturday trips to the butcher's, when her mum would buy enough to 'feed a pack of wolves'. Mum would growl and Marie would hide behind Imogen, crying, 'Can I be the baby wolf?'

'No, you can't,' said Imogen to her memory-sister.

She reached a small square with a fountain. The fountain was made of stone birds standing on each other's backs to form a pyramid of wings and legs. Some of their heads were missing, but the stone birds were still recognisable as velecours. Water was supposed to spout from the beak of the bird at the top, but there was no water in the fountain today.

In the distance, Imogen heard barking. People looked about to see where the noise was coming from. A woman ushered a group of children inside, shutting the door behind them. Imogen sat on the doorstep, tucking her feet out of the way of passers-by.

The barking got louder and faces appeared at the windows around the square. There was a disturbance in the crowd. It ran down the main street like a spark along a fuse. People shouted and stepped aside. Then, just before the spark hit the square, the crowd parted. A human firework jumped out, rolled across the ground and stood up – all in one fluid movement.

Imogen had never seen someone move like *that* before. The human firework was a thin woman dressed in green, with her hair tied up in two bunches. In one hand, she grasped a dead rabbit. Imogen recognised her at once. It was the woman she'd seen feeding the velecours.

A voice from above shouted, 'Lofkinye, they're coming for you. Better run!'

But it was too late. Dogs hurtled down the main street, all fangs and muscle. The woman turned to leave, but the animals blocked her way. She sprinted to the fountain and climbed up, lifting her ankles out of reach of the dogs' snapping jaws.

A flash of red and the clatter of hooves announced the arrival of the dogs' masters. Imogen stood up on tiptoes to get a better view between the grown-ups.

The two men on horseback wore the crimson jackets and plumed helmets of the Royal Guards, the king's men. One was skinny and one was plump, but other than that they looked very similar. They cantered round the fountain, forcing onlookers to press tighter against the

houses. The woman climbed further up the fountain, rabbit still in hand.

'The game's up,' called the thin guard. 'You know it's illegal for lesni to hunt and *I* know you didn't get that bunny from the butcher's. Why don't you come down, save us destroying this nice fountain?' The woman's eyes darted from the man to the crowd. Her face was full of tension. Eventually, she nodded.

'Jan, hold back the dogs,' said the thin guard. His partner called the dogs to heel. They obeyed unwillingly, eyes still locked on their prey.

The woman lowered one foot. She felt around for the back of a stone bird. Finding it, she moved her other foot to join the first.

'That's it. Keep going.' The skinny guard turned to the other and grinned. 'I told you the lesni obey orders. You just have to be firm, show 'em who's in charge.'

But, as he turned back to the fountain, his face fell. The woman had dropped the rabbit and was jumping, skirt billowing, fists raised. The thin guard opened his mouth. The crowd held its collective breath. The woman landed on the back of the horse with a thud. She grabbed the guard from behind. The horse turned a full circle and bucked, but both riders stayed on.

The dogs fought over the dead rabbit, tearing it to pieces in a matter of seconds.

Struggling free from the woman's grip, the guard reached down to his boot and pulled out a blade. This time the horse reared on to its back legs. For a split second, it looked like the poster for a great romance. Imogen stared, open-mouthed. Then the riders hit the ground.

Imogen didn't see much of what happened next. People were screaming and trying to leave the square. The dogs were out of control, tearing at clothing and skin. Imogen ran past the fountain, heading towards the street she'd come down, but, just like all the other streets feeding into the square, it was packed with people fighting to get away.

Imogen turned to see the human firework and the guard wrestling on the ground like an eight-limbed monster. The guard had lost his dagger. With one arm, he reached for it; with the other, he held the woman by her hair. A little black box tumbled out of his pocket and landed next to the blade.

Imogen didn't want the guard to hurt the woman. All she'd done was hunt rabbits. It didn't seem fair for her to get chased and arrested while Blazen got praise and free beer. Imogen hurried to the dagger and the guard looked up. His helmet had fallen off, revealing an oily comb-over.

'Give that to me,' he growled.

Imogen picked up the dagger and the box. She had no intention of helping the guard. He didn't seem nice at all. As she straightened, she noticed an alleyway, barely half a metre wide, between the houses.

'Give it to me now,' roared the man, 'or I'll have you disembowelled!'

Imogen shook her head.

Giving up on the dagger, the guard turned and seized his prisoner with both hands. The woman scrambled to get free.

But Imogen could linger no longer. The second guard was coming her way. She fled with the dagger in one hand and the little black box in the other.

Chapter 29

Imogen hurtled down the alleyway. Behind her someone was shouting. It was the other Royal Guard.

'Stop in the name of the king!' he yelled, but Imogen kept on running.

The alley narrowed and the walls grazed her shoulders. She shoved the box into her tunic pocket and glanced back. The guard was chasing her, but he was too broad to fit down the alley head-on. He moved sideways like a crab, with one claw extended in her direction.

Eventually, Imogen also had to turn to the side. Ahead, a vertical bar of light reduced the world to two walls and an exit. It was hard to judge the width of the gap at the end. She hoped she'd fit.

When the walls were so close that Imogen couldn't turn her head to look behind her, the guard stopped shouting. The odd grunt told her that he was still there. She took a deep breath, feeling the walls on either side pushing back against her torso. That bar of light wasn't far away.

Her left hand was the first thing to emerge. She wrapped

her fingers round the corner of the wall, easing herself out on to the sunlit street. Her tunic snagged on the stonework and a bit of it ripped off as she tugged herself free.

The street she stood on was calm. Peaceful even. A couple walked hand in hand. A woman hung white linen from a window and a cat was cleaning itself on the opposite side of the lane.

Imogen glanced back down the dark corridor. The guard's sweaty face was just visible. He looked like a rat stuck up the spout of a watering can. As Imogen turned to leave, she *almost* felt sorry for him. *Almost.*

She checked that the little box was still in her pocket and tied the dagger to her ankle. It was good to be armed for the journey. She hoped that the woman had got away too.

As she strode away from the alley, Imogen walked with a spring in her step. She was heading towards the outskirts of Yaroslav, towards the forests, towards home.

CHAPTER 30

Imogen stood at the city gates. She knew she needed to start walking now if she was serious about getting home. She didn't fancy being in the forests after dark. Not now she knew about the skret. Not now she'd lost Marie.

If she walked quickly, she might get half an hour before she needed to turn back . . . or found the door. Perhaps she could use the dagger to prise it open.

There was a man leaning against the city walls, gazing out across the meadows to the forests beyond. Even though the sun hadn't set, it was dark underneath the trees: a green-and-gold filtered twilight zone.

The man was wearing a velvet jacket and a fur-lined cap. *Perhaps he knows the fastest route through the meadows,* thought Imogen, and she cleared her throat, preparing her most grown-up voice. The man must have heard because he glanced her way. One of his eyes was missing.

'Oh,' said Imogen. That wasn't how she'd meant to begin. She tried again. 'Excuse me, but do you know the fastest way to the forests?'

The man raised his two eyebrows above his one eye. 'Of course,' he said. 'But whatever you're running away from, there's far worse out there.'

'I'm not running away,' said Imogen, defiant.

'Then why are you dressed like a boy?' The trace of a smile crossed the man's face.

Imogen looked down at the clothes that she'd borrowed from Miro. 'I'm not scared of the Kolsaney Forests. I can look after myself.' But even as the words escaped her lips, she knew it was a lie. She was tired, she hadn't eaten since breakfast and she was terrified of the skret. Perhaps the man had a point. Perhaps it was getting late.

She rested her back against the wall and squinted up at his face. The hole where his eye ought to be was framed by half-shut lids and the skin was bunched like a segment of grapefruit.

'Did the skret do that to your eye?' asked Imogen.

The man shook his head.

'What then? Something from out there? Is that why you're afraid of the forests?'

'It wasn't an animal.'

'A person?'

'Sakra! You ask a lot of questions. Why don't you run home to your mother?'

Imogen crossed her arms and narrowed her eyes. She

hated being told what to do. 'Perhaps I will,' she said. 'I shouldn't be talking to strangers anyway.'

'You're the one asking for directions! I stand on this same spot every evening. What makes you so sure *you're* not the stranger?'

Imogen opened her mouth to defend herself, but, once again, she realised the man had a point. 'I'm sorry,' she said, unfolding her arms. 'That was a bit rude ... But why do you come here every day?'

The man sighed. 'All right. I'll tell you. I come to look at the forests. I used to live there, among the trees.'

'I thought you said it's unsafe?'

'Who's telling this story?'

Imogen stared at her feet. 'You are.'

'My home wasn't a house. Or not what you město would call a house. I'm one of those lesni you cross the street to avoid.'

Imogen didn't know what město or lesni were, but she sensed that the man didn't want to be asked any more questions so she kept her mouth shut.

'I make things from wood.' He held up his hands as if that proved his point. 'I make boxes that sing, wind-up ornaments, clocks and more. I made my finest timepiece for King Vadik: a clock that could read the stars. But when Vadik died, his younger brother, Drakomor, took the throne and he wanted me all to himself. Drakomor offered me a permanent position at the castle. I'd be called Chief Clockmaker, or some stupid title like that, but I didn't want to live in that tomb. It's unnatural. So the king took my eye.'

Imogen gasped. 'No!'

'It wasn't him *personally* that did it. It was one of the Royal Guards, but I've no doubt that Drakomor was behind it ... The things that man's done ... Surely the stars have a punishment in store.'

'Miro's uncle – I mean, *King Drakomor*, took your eye because you turned down a job?'

'He didn't want anyone else to have a clock like his. Sometimes I'm surprised that he didn't take them both. I bet he was hoping that I'd learn my lesson – that I'd come and work for him after all.'

A group of young men carrying scythes strolled in through the city gates. They looked tired, but they talked and laughed as they passed.

'That's horrible,' said Imogen. 'That's a horrible thing to do ... But the forests are still there. You don't have to live in Yaroslav.'

'Ah, that's the brilliant part,' said the man, shaking his head. 'Ever since King Drakomor was crowned, or around about then, the skret started playing up. Eventually, the forests became unsafe and I fled, along with my family and the other lesni. It's ironic really. All that fuss I made about not wanting to leave home and a load of marauding skret made me do it anyway.'

He fiddled with his embroidered cuff, studying it as if the answers to his problems were stitched into his sleeve. Imogen didn't want to believe him. It was such a shocking story. But he didn't look like he was joking and she couldn't think why he'd lie.

Little white moths fluttered across the fields, towards the city, and a girl with long plaits came running out of the gates. 'Father, you're still here!' she cried, trotting up to the man. 'It's almost dark.'

'I was just telling the tale of my star-reading clock.'

The girl rolled her eyes. 'Not that one again! I've heard it a million times.'

'Lucky you,' said the man. Affection shone from his face as he looked at the child and Imogen felt a flicker of sadness. Sometimes her mum looked at her in that way.

'Right, I think I should be leaving,' said the clockmaker, holding out his hand. Imogen shook it. His skin was as rough as bark.

'My name's Imogen,' she said. 'What's yours?'

'Andel and this is my daughter, Daneetsa.' The girl gave a solemn nod.

The sun was touching the tip of the tallest mountain as

Andel and Daneetsa turned to leave. They'd linked arms. They looked happy. Imogen blinked back the tears. There was no point in crying for her mum.

'Hey, Imogen,' called Andel. He was about to step through the gates. 'Save your parents some worry and get yourself home. It's too late to be running away.'

Imogen nodded and gave a half-hearted wave. *But I wasn't running from home*, she thought. *I was running towards it.*

CHAPTER 31

As the evening bells tolled, the people of Yaroslav went about their nightly ritual – locking doors, putting out fires, tucking children into bed. But Imogen was nowhere near a bed. She was crossing Kamínek Bridge with an empty stomach, a knife fastened to her ankle and a little black box in her pocket.

She had failed to find her way home. She had failed to even start looking. Andel's story about 'marauding skret' had put her off the forests. As Marie would have said, she was 'too chicken'.

The problem was that Imogen didn't have a Plan B. She had avoided running into the skret amid the trees, but that was only postponing the inevitable. She had no intention of returning to that stab-you-in-the-back sister and stuck-up prince. They wouldn't catch her banging on the castle door, begging for forgiveness. No way.

She climbed on to the low parapet that ran along the edge of the bridge. The statues stood beside her. The nearest was a hooded priest, with one foot sticking out from underneath his robe. His big toe had been rubbed smooth by hundreds of fingers.

Miro had told her about that statue: 'The peasants have some funny ideas. They believe that if they touch the old man's toe their families will be protected against evil.' He had laughed. Clearly, his family were above such superstitions.

But there, around what was visible of the priest's ankle, were a load of scratches. Skret claws had been at work. Imogen touched the stone toe.

She sat down on the wall next to the statue of a mighty warrior. One leg was missing, but he still looked ferocious. Then she untied the dagger from her ankle and put it next to her. Couldn't have that falling off the side of the bridge. Holding on to the warrior's remaining leg, she swung herself round so that her feet dangled above the slow-moving water. It was just about visible in the dark, curling round the rocks below.

'Think, Imogen, think!' she said out loud. There must be a safe place in Yaroslav to hide from the skret, a cubbyhole to tuck into. She walked through the city in her mind, exploring the streets she had come to know, but could think of nowhere suitable.

Perhaps, if she sat still enough, the monsters would mistake her for a statue and pass her by . . . but the warrior's missing limb suggested that even basalt people weren't safe. Imogen shivered.

She took the box out of her pocket and shook it, holding it close to her ear. It gave a faint clink. She opened the lid. There was a glint of yellow – a pair of gold rings were nestled inside. That was strange . . . What were the Royal Guards doing with jewellery?

Imogen put the rings on. They were both too big for her fingers, but the smaller one fitted her thumb. She thought, with more than a little bitterness, that if Marie had been there she would have let her keep one.

The first skret cry rattled out across the city. A flock of birds took off like a many-winged creature and Imogen's self-pity vanished with them.

Fear, it turned out, trumped most emotions.

Chapter 32

While Imogen sat on Kamínek Bridge, the other two children sat in the room at the top of the second tallest tower. Miro watched as Marie moved her food round her plate. 'You said you liked bread dumplings.'

'I'm not hungry,' said Marie.

'What do you want to do tomorrow?' he asked. 'I was thinking we could ride the velecours?'

Marie shrugged her shoulders.

'Or we could play hide-and-seek, but this time in the library!'

Marie pushed her plate away. 'Hide-and-seek is no good with two people,' she said.

Miro didn't understand. Why couldn't they carry on having fun, like they had before? After all, it was Imogen's fault that she was out there alone, not his.

A servant cleared away Miro's plate and the fifth course arrived – jelly in all the colours of the rainbow, with whipped cream on top and fruit at the bottom.

Suddenly, the clock started chiming and both children

turned to watch. The little door opened and out came a miniature heart. It was painted in intricate detail – every artery and vein accounted for, every beat in time with the second hand.

When the heart had done its turn, it rolled back inside the clock.

'I thought Imogen would be back by now,' said Marie.

'Ooh, this is my favourite,' said Miro, starting the jelly.

'Did you hear what I said?'

'Of course, but I don't see what I can do about it.'

'We should go and look for her.'

'She could be anywhere.' Miro spooned whipped cream into his mouth. 'She could even have left the city.'

'But what about the skret?' said Marie.

On cue, there was a scream from the city streets below – a wild howl that flew in through the open window and whirled round the room before dying down near the fire. Miro ran to close the curtains.

'What *about* the skret?' he said. 'I thought you and Imogen had fallen out. I don't see why you should waste your time being worried. She's not your friend any more. She broke our pact.' He came back to the table and helped himself to a slice of orange and cinnamon cake. He'd tackle that after the jelly.

'You've *really* never had friends before, have you?' said

Marie, standing up. 'That's not how it works. Anyway, she's not my friend. She's my sister and I'll go out to find her alone if I have to.'

Miro stared at his guest. She looked funny, with her wild red hair and the oversized, borrowed clothes, but he could see that she was serious. 'Fine,' he said. 'It's too dangerous out there now, but I've got an idea. I'll send Yeedarsh to look for her.'

'Yeedarsh? You mean that old man who wanted to throw us in the dungeons?'

'That's the one.'

'But he's ancient!'

'True, but he has a secret weapon. Something even the skret are afraid of.'

Marie studied his face. 'What kind of secret weapon?'

Miro smiled. 'She's called Medveditze.'

CHAPTER 33

'Can I look now?'

Anneshka tapped the floor with her slipper, checking she had climbed the final step.

'Not yet. Wait here one minute.' King Drakomor's fingers guided hers to the wall.

It was strangely warm up here, and quiet too. So quiet that Anneshka thought she could hear the drumming of her heart.

'You asked to see the most valuable object in my collection,' said Drakomor.

'Yes, but do I really have to wear this blindfold?'

'I've never shown this to anyone before,' he said. 'I want it to be special.'

A door opened and even warmer air whooshed over Anneshka's face. Drakomor guided her forward.

'Now?' she asked.

'Almost. Be patient, my love.'

'It's so hot in here.'

'I'm afraid that can't be helped.'

And then she heard it. But not with her ears. She heard it in the knotty part between her ribs: a sound-feeling that made her bones vibrate. 'I've waited for long enough,' she said and she pulled off the blindfold.

The room at the top of the tallest tower was empty, apart from a pedestal that was covered by a cloth. It was dark too, with only one torch by the door.

Anneshka walked round the room and peeped out through a window. She tapped on the glass, scaring away a pair of moths. She couldn't see her parents' house. At this time of night, the only thing that was clearly visible was the second tallest tower, with its candles burning bright.

Drakomor clapped his hands and Anneshka turned. Something about him reminded her of a tacky illusionist. He pulled the cloth off the pedestal with a flourish.

'May I?' she asked, already stepping closer.

The object on the pedestal glowed ruby red. It was the size of a man's head, but within its polished surfaces whole galaxies seemed to swirl. It pulsed. Just a few beats per minute. Just enough to let you know it was there.

'It's beautiful,' she said, really meaning it.

'Thank you. *This* is the crowning jewel of my collection, but you're the first . . . I mean . . . I haven't shown it to anyone else.'

The stone's heat made her face prickle. She slipped off a glove and put out her hand. Stuff the colour of clotted blood and exploded stars passed under her fingers. 'Be careful!' said the king, reaching for her arm.

'Don't,' she snapped.

Anneshka stroked the stone with her index finger. A pulse travelled up her arm, along her collarbone and down her spine. The wind outside picked up. She pushed her whole palm against the hot surface.

'That's enough,' said Drakomor. 'You'll burn yourself.' He leaned over her shoulder.

Outside, the wind tore through the city. Anneshka saw her face in the stone; a future-queen looked back out. Every feature was perfectly symmetrical, with suns for eyes and Milky-Way skin.

The wind careered round the tower, circling and circling and calling her name. Another pulse. She closed her eyes and the world trembled. She let go.

'Anneshka – your hand – you've hurt yourself. Why did you do that?' Drakomor cradled her hand in his, looking from her blistered skin up to her face and back to her hand again. She put the glove on.

'How did you get it?' she asked.

Drakomor looked confused.

'The heart of the mountain. I know what that is. How did you get it?'

'It . . . it was a gift.'

'A gift?' She tried to make him look her in the eye.

'Look, my love, we should get you to the kitchens. Put some balm on that burn.'

'Tsh! Stop fussing!' And then more gently: 'Please, tell me how you got it. Then we'll go back down.'

Drakomor ran his hands over his face. When he finally looked at her, he was wearing a strange expression.

'Láska, don't fret,' she said. 'You don't need to be afraid.' She put her non-blistered hand to his cheek.

'I'm not afraid,' he said.

'Then what?'

'I don't have the word for it. It makes me feel sick. Just thinking about it makes me feel sick. I should never have brought you up here.'

'Share it with me,' she cooed. 'Let me help you. After all, we're family now – or we will be soon.'

He sighed. 'You have to promise not to tell anyone. Not even your mother.'

'I promise,' she said. 'We're in this together. Just the two of us.'

She encircled him with her arms and he spoke into her shoulder.

'It was the evening of Zimní Slunovrat – back when all of Yaroslav used to put on those disgusting masks. Do you remember? It was hard to tell the people from the skret and the skret from the people.'

'I remember.'

'My brother, Vadik, was still alive. King Vadik and his closest advisors celebrated Zimní Slunovrat at the top of the Klenot Mountain, with the skret, as was tradition.'

'Go on ...'

'Well, you know how skret banquets go. That vile oily stuff they drink. They were all rotten from it. Most of the court were too, but I'd had enough of making small talk.

'Vadik and his wife were deep in discussion with the Maudree Král. Vadik saw me across the cave and shot me one of his crowd-pleasing smiles. Everyone loved that smile. There was something so unkingly about it. It belonged to a boy.

'But I didn't smile back. The Maudree Král may call himself a king, but the mountains are no kingdom. Why should my brother simper for that fiend?

'I couldn't endure it, so I grabbed a torch and slipped away; away from the fire they keep burning all winter ... away from the merrymaking. I was going home. That was always my plan.'

Anneshka gave him an encouraging squeeze.

'But I got lost in those twisting tunnels and lonely

grottoes. And instead of getting out I found myself going deeper into the mountain.

'I could see my own breath freezing in front of me. The ceilings of the caves were lined with icicles. Sometimes the floor too. It was too slippery so I crawled and the further I went, the colder it grew. Eventually, it was too cold to think straight. I began to panic. I wouldn't have been the first to die inside the mountain.

'When I felt the cold dying away, I thought I was back at the great hall. I thought I'd see Vadik. He would ask me where I'd been and I would make something up to save face. He'd laugh and clap me on the back, knowing the truth but not needing to say it.

'But I wasn't just round the corner from the feasting cave. I was at the mountain's core. The warmth I felt wasn't from the skrets' fire, but from the mountain's heart.'

Drakomor stared into the stone with greedy eyes.

'I was familiar with the lesni stories. They'd talked about a stone that had fallen from the stars for as long as I could remember. The Sertze Hora. That's what they called it. They said it made the mountains tall, the forests deep and the valley rich with life. They said it lived at the heart of Klenot Mountain. But I thought it was all – well – just stories.

'When I found the Sertze Hora, it was lying on the

ground as if it had been dropped. Can you imagine? An incredible jewel, just waiting to be found ... The ice around it had melted away. And that feeling. That thunder it makes. It has a rhythm, just like a real heart. You must be able to feel it?'

Anneshka nodded.

'I slipped off my cloak and wrapped it round the stone, carrying it close to my chest like a swaddled infant. The beating travelled through me. Even my jaw shook. And my heart! I've never felt anything like it. It was as if it was trying to thump its way out ...'

'Go on,' said Anneshka.

'I don't know how long it took me to escape. All I know was that it was still night when I stood at the foot of Klenot Mountain and I was sweating like a beast. Even through the cloak, the Sertze Hora burned.

'I did look back at the summit of the mountain. I did think of my brother. I could still see the faint glow from the skret fires. The celebrations were continuing without me. But I didn't want to linger in case I was being watched. I thought I saw blinking in the trees. Even the moon stared at me like a giant eye with the lids pinned back.

'I ran through to the place where our horses were tied and I rode back to Yaroslav with one hand on the reins and one holding the stone. I only stopped on Kamínek Bridge because something caught my eye, something in the water. A scornful face looked up. *What have you done?* it seemed to say. But it wasn't a human face. It was one of those stupid Zimní Slunovrat masks. Someone must have dropped it.

'I tied up my horse and crept into the castle through the servants' entrance, passing the room where Miroslav used to sleep. His nurse was with him. I could hear her snoring. I ran to my room and bolted the door.'

Drakomor stopped. Beads of sweat were forming on his face and running down his neck. Anneshka picked up the cloth and covered the Sertze Hora.

Drakomor allowed himself to be steered to the window like a child who had woken from a bad dream.

'Here,' said Anneshka, 'some air will do you good.'

'It's not finished,' he croaked. 'I mean, I'm not finished. I didn't let anyone know. Didn't let those who knew speak. But I want you to know. I'm tired of being the only one . . .' His hands were shaking. 'My brother . . . he didn't come back that night.'

'What?'

'He didn't come back as he'd left. The Royal Guards called me to the North Gate before dawn. The city was still asleep.

'I could feel the guards' eyes on me. I wished they would look down. They should have looked down! There were sacks outside the gate, like the ones they transport meat in. They were turning the soil red.

'I didn't want to open them. I got a guard to do it. He slit the closest sack and vomited. I sent another guard. I asked him what was in there and he said it. No fancy language. No cushioning the blow. "It's your brother, my lord."

'My brother. My brother was in there and they'd made such a mess of him. His face – just like my face. No more famous smiles . . . and his chest was open.' Drakomor sank to the floor. 'They'd taken his heart.'

'Are you sure no one else knows?' asked Anneshka. 'No one else knows how King Vadik really died?'

Drakomor looked up. 'Don't you understand? The skret killed everyone who was there that night, apart from me.'

'But what about the guards who saw the bodies?'

'I sent them away – beyond the mountains.'

Anneshka stroked his hair and looked out of the window. The candles in the second tallest tower were still burning bright.

'Good,' she said. 'That's very good.'

CHAPTER 34

Imogen stood in the middle of the bridge. Thirty black statues looked on. The priest with the lucky toe. The warrior with the missing leg. An array of powerful men. None of them would help her now.

The rings were back in her pocket and the dagger was in her hand. She was still. If she had been a deer, her ears would have been moving. She was listening. She wanted to be sure . . .

There it was. Another skret cry sent adrenalin fizzing through her body. Her feet decided which way to run. They took her towards the castle, towards the light. Moths fluttered in every direction, but none of them was familiar. None of them was *her* moth.

Imogen knew the city streets better than the first time she'd run from the skret, but she still came to dead ends. She still took wrong turns. She hesitated in front of a house decorated with so many skret teeth it gleamed. Left or right? Right or left? A blood-curdling scream. Closer this time and to her right. Left it was, then.

The moon was full and, when it appeared between the clouds, Imogen could see by its light. When it was hidden, Imogen thought the darkness would swallow her whole.

Things moved in the shadows, always in the margins of her vision. She shook her head. It was just her imagination. Surely the skret couldn't have caught up so quickly . . .

She ran down the centre of the street, as far from the dark edges as possible, but a cloud covered the moon and she had to stop. Something was definitely there. She turned to face it, holding the dagger at arm's length, gripping the hilt with both hands. There it was. A fluttering.

A silvery grey moth flew out of the blackness. Imogen lowered her dagger. She'd know those antennae anywhere.

'It's you!' She rushed towards the shadow moth. No time for pleasantries. Her guide flitted on ahead and Imogen followed willingly.

Skret cries echoed down passageways and ricocheted off rooftops. It was impossible to tell which direction they were coming from. But that didn't matter. Imogen's moth was back. She was about to be rescued.

She was so relieved that it wasn't until the moth led her down a tunnel-like alley, into an enclosed courtyard, that Imogen had the bad thought. What if her moth was not friend but foe? What if it had never been 'her' moth at all? It had taken her through the door in the tree, into skretinfested forests. What if it had always known it was leading her towards danger?

The only exit from the courtyard was the alley that she had just come down. On the other side of the courtyard there was a statue. Imogen was used to Yaroslav's statues – the place was littered with them. Miro had often joked that if only the stone soldiers of Yaroslav would come to life, the skret problem would be solved. But this statue was different.

It was bigger than Imogen, but not as big as a grown-up, with arms that finished too close to its knees. The shadow moth settled on the statue's bald head. Heart thudding, Imogen followed.

Up close, it was clear that the statue had been made by a skilled artist. The huge, circular eyes were like those of the deep-sea fish on telly. The hooked claws belonged to the stuff of nightmares. And that face! It was captured mid-snarl: a skret.

Imogen stood in front of the monster. Even though she knew it was made from stone, she could have sworn its eyes flickered. Sitting on its palm was another moth, but this one wasn't alive. It was part of the statue. It had the same wings, buggy eyes and long antennae as the real shadow moth and it looked like it was the skret's friend. Imogen's hand shot to her mouth. 'No!'

The real skret, the creatures made of fleshy stuff not stone, were closing in. She could hear them calling. She looked up at the statue's head, but her moth wasn't there. She ran round the courtyard, her breath coming shallow and fast. Her moth was nowhere to be seen.

'How could you?' she cried. In answer to her question came the screech of a skret. It approached down the alley, half masked by shadows. Imogen hammered on the door of the nearest building. 'Help me,' she screamed at the top of her voice. '*Heeeeelp!*'

The sound she heard next wasn't human. But it wasn't a skret either. A colossal roar made every window in Yaroslav tinkle and every shutter shake. It was a roar that belonged to the forests and mountains; a roar that stripped away all but a thin core of instinct. And that instinct said, 'Run!'

But where could she run to? The skret lost no time scuttling into the courtyard, scaling the nearest building and disappearing over the roof. In the hole that the skret left behind, something else had appeared. That something almost filled the alley – shoulder blades up near the arched ceiling. Imogen trembled. The dagger in her hand trembled too.

The thing stepped into the courtyard. It had two heads. As the moonlight fell across it, Imogen saw that the heads were attached to two separate bodies. One, covered in a black hood, belonged to the old servant called Yeedarsh. The other belonged to an enormous brown bear.

Throwing back its head, the bear roared again.

CHAPTER 35

Imogen dropped the dagger. 'Yeedarsh?' she said in wonder. His face looked as pale and as old as the moon. 'It wasn't my idea to come looking for peasants at this hour,' he said, scowling.

'Yeedarsh!' This time she said it with pure joy.

'But, if the young prince wishes it, I must obey.'

Imogen approached cautiously, not wanting to make any sudden movements. The bear's giant head turned towards her, its golden eyes making perfect orbs in the darkness. It wasn't wearing a chain or a muzzle, not like the dancing bears Imogen had seen in the books in the castle library. And it was big. Bigger than Imogen had ever imagined a bear could be. Its back was higher than the old man's head and its paws were as large as serving dishes.

'Is it safe?' said Imogen, staring at the animal.

'Who, Medveditze? Oh yes. She's used to humans.'

'*Med-vee-deet-saa.*' Imogen repeated the name slowly.

'Enough gawping,' said the servant. 'Do you want to be rescued or not?'

Imogen nodded.

'Right then,' said Yeedarsh. 'It's a bit of a walk back to the castle and there are plenty of skret about. Make sure you stay close. I can't see Prince Miroslav being happy with me delivering just a part of you.'

Imogen did as instructed. Yeedarsh walked slowly, but the skret seemed to have vanished like bats before dawn.

'Where have all the skret gone?' asked Imogen, looking over her shoulder.

'Oh, they're still here. No doubt they're hiding between the chimney pots. They're afraid of my Medveditze.' The old man gave a dry laugh.

'Skret are afraid of bears?'

'It's the only creature they respect.'

Imogen watched Medveditze's lumbering gait. Her paws made silent contact with the ground. Occasionally, the bear turned to look at Yeedarsh, perhaps to check that he was keeping up.

'Where did you get her from?' said Imogen.

'I rescued her,' said the old man, unable to keep the pride out of his voice. 'Her mother was killed when she was a cub.'

'How sad ...'

'It's not sad. That's how it goes with bears. They fetch a good price.'

'Well, why didn't you just get Medveditze stuffed if money is all you care about?'

'I didn't say that's all that I care about.'

They walked in silence for a few minutes, but Imogen couldn't stay quiet for long. Her head was crowded with questions.

'Is Medveditze big for a girl bear?' she asked.

'One of the biggest.'

'How big do bears get?'

'Not as big as they used to.'

'Why?'

'As Yaroslav has grown, they have shrunk.'

'Can I touch her?'

'Enough questions! She's not a plaything.'

'I'll stop talking, I promise.'

Yeedarsh paused. 'If she growls, let go of her and look away.'

Imogen stretched out her arm and brushed the tips of the bear's fur with her fingers. It was coarser than she'd expected. She stroked it with her palm. The bear didn't respond. She put her hand into the fur and her arm disappeared up to the elbow. Medveditze looked back at her. 'Sorry,' said Imogen, removing her hand. The bear gave a snort, which could have meant, *Don't mention it*, or, *I'll tear you limb from limb*.

As they approached the castle, Imogen began to play the scene where she was reunited with Marie in her head.

Marie would be so impressed that she'd fought off the skret. Imogen was determined not to apologise. Perhaps they wouldn't have to talk about the argument at all. Perhaps they could just carry on as if she'd never left.

Yeedarsh fumbled for his keys.

'Yeedarsh?' said Imogen.

'Hmm.'

'You know the place where you found me – the courtyard.'

He ushered her inside. 'Yes, I know it. Keep your voice down.'

'Sorry . . .' She lowered her voice to a whisper. 'You know there's a statue of a skret.'

'Get to the point.'

'It was holding a moth.'

'So what?'

'It's just that I've seen a moth like that before.'

Now she had his attention. 'Go on.'

'I was curious . . . Why was the moth with the skret? What kind of moth is it?'

His beady-eyed stare made her uncomfortable. 'Curiosity killed the wildcat.'

'That's not the saying. It's—'

'It's not a saying, idiot child. It's a fact.'

'Okay. I . . . I guess I'll go to bed now. Thanks for coming to get me.'

'Oh, no you don't.' Yeedarsh grabbed her by the scruff of the neck. 'You're coming with me.'

'But I'm tired!'

'So am I, little peasant, but, if you've seen the moth that I think you've seen, it could be important. So, tired as I am, we're going to the library.'

CHAPTER 36

The king's collection was scattered throughout the castle, and the library was no exception. Globes charted unfamiliar lands. Tables were strewn with snake heads and amulets.

These objects were the stars of the show. The books that lined the walls, from the floor right up to the high ceiling, were just a backdrop. King Drakomor didn't collect stories.

Yeedarsh tutted as he walked past the chessboards. Black and white pieces were strewn across the floor, as Imogen and Miro had left them. Yeedarsh stooped to pick up the black king. His knees creaked. 'It's always the way,' he said, placing the king in the middle of the board.

Medveditze stood by the door like a furry bodyguard. Imogen waited.

'You pick up the chess pieces,' said Yeedarsh. 'I'll light the torches.' Imogen did as she was told. When the old man had lit every torch in the room, he pointed to the ceiling.

'Can you read?' he asked.

'Of course.'

'Good. Climb up there and fetch me the black book called *The Book of Winged Things.*'

'What?'

'Or I'll get you and your little friend thrown out. Miroslav is only allowed to keep you so long as the king allows it, and guess who has the ear of the king . . .' He tapped his ear. There were hairs poking out of it.

'Okay, okay.'

Yeedarsh tied a bit of cloth in a knot and handed it to Imogen. 'Use this to carry the book,' he said. Imogen put the makeshift bag round her neck and looked up at the bookshelf. The ceiling was a long way up and her feet were sore from running from the skret.

'Come on, we haven't got all night,' said Yeedarsh. Imogen wanted to say that they had, but she bit her tongue.

She climbed slowly, searching for spaces where the books weren't too big or too densely packed – spaces where she could fit a hand or a foot. A spider's web broke on the crown of her head. The web's creator scurried off.

When she was about halfway up, she paused to catch her breath. It was hard to see up here, away from the torches, but her eyes were adjusting. The books in front of her nose had strange names: *The Witch of the Kolsaney Forests*, *A Myriad of Mushrooms*, *Blue Blood of Yaroslav*.

'Which shelf is it on?' she called down.

'The top one.'

Her left foot nudged something and she fumbled for a foothold. An ornament fell, smashing close to the old man. He cursed and shuffled away from the broken glass.

'What's the book called again?' said Imogen.

'*The Book of Winged Things*.' His voice sounded distant. She didn't dare look down.

And then she saw it. A shiny black poisonous toad of a book. The title was etched down its spine in green.

Imogen hesitated just long enough to wish she was at home. She wished for her familiar bedroom. She wished for crumpets and chores and the smell of Mum's perfume. She wished she wasn't so high up.

She put the book in the cloth around her neck and began her descent. The book banged against her knees as she climbed. A few minutes later, she stepped on to the floor and handed Yeedarsh his prize. 'What is it?' she asked.

'An encyclopaedia of moths. Every single nasty species.'

Imogen inched closer. It wasn't like any encyclopaedia she had seen before. There weren't many words, just a few sentences per page, scrawled in wonky handwriting that bunched at the page edges. Most of the space was taken up by detailed illustrations of moths. But despite the detail they looked lifeless. At first, Imogen put it down to the shading. The artist hadn't coloured in the right places to make the insects look three-dimensional. A bright purple moth was the size of a fingernail. A midnight-blue one had oversized antennae. The page had been extended to show their full length.

And then Imogen realised that they weren't illustrations at all. They were real moths that had been flattened and sewn into the book. Some of them even looked like they had been killed *by* the book – as though the author had slammed the pages shut on the insects as they flew, pressing them like flowers.

Tiny blots of blood and smudges of shimmering wing-dust confirmed that her suspicions were correct. It must have taken a long time to collect them all.

'Aha!' cried Yeedarsh, triumphant. He pointed to the page with a yellowing nail. 'Is THAT the moth you saw?'

The moth's body was covered in fine fur. It had long antennae and grey wings that glistened if you looked at them from the right angle. Imogen recognised it instantly. 'Yes, that's my moth!' It was horrible to see it like this: a specimen in a book. Next to it there were two words in spider-leg writing:

Mezi Můra

'What does that mean?' said Imogen.

'Trouble,' said Yeedarsh. 'Mezi Můra are an ill omen. I didn't think there were any left ...'

'What's an omen?'

'Don't your peasant parents teach you anything? I suppose you don't even know your shneks from your slimarks?'

Imogen blinked.

The old man rolled his eyes. 'Skret have a kinship with moths,' he said. 'Moths like the dark. Skret like the dark. Moths creep and crawl. So do the skret.'

'Moths are their friends?'

'If monsters can have friends, yes. The Mezi Můra are the skret's favourite species. They bring people bad luck.' Yeedarsh wrinkled his nose. 'A favourite beastie – have you ever heard of anything so disgusting?'

Imogen glanced at Medveditze, thinking she seemed very much like the old man's favourite.

'They might not look like much,' continued Yeedarsh, 'but the Mezi Můra are smart. They're always making plans. Always up to no good.'

'What about the other moths?' said Imogen. 'They can't *all* bring bad luck.'

'No,' said Yeedarsh. 'Most of them are too stupid to do any harm. Back in the old days, they used to carry messages. These days, they're little more than a flappy pest.' Yeedarsh slammed the book shut. 'But . . . it's possible that your moth has been sent for a reason. The fact that it's a Mezi Můra is very troubling indeed. So, next time you see it, be sure to squash it flat.'

He put the book on the bottom shelf and shuffled over to the door. Medveditze was scratching her back against a giant sculpture of a naked woman. Imogen didn't move. Her moth. Had it been tricking her all along? Had it really meant for her to be skret supper?

'Come on, peasant,' said Yeedarsh. 'It's time for bed.'

CHAPTER 37

It was just before dawn when Imogen opened the door at the top of the second tallest tower. She was exhausted. She was planning to slip under the quilt and catch a few hours' rest before the others woke up. What a surprise Miro and Marie would have when they saw her there.

But Marie wasn't asleep. She was sitting by the fireplace with her hair sticking out at all angles and her bloodshot eyes fixed on her sister.

'Oh,' said Imogen. 'You're awake.'

'Shhh!' Marie eyeballed a pile of sheets at the bottom of the bed. The sheets snored softly.

Imogen hadn't expected it to be like this. 'Why are you awake?' she said, whispering this time.

'Why do you think?' said Marie.

Imogen thought about leaving – going back out of the door, down the stairs and away from that stern face. But she was so tired.

She slumped into the chair on the other side of the hearth

and put her feet up. She hoped she looked indifferent. 'So, what happened?' she said. 'Did you have a nightmare?'

'No.'

'Miro hog all the covers?'

'You know why I'm awake, Imogen. You and your stupid temper. Stomping off just because you didn't get your way. You could have been killed!'

'What do you care?' snapped Imogen. 'You clearly prefer Miro to me. Bet you don't even want to go home. Bet you don't remember what home is!'

'Of course I want to go home, but home isn't much good if you've been killed by skret. Mum doesn't want us to be eaten by monsters – that's what you said when we first arrived! Remember?'

Imogen couldn't bear this. Who did Marie think she was? 'Well, I *am* alive, aren't I?' she said. 'No thanks to you.'

'Oh yes. And who do you think sent Yeedarsh?'

Imogen stared intently at the candles on the mantlepiece.

'Do you think he wanted to go out there at night?' said Marie. 'Do you think he cared whether you were okay? Because I'm telling you – he didn't.'

'I was doing fine,' said Imogen, the blood rising to her cheeks.

There was a long pause.

'You sent Yeedarsh to rescue me?'

'I got Miro to send him. I was worried about you.'

Imogen fiddled with a stray thread sticking out from her tunic. 'I suppose that's . . . I suppose I . . . thank you.' She snapped off the thread. 'And I'm sorry.'

The corner of Marie's mouth twitched. 'That's okay.'

The morning bells tolled and the girls turned to look at the clock. A miniature planet flew anticlockwise, looping round all five of the clock's hands. The hatch popped open and a wooden skeleton came out. It danced a wonky jig, took a bow and trundled back in. Imogen thought about the one-eyed man she'd met, the one who said he made clocks. Had he made *this* clock?

'I preferred it when it did the hunter,' said Marie, breaking Imogen's train of thought. 'So what did you do out there?'

'Oh, you know, fought off a few skret. Showed them who's boss.' Imogen felt around for the dagger. She didn't have it.

'You fought skret?' said Marie.

'Uh-huh.'

'Wow. What else did you do?'

'I found this.' Imogen got up and handed the black box to Marie.

'There's gold in here,' said Marie.

'I know.'

'Whose is it?'

Imogen shrugged. 'One of the Royal Guards dropped it, but there's something else . . .'

She waited until Marie had finished inspecting the rings. She wanted her sister's full attention. 'You know when you followed me through the door in the tree?'

Marie nodded.

'Well, I was following someone too,' said Imogen.

'I didn't see them.'

'You wouldn't have done. It was a moth.'

'A moth?'

'Yes. But it wasn't like other moths. It was out in the daytime – in the rain. And it was like it knew me, like it wanted to show me something. I suppose I thought it was my friend.'

'You thought an insect was your friend?'

'Let me finish. Last night I saw the moth again and now I'm not so sure about it being friendly. It led me to a statue of a skret, and Yeedarsh made me look it up in the library. He says that my moth is the skret's favourite and seeing it is a bad omen. That means bad luck.'

'The skret's favourite . . .' said Marie. 'So what are we going to do?'

'I'm going to bed.' Imogen kicked off her boots.

'And after that?'

'Breakfast.'

'Imogen!' cried Marie. 'Don't you see? If the moth was

sent by the skret and the moth led you here, then the skret must know about the door in the tree. They must know how we can get home.'

Marie looked at Imogen as though she was waiting for the penny to drop.

Imogen narrowed her eyes. 'Oh, you're right,' she said at last.

'So we need to talk to the skret,' said Marie.

'But how? We'd have to find one. We'd have to find *the* skret that sent the moth.'

'Don't they have some kind of ruler?'

'He's called the Maudree Král,' said a voice from under the sheets.

'Where does he live?' said Marie.

'In a cave at the top of Klenot Mountain,' said Miro.

'Can we meet him?'

'Impossible.'

'A door in a tree is impossible,' said Imogen, 'and we *need* to meet the king of the skret.'

'And you have to help us,' said Marie. 'Because you're our friend.'

Under the covers, Miro sighed.

CHAPTER 38

O n the final morning of her visit, Anneshka sat in the
king's study. She'd found a spot in the corner of the
room where the torchlight was good enough to do her
needlework.

Drakomor was inspecting his collection of ancient coins.
He sat at his desk, stacking the coins into towers.

The couple hardly spoke, at ease in each other's company.
A knock at the door disturbed their peace. 'Who is it?'
called the king.

'Petr and Jan Voyák of the Royal Guards, Your Highness.'

'Let them in.'

Two men came into view. They edged round the king's
collection with all the daintiness of a pair of ballet-dancing
hippos. When they stood in front of Drakomor's desk,
they bowed. They didn't notice Anneshka, sitting in the
corner between a marble pillar and a giant sculpture of a
hand. She kept as still as a hunting cat.

She recognised the man with the round belly. He'd
delivered the invitation to her parents' house. She didn't

know the thinner man with the greasy comb-over.

Drakomor removed his monocle. 'Petr and Jan,' he said, 'I expect you've come back from the jeweller's with the rings? I am so looking forward to seeing them all polished and shining like new.'

Even from her hiding place, Anneshka could see that something wasn't right. The thin man had a black eye and they both looked uncomfortable.

'Don't dither,' said the king. 'I've waited long enough.'

'Your Highness, we have some bad news,' said the fat guard.

'What kind of bad news?'

'It's about the rings . . .'

'What about them?' The smile was slipping from Drakomor's lips. He turned to the thin man. 'Come on, Petr. You're the Chief of the Royal Guards. Don't hide behind your brother.' Petr swallowed. Neither guard spoke.

'What's going on?' snapped the king. 'Got dumplings stuck in your throat?'

'Sorry, Your Highness. No, Your Highness,' said Petr. 'The rings have been stolen.'

Drakomor sat back in his chair and ran his fingertips along his moustache. He let the silence stretch out.

The fat one, who must have been Jan, broke first. 'We were ambushed!' he cried. 'There was nothing we could do.

We were arresting a lesni woman for hunting when they sprang on us without warning.'

'How many were there?' demanded the king.

Petr smoothed down his comb-over with both hands as if that was the real cause of his distress. 'One, Your Highness,' he said.

'One?' The king stopped stroking his moustache. Anneshka suppressed a smile.

'But she was very quick,' blurted Jan. 'I've never seen anyone run down an alley so fast.'

'She?' The king slammed his hand on the desk, making the coin towers tremble.

'We caught the woman, Your Highness. You don't need to worry about that.'

'So you *do* have the rings?' The guards looked at each other.

'No.'

'Well, who does?'

When Petr spoke, it was in a voice barely above a whisper: 'A little girl.'

The king's fist smashed into the coin towers. Money flew in all directions.

'Are you seriously telling me,' he bellowed, 'that my finest soldiers were outsmarted by a child?'

The king pointed at the coins. 'Pick them up.' The men

dropped to their knees. 'And what did she look like, this amazing little girl? This child with the strength of one thousand men? Would you recognise her if you saw her in the street?'

'Oh yes, Your Highness.' Jan nodded furiously. 'She was dressed like a boy, with short hair and trousers. Must've been some kind of disguise.'

'And the woman that you caught. What do you know about her?'

'She's a lesni poacher, Your Highness,' said Jan. 'Caught hunting rabbits.'

'I want to make an example of her,' said the king. 'But, before we do that, the child must be found. I don't care if you have to round up every girl in Yaroslav and burn every house to the ground. You can say that the child will be spared. Offer a reward. That ought to get tongues wagging.'

'The girl won't be punished?' said Petr, looking up with surprise.

'That's not what I said.'

'Very good, Your Highness.'

'And if you don't find the child – if my brother and his wife's rings don't turn up – you can be sure that I will be holding you idiots responsible.'

The guards placed the coins on the desk and got to their feet. They saluted out of time with each other.

'Why are you still here?' demanded the king. 'I want word putting out about the reward, along with a description of the girl. There's no time to lose.'

'There was one other thing, Your Highness.' Jan reached into his pocket. 'She left this behind.' He pulled out a shred of cloth and handed it to Drakomor.

When the guards had left the study, Anneshka walked over to Drakomor's desk. He looked like he'd forgotten she was there. His face changed when he remembered. 'Sorry you had to witness that,' he said.

'No need to apologise. I actually quite enjoyed it,' said Anneshka. 'You were very . . . regal.'

She took the scrap of cloth from her beloved. It was dark blue, embroidered with stars. 'A fine cloth,' she said, feeling the velvet.

'The finest,' agreed the king. 'In fact, it looks familiar. I think Miroslav has something similar . . .'

Anneshka seized her chance. 'That reminds me,' she said. 'I've been thinking about the prince.' The king looked uncomfortable, but Anneshka kept going. Who knew when they'd be alone again. 'I've been thinking that perhaps something ought to happen . . .'

'Happen?'

' . . . to him.'

CHAPTER 39

Yeedarsh could tell by the way Anneshka looked at him out of the corners of her violet eyes that she despised him. But that wasn't a problem. He felt little love for her. Every step she took was too graceful. Every glance was loaded with meaning. Her hands were tipped with fierce pointed nails and her face was shaped like a cat's. Yeedarsh sometimes imagined he could see her tail swishing – the tip of it flicking at the bottom of her skirts.

The king hadn't told Yeedarsh much about Anneshka. He hadn't announced that he planned to marry her. He hadn't even said he was considering it, but he didn't need to. Yeedarsh could see that he'd fallen for the woman. He could see that she was beautiful too, but Yeedarsh was a traditionalist at heart. And the tradition had always been for the king of Yaroslav to marry a princess. Anneshka was not a princess. Not even close.

So during the midday meal, while Anneshka was packing for her return to her parents', the old servant voiced his concerns about the lady's ancestry. He did it as delicately as he could.

'I don't know why you're worrying,' said the king, removing bits of egg white from his moustache. 'Have I announced an engagement?'

'No, Your Highness, you haven't, but please hear me out. You know I have served your family well. Ever since you were a boy—'

'Yes, Yeedarsh. Pass me the salt.'

Yeedarsh did as instructed. 'I only tell you out of duty. Out of loyalty . . .'

'I understand,' said the king, 'but really don't trouble yourself.'

Yeedarsh hesitated for a moment. 'There was something else I wanted to mention,' he said. 'There has been a sighting of a Mezi Můra. I fear it's a bad omen.'

'Nonsense,' scoffed the king. 'The Mezi Můra is a rare butterfly, not a witch riding a goat backwards. I don't hold with such superstitions.'

'With the greatest respect, Your Highness, the Mezi Můra is a moth. A very clever moth.'

'Don't patronise me.'

'It brings bad luck.'

'Yeedarsh, there are moths everywhere in this city. They'd eat my fur collection if I let them inside, but that's another story . . .'

'I hear that the rings have gone missing,' said the old

man. 'The ones King Vadik and Queen Sofia used to wear.'

'Who told you that?' snapped the king.

'News travels fast in the kitchens.'

'Well, perhaps you had better get back down there.'

Yeedarsh nodded and gathered the king's breakfast things. He walked towards the door slowly. Balancing trays was not as easy as it used to be.

Had he been a little bit faster, he would have opened the door sooner. Had he opened the door sooner, he might have seen a pair of dainty feet in jewelled slippers standing in the corridor. But that's not how it happened and the jewelled slippers disappeared round the corner unseen.

CHAPTER 40

News of Yeedarsh's death spread quickly. The serving girl who found his body screamed until three guards appeared.

'What's going on?'

'Hey, look, it's old Yeedarsh.'

'Look at all that blood.'

'Weren't you supposed to be patrolling this wing?'

'I thought you were.'

'I was not. This is the West Wing. I never do the West Wing.'

The youngest guard bent down to pick up a foot. 'We can move him outside. Say we found him there.' The foot came off in his hand. The serving girl fainted.

It turned out that none of Yeedarsh's limbs were attached where they ought to be. The guards concluded that it was a skret attack. The skret had a thing about cutting people into pieces. What the men couldn't work out was how the monsters had managed to break into the castle. It had never happened before.

The guards knew they would be in trouble with the king if he discovered what had happened on their watch, so they picked up Yeedarsh – one piece at a time – and reconstructed his body in a street that ran alongside the castle. Then they cleaned the blood from the castle floor. It was decided that the youngest guard should break the news to the king. They all agreed, apart from him.

The only thing they hadn't factored into their plans was the unconscious serving girl. When she came to, she ran to the head cook. She told the cook everything over a cup of warm milk and brandy. 'Skret murdering servants inside these very castle walls?' said the cook, her chins wobbling with outrage.

The serving girl nodded.

'Well, if *we're* not safe,' said the cook, 'no one is . . .'

The head cook was married to the king's blacksmith. The king's blacksmith told everyone at his local. They, in turn, told their families and, within a few hours, the whole city was alive with whispers that the castle had been breached.

Eventually, the news reached the king. He had the young guard who had delivered the false news sent away, beyond the mountains.

Chapter 41

Miro prepared the room at the top of the second tallest tower for his visitor. The fire was lit. Gingerbread biscuits were carried up from the kitchens and a pot of orange honey wine, called medovina, was kept warm above the flames.

Imogen helped as best she could, but her mind was elsewhere. She couldn't stop thinking about the king of the skret. Did the monster really know how they could get home? Would they make it up the mountain, to the caves where he lived? She'd never climbed a mountain before . . .

The clock struck midday and the tower door flung open. Blazen Bilbetz entered, huffing and puffing and wiping sweat from his brow.

'My prince!' he boomed, flopping the top half of his body forward in a mock bow.

'Have a seat,' said Miro. Imogen wondered if he'd noticed the hunter's sarcastic tone.

Blazen's shoulders didn't fit between the wings of the chair so he perched on the edge of the seat. 'That staircase is one hell of a climb,' he said, eyeballing the pot over the fire. 'I hope you didn't call me up here for herbal tea ... Are those buvol horns?' Blazen picked up a drinking horn. 'Killed a load of them in my youth ... fearsome things they were.'

Miro took a seat by the hunter. 'This is Imogen, who you've met before,' he said. 'And this is Marie, who you haven't.'

'Why, that one's as ginger as a fox,' said the giant, chuckling. Marie's cheeks turned pink in an instant. The three children sat in silence, waiting for the laughter to stop.

Imogen offered Blazen some medovina. He rubbed his hands together. 'It's not my normal tipple, but I suppose I could try it.' Imogen spooned the orange liquid into a horn and handed it to Blazen. He drank it in one gulp.

'So what is it you're after?' said the giant. 'A new wolf rug? Antlers for the hearth?'

'Neither,' said Miro.

'I'm not going looking for that door again. I'm a hunter of monsters and beauteous things, not bits of wood.'

'Don't worry,' said Miro. 'We're not going to ask you to look for the door.'

The giant helped himself to biscuits, picking up four at a time.

'Imogen and Marie are planning a trip up Klenot Mountain,' continued the prince. 'They intend to meet the king of the skret, the Maudree Král.'

Blazen spat out the biscuits. 'They want to do *what?*'

'They're in need of a guide.'

The hunter pretended to look over his shoulder. 'Well, I don't know why you're all looking at me. I'm not going up that mountain. You've seen what happened to me with the stairs.' He chuckled, patting his rounded stomach.

'I'm serious,' said Miro.

'So am I! There's no way I'm making a journey like that. Being in the forests is dangerous enough . . . In case you hadn't noticed, boy, the skret are hunting people like rabbits. If the bunnies are stupid enough to wander into the beasts' den, they'll be skinned like the rest.'

'But you're the man that killed one hundred bears,' said Miro, a little plea creeping into his voice. 'You banished the mountain witch, released her prisoners and married her daughter before it was even time for lunch.'

'That one didn't work out so well,' the hunter muttered into his beard.

'Surely, Blazen Bilbetz, the fiercest warrior Yaroslav has ever known, isn't afraid of a few skret . . . are you?'

'There'll be more than a few.' Blazen shifted in his chair, making it squeak. 'And it only takes one to kill you. Just look at what they did to Yeedarsh!'

'I know,' said Miro, and he started fiddling with the rings on his fingers. 'I heard about Yeedarsh. My uncle will make them pay. You can count on that.'

'Bet Yeedarsh didn't see *that* coming,' said Blazen, puffing up his cheeks and shaking his big head. 'Bet he didn't even have time to scream.'

Miro looked back at the giant. 'But you're not Yeedarsh.'

'I'm not as young as I was. Is a man not allowed to mellow in his old age?'

'Mellow?'

'You know, put his feet up. Enjoy his past glories from the comfort of the Hounyarch.'

'Past glories?' Miro looked like a balloon that the air was being let out of. 'I thought you would do it. I thought ...'

'Well, people aren't always what you expect,' said Blazen. 'Take you, for example. When we first met, I just thought you were a rich kid – not *the number-one* rich kid, not the prince of Yaroslav! We're all fooling someone. The sooner you learn that the better.'

There was an uncomfortable silence. Blazen refused to make eye contact. Instead, he stared resolutely out of the window. Imogen followed his gaze. She could see the top of the tallest mountain.

'It's the wrong time to go,' said Blazen. 'You know that, don't you?'

'What do you mean?' asked Marie.

'It's autumn ... not far off winter.'

'We can't wait until next summer to go home,' said Imogen.

The giant stroked his beard, massaging in biscuit crumbs. 'Let me tell you a story,' he said and he didn't wait for permission to begin.

'Last winter, a man appeared in the fields outside Yaroslav. In the evening, he wasn't there. In the morning, he was. His cart was dripping in meltwater. The horse was one of those fluffy ones – the type that sometimes come from beyond the mountains. It was just standing there, eating grass, like horses do, and the man was curled up in the back of the cart. He was old and frostbitten. He'd been dead for hours.'

'What happened?' asked Imogen.

'He'd tried to cross the mountains at the wrong time. Must've got caught in a blizzard – frozen to death. He'd probably done that route one hundred times before, because the horse knew the way and it pulled the cart down the mountains, through the forests and across the fields to Yaroslav's walls. Not a bad effort for an overgrown rabbit.'

'I remember that man,' said Miro. 'My uncle told me about him. He said he was a merchant.'

'Yeah, that's right.'

'My uncle said he'd suffered for his stupidity.'

'Your uncle's right,' said the giant. 'There are many more like him along the icy mountain paths.'

Blazen squinted at the children with his piggy eyes. 'So ... still want to go?'

Imogen and Marie nodded.

'What about you?' said Blazen, turning to Miro. 'Are you stupid too?'

'I already told them not to go,' said Miro, pulling a blanket from the back of his chair and wrapping it round his shoulders. Just talking about the mountains seemed to make him feel cold. 'I told them the Maudree Král is more likely to kill them than help them.'

'That doesn't answer my question,' said Blazen. 'Are you going with them?'

Miro hesitated. Imogen wanted to say that he hadn't been invited, but she bit her tongue. 'I belong here,' said the prince.

'You mean you'd miss your servants and your comfy bed?' said the giant. 'I don't blame you.'

'I know how to forage and sleep in the open,' cried Miro.

Blazen laughed and slapped his thighs as though he'd just heard the world's best joke. 'No, you don't! You're about as ready for the wilderness as a jam-filled doughnut.'

'That doesn't even make sense.' Miro pulled the blanket tighter round his shoulders.

'I remember what you said when we were hunting for that blasted door,' said Blazen, still chuckling. 'You said you were the furthest from Yaroslav you'd ever been. And that was when we were in the forests' outskirts. You'll have to go much deeper and higher than that to meet the Maudree Král—'

'I have other duties to attend to,' said Miro. 'You can't go running away when you're heir to the throne. Uncle would never allow it.'

'All right, all right,' said Blazen, wiping tears of laughter from his eyes. 'You're not going. I get it.'

'And you neither,' said Miro.

'No. Me neither,' said the giant.

'I told you the hunter's a coward,' said Imogen. 'We'll just have to find someone who isn't.'

Blazen looked her up and down – shifting from merry to malign in the blink of an eye. 'You ought to be careful,' he said. 'I haven't forgotten what you did to my zpevnakrava.'

'What's a zpevnakrava?' said Marie.

'It *was* the finest musical instrument in the land,' said Blazen, 'until girlie stuck a knife in it.'

'Well, *I* haven't forgotten that you failed to find the door in the tree,' said Imogen, narrowing her eyes. 'All that riding around in the forests and we're still no closer to getting home.'

'I'll tell you something, girlie . . .' The giant leaned

forward, making his chair squeak for mercy. 'You look a lot like the description the Royal Guards are putting about.'

'What description?'

'The description of the child that stole King Vadik and Queen Sofia's wedding rings. The Royal Guards said she was about your size. Same short hair. Same freckled face. Same silly little outfit with the silly little stars.'

'I don't know what you're talking about,' said Imogen.

'That's funny because you look like you do. There's a hefty reward on your head. Wouldn't mind getting my paws on some of that gold.'

Imogen glared at the giant. He didn't blink.

'More biscuits?' asked Marie in her chirpiest voice.

'Oh, all right,' said Miro. 'I'll buy your silence.'

Blazen turned to the prince. 'How much are we talking? They're offering three hundred crowns for information about her.' He pointed at Imogen with a biscuit.

Miro walked over to the chest by his bed and rummaged around. 'Two bags,' he said. 'It's all I have left.'

'That will do.' Blazen held his drinking horn out for more medovina. Marie filled it up.

'This is the second time I've had to pay you off,' said Miro, depositing the bags of gold at the hunter's feet. 'Can I assume it will be the last? No one must know where Imogen and Marie have gone. I don't want them being chased by Royal Guards up Klenot Mountain.'

The giant nodded, slipping the bags into his pockets.

'And if you won't take my *friends* –' Miro said the word carefully – 'up the mountain, do you know someone who will?'

Blazen thought for a moment. 'There is one . . .'

'Oh yes?'

'I'm not saying she's any braver than me, but she is younger and she knows the forests well.'

'Who?'

'Her name's Lofkinye Lolo. We used to go hunting together . . . back in the old days.'

'Where is she now?' said Miro.

'Beneath our feet, of course.' Blazen stamped on the floor.

'Dead?'

'No!' said Blazen. 'In your stinking dungeons. But girlie must know her already! She's the woman that was getting duffed up when girlie stole the rings.'

CHAPTER 42

Yeedarsh's funeral ended with cathedral bells. Anneshka watched the priest as he said goodbye to the mourners and thanked them for coming. The Royal Guards left first, followed by the friends of the king, then a small party of servants and, finally, the prince.

The priest patted Miroslav on the head and said some comforting words. The boy nodded and walked away, towards Castle Yaroslav.

'The child has known Yeedarsh since he was an infant,' explained the priest, tucking his hands inside the sleeves of his robes. 'It's hard for him to see the old man go like this. Especially after losing his parents. Very hard indeed.'

'Who were those people that were sent away before the ceremony?' asked Anneshka.

'Just some curious townsfolk,' said the priest.

'They were shouting. They seemed more than just curious.'

The priest shook his head. 'They want revenge, I suppose. They want to see the skret punished for what they've done.'

'But Yeedarsh isn't the first to be killed by the skret,' said Anneshka.

'He's the first to be killed inside the castle walls. It looks like the skret are winning ... And it looks like we are not.'

'I see ...' Anneshka glanced at the altar, where the king was standing over Yeedarsh's coffin. 'Father, would you mind leaving us for a minute? I need to have a word with the king.'

'Not at all.'

Anneshka pushed the cathedral door closed behind the priest and turned to face Drakomor. It was just the two of them now.

Her skirts kissed the floor as she walked down the aisle.

'His soul may be with the stars,' said Drakomor, with a voice full of emotion, 'but it's fitting that his body rests here. My ancestors have been buried in the cathedral since time began and Yeedarsh has been serving our family for nearly as long.'

'I heard that you sent the guard away,' said Anneshka. 'The one that found Yeedarsh. The one that was supposed to be patrolling the West Wing.'

'What of it?'

'I would have had him executed. Someone has to pay.'

'You were at your parents' house,' said the king, visibly taken aback.

'It will be so much easier when I'm with you all the time.'

Their eyes met across the coffin and Anneshka held his gaze. 'You do know that people are blaming you, don't you? They're saying you can't even protect your own home.'

'Perhaps I can't. The skret are getting bolder by the day. Just look at what they've done to Yeedarsh . . . It's so *monstrous*. How could they do this to a harmless old man?'

'"Harmless" isn't the first word that springs to mind,' muttered Anneshka.

'What?'

'We're at war, Drakomor. What do you expect your enemy to do? They kill us. We kill them.'

'Weren't you listening when I told you what they did to my brother? These are no ordinary enemies. These are monsters we're fighting.'

'Láska, I know you're upset,' said Anneshka, 'but you need to understand the skret if you're going to defeat them. They're more similar to us than you think. They eat and sleep, just like we do.'

'They sleep in the day.'

'They mourn, fear, hate – even worship.'

Drakomor was looking at her like she was out of her mind. 'Worship?'

'The Sertze Hora – the stone you keep in the tower – is precious to them in a way that goes beyond reason.'

'What do you mean?' said the king.

'Come on . . . you must have worked it out by now.'

'Worked out what?'

'Why the skret come here every night. You told me that it began five years ago, around the time your brother was killed. Around the time when you took the heart of the mountain and stuck it up in that tower. Isn't that a bit of a coincidence?'

'The skret weren't doing anything with the Sertze Hora,' snapped Drakomor. 'It was just lying there.'

'I know, I know,' she said soothingly. 'But perhaps they still think of it as theirs and that's why they turned against Yaroslav. That's why they visit every night. They want it back. Surely the thought has crossed your mind?'

'They can't have it back.'

Anneshka left a respectful pause. From the walls of the cathedral, angels watched with painted smiles and knowing eyes. It seemed to her that they were only pretending to play their instruments.

The king sank down into a pew. 'I don't know what to do,' he said. Anneshka sat next to him, taking his hands in hers.

'Yaroslav needs some good news for a change,' she said. 'Something to celebrate.'

'But what?'

'A wedding.'

'You think it's time?' said the king. 'We haven't even got the rings ...'

'They'll turn up. Especially with the reward you've offered. Let's announce it. Let's announce our wedding. We can be ready within ten days. Perhaps just a week. It'll be the perfect distraction from all this nasty skret business. You can send word up the mountain too. Tell the Maudree Král that we're starting afresh – that we want to rebuild the old ties between the people of Yaroslav and the skret of Klenot Mountain ...'

'I'm not having skret at our wedding feast.'

'That's not what I'm proposing, láska.'

'What then?'

'Yes, the skret will receive an invite. Yes, they'll come to celebrate. But they won't even taste a drop of our wine. Won't even sniff the soup.'

The king stood up and started to pace in front of the coffin. 'Now there's a thought ... we could build a trap ... and the people will see it.'

'Exactly! What better way to demonstrate how well you protect Yaroslav from the skret? What better way to prove that you're in charge and avenge your brother?'

'I can't believe it,' said Drakomor. 'Not only have I got the prettiest bride in Yaroslav, but the smartest one too.'

Anneshka gave a smile sweeter than a sugar mouse.

CHAPTER 43

After Yeedarsh's funeral, Anneshka sat in the room at the top of her parents' house. She'd changed out of her mourning dress and her mother was brushing her hair.

'It's happening just as Ochi predicted,' said the older woman. 'I knew it was worth paying that witch to read your stars . . . Now remember, the king won't want a wife that talks too much and wakes too late. Or wakes too early and talks too little.' She jabbed at Anneshka's ribs. 'Have you been eating properly? The king won't want his wife to be as bony as a bird.'

The brush snagged on a knot and Anneshka flinched. 'Don't make a fuss,' said her mother and she pulled at the hair until Anneshka thought she'd tear it out. 'The king won't want a wife that jumps every time he raises his voice.'

'I know perfectly well what the king does and doesn't want,' snapped Anneshka, taking hold of her hair and yanking it out of her mother's hands. 'I don't need you any more, you old dragon.'

Anneshka's mother trembled with rage. 'You ungrateful

child!' she screamed. 'The things I've done to prepare you for your destiny! The sacrifices I've made!'

She lashed out, but Anneshka stepped back and her mother's hand swiped at thin air.

Anneshka smiled. She didn't have to put up with this any more. She walked out of the house with her hair hanging down her back like liquid gold.

When she arrived at the castle, the bells were ringing for dusk. Her parents' house was over a mile away, but Anneshka fancied she could still hear her mother wailing.

'My name is Anneshka Mazanar,' she told the guard at the entrance, 'and this is my home.'

CHAPTER 44

That night Imogen had another dream.

She was back at home. There was laughter coming from Mum's bedroom. She opened the door to find Mum and Marie building a den. There were extra pillows and duvets on the bed, and blankets were strung up between the headboard and the curtain rail, like sails on a ship.

Mum switched on the fairy lights, giving the room a pinkish glow. 'Come on, Imogen,' she said, 'there's room for one more.'

Imogen climbed on to the bed and Marie made space for her in the middle of the duvet-nest. It was lovely. Like being inside a cocoon.

'I broke up with Gavin,' said Mum, putting a stack of books on the bedside table and settling down next to the girls. Imogen searched her mum's face for signs of tears, but couldn't see any.

'Gavin the banker?' said Marie.

Mum laughed. 'Yes. Gavin the banker. There's only so much talk of interest rates a woman can take ...'

Imogen could hear the rain outside and feel the warmth of her mum's body through the duvet. She snuggled closer.

'I think we should celebrate with a story,' said Mum. 'Which one do you want?'

'The one about the princess in the tower,' said Marie.

'No! The one about the dead things that won't stay dead,' said Imogen.

'Imogen, you know that one frightens your sister.'

'She can always leave.'

'Hey!' cried Marie, yanking the duvet. 'That's not fair!'

Mum reached over and smoothed Marie's hair. 'I have a story to suit you both. It's about a very long journey.'

'A journey to where?' said the girls in unison.

'Well, if you let me tell it, you'll see.'

Mum read for what felt like hours and Marie dozed off, but Imogen didn't want to sleep. She wanted to hear what happened next. She could really picture the hero setting out on his quest.

She imagined that the duvet was a vast, forested landscape, with snowy mountain peaks. The hero walked along a ridge. Between two folds in the covers, Imogen imagined that there was a valley. At the bottom of the valley, she could see a city surrounded by a wall, and at the heart of the city there was a castle with towers. Imogen wasn't concentrating on the story any more. She leaned in, trying to get a better look.

'What is that place?' she said.

Mum looked over the top of the book. 'What place?'

'The city.'

'Darling, have you been asleep? There's no city in this story.'

There was a light coming from the second tallest tower.

'But it's right there – in the duvet.'

Mum put her hand on Imogen's forehead. 'Are you feeling okay?'

Imogen looked at the mountains surrounding the city. The biggest one had jagged rocks at its peak. That was Klenot Mountain. That was the one they had to climb. Suddenly she felt very cold.

'Come here,' said Mum, pulling Imogen closer and tucking the duvet round her neck. 'You must be coming down with something. It's a good job we're already tucked up in bed.'

When Imogen woke up, she thought she could still feel the warmth of her mother's arms.

She opened her eyes. It was morning and Miro was sitting by the fireplace, holding the little black box. Marie was asleep. She'd turned herself upside down in the night.

Imogen felt a sob rising in her chest. She stifled it, curling into a ball. Her mum wasn't there. Her mum might never be there again. It had all been a dream . . . And yet it was also a memory. Her mum really had dated a banker called Gavin and she really hadn't seemed sad when it ended. Imogen hadn't been sad either.

It had been a long time since she'd thought of that day. They'd made a den in Mum's big double bed and stayed there all afternoon. Imogen remembered asking: 'Is that it? Are you done with boyfriends now? Will it just be the three of us?'

Her mum had replied: 'It will always be the three of us, Imogen. No matter what.'

Well, it wasn't the three of them now, was it?

Imogen sat up and pushed the covers off her legs. Lying in bed wouldn't help her get home. She would just have to get up that mountain. *If* the skret king was friends with the shadow moth and *if* he knew about the door in the tree, then perhaps there was hope.

'Good morning, Miro,' she said, striding over to his seat by the fire. 'Today we're going to ask Lofkinye Lolo to be our mountain guide!'

Miro didn't reply. He had taken the rings out of the little box and he was turning them over again and again. 'What are you doing?' said Imogen, annoyed.

'I'm going to give the rings back to Uncle,' said Miro.

'But Blazen promised to keep his mouth shut. No one will even know we've got them.'

'It's not right. Uncle Drakomor is looking for them.'

Imogen wanted to reply, but she was interrupted by the chiming of the clock. Mechanical stars circled its face. The hatch opened and a wooden figure stepped out. It was a woman in a pouffy dress. She floated forward and blew a kiss.

'It's a princess!' said Marie, suddenly awake.

'No, it's just a woman in a wedding dress,' said Imogen. The figure glided back into the clock.

Imogen turned to Miro. 'Haven't you heard of *finders keepers*?' she asked. 'It means that if you lose something it's not yours any more and, if you find it, you get to keep it.'

'But Uncle didn't lose the rings,' said Miro. '*You* stole them.'

Marie put her head on one side. 'I suppose that's true.'

Imogen wasn't so sure. 'Didn't you say they were your parents' wedding rings? You've got just as much right to them as he has.'

'Uncle looks after them for us both.'

'Fine,' said Imogen in a voice that sounded not fine. 'Off you go, then.'

Miro stood up to leave. 'We'll go and speak to the woman Blazen recommended when I'm back,' he said. 'Once you've got her, you won't need me any more. You'll be on your way home.' He turned to Marie. 'Both of you.'

'Good,' said Imogen. 'I can't wait.'

CHAPTER 45

Miro walked to his uncle's study. After his parents had died, he used to sit in that room with Uncle Drakomor and go through his father's stuff, poring over letters and keepsakes.

Sometimes Drakomor would open the little black box and hold up the wedding rings so they shone in the firelight. He'd tell Miro stories about his father. They always began: 'Many years ago, when the stars were old and the moon was young . . .' He'd tell the stories over and over again, polishing them until they gleamed in the firelight too and Miro thought he could see familiar figures flickering among the flames. He loved those evenings.

But, in recent years, Miro had grown wary of his uncle's study. This was the place he got called to if he'd done something wrong. Miro couldn't help feeling that his uncle cared more and more for his collection and less and less for him.

When Miro had been caught stealing from the kitchens, his uncle dismissed his favourite cook. When Miro damaged a priceless teapot, he spent a month alone in his tower. When he failed to improve his algebra, his tutor was sent beyond the mountains and never heard from again. That was his uncle's style: death by isolation.

There were two guards outside the king's study. As usual, they ushered Miro inside. As usual, he had to squeeze past the king's treasures. But then things got less usual. Uncle Drakomor had company. Standing behind him, as he sat at his desk, was a woman. A woman Miro had never seen before.

His uncle's visitors were normally fusty old aristocrats with droopy moustaches and even *they* weren't allowed in the study. This was a private space. The woman raised an eyebrow, as if to say, *And who are you?*

'I don't think you've been properly introduced,' said the king. 'Miroslav, this is Anneshka Mazanar.' The woman bowed her head. 'Anneshka, this is my late brother's son.'

The woman had yellow hair and almond-shaped eyes. Miro thought she was pretty. He wondered if his uncle thought so too.

Miro must have been staring because his uncle said, 'Go on, give the lady a bow.'

'Why is she in your study?' The words came out of Miro's mouth before he could stop them.

'Miroslav!' cried his uncle.

'It's perfectly all right,' said the woman. 'You and I will be seeing a lot more of each other from now on.'

She walked round the desk, slowly and purposefully, towards Miro. She bent down so her face was level with his. Her eyes were a fantastic blue, almost purple. Miro couldn't stop looking at them, but they weren't looking at his face. They were looking at his tunic, which was cut from the same material as a lot of his clothes – a dark velvet embroidered with gold stars.

'This is a lovely thing,' purred the woman, touching the edge of his sleeve. Miro wasn't sure whether to say thank you. It didn't feel like she was talking to him.

'What's that?' asked Drakomor.

'I said, this is a lovely outfit your nephew has. Don't you think?'

'Oh yes, very nice.'

She walked back to the desk and Miro realised that he had been holding his breath. She whispered something into the king's ear and now *he* was looking at Miro's tunic too.

'I can come back another time . . .' said Miro.

'No, no, Miroslav,' said the king. 'Say what it is you've come to say.'

'Right.' Miro took a deep breath and blurted out his story: 'I was walking along a corridor in the East Wing – just the other night – you know the corridor with the big tapestry and the—'

'Yes, I know, boy. What's your point?'

'Well, I found this thing there and I think it might be what you're looking for?'

He reached into his pocket and removed the black box.

'What's that?' snapped Drakomor. Miro placed the box on the desk so his uncle could see. 'The rings!'

'Are they the ones that were missing?' asked Miro, trying his best to sound innocent.

The woman was craning her neck over the king's shoulder to get a better look. He passed her the box. She slipped the smaller ring on to her finger. Miro wanted to stop her.

'What do you think?' she asked, holding out her hand.

'It suits you!' said Drakomor. 'A perfect fit.' He turned back to Miro. 'What's wrong with you, boy? Why do you even have to ask? Don't you remember your own parents' wedding rings?' Miro clenched his fists. He wanted the woman to take off his mother's ring.

'Your uncle asked you a question,' said the woman. Miro shook his head. The king rolled his eyes.

'While you're here,' he said, 'there's something I may as well tell you.' The woman put a hand on Drakomor's shoulder and gave it a squeeze. The ring flashed on her finger. 'Anneshka and I plan to get married.'

There was a pause while the grown-ups waited for Miro to speak.

'I believe the customary response is "congratulations",'

said the king. Miro opened his mouth. He tried to say it, he really did, but the word stuck in his throat like a long fish bone. 'We'll be telling the servants soon, but I thought you should be the first to know.'

'Won't that be nice?' said the woman. 'You'll have a mother again.'

Drakomor picked up the remaining ring and held it up to the candlelight. Miro dug his fingernails into his palms.

'I'll go now,' he said, but the grown-ups were talking to each other in excited whispers. They didn't seem to notice Miro any more. He slipped away quietly, disappearing between the enormous stone and a fossilised troll head.

CHAPTER 46

Imogen and Marie waited for Miro to return from his uncle's study for hours. They read books. They ate cake. They even made the bed. But eventually they began to wonder what was going on.

'I thought he'd be back by now,' said Imogen.

'He said we'd go to the dungeons,' said Marie. 'He said we'd ask Lofkinye Lolo to be our guide.'

'Perhaps he chickened out. Dungeons do sound a bit scary.'

'That would be bad. That would be really ... What's the opposite of brave?'

'Lily-livered,' said Imogen. 'That's what he is! Have you ever seen him do anything that puts his neck on the line?'

'He did rescue us,' said Marie, 'when we first got here and the skret were coming.'

'He let us into the castle. I'm not sure I'd call it a *great* rescue.'

'He cut his thumb and made a pact. That was brave. There was blood and everything!'

'That was odd. That's what that was.'

Marie pressed her lips together, thinking. 'Didn't he save you from Blazen Bilbetz when you broke his bagpipes?'

'That?' scoffed Imogen. 'All Miro did was pay. You don't have to be brave to pay. You just have to be a prince. Let's go to the dungeons without him.'

'Do you think they'd let us in?'

'No,' said Imogen, kicking the nearest chair. 'This is *so* annoying.'

'We'll have to go and look for him,' said Marie.

'Oh, all right.' Imogen rubbed her toe and scowled. 'I suppose we haven't got any choice.'

The sisters climbed down from the second tallest tower and set off in different directions. Imogen started in the West Wing, sending Marie to the North.

The corridors seemed to run on forever, connecting room after room like a massive rabbit warren. Imogen opened every door and checked under every table. Some of the places were familiar; others were unexplored. None of them contained the prince.

The girls regrouped in the library. 'No luck?' asked Imogen.

'No,' said Marie. 'There were voices in the king's study, but the guards said Miro left hours ago.'

The girls searched the South Wing together. The prince hadn't shown them this part of the castle. They ran from room to room, calling Miro's name. Eventually, they came to a staircase that was flanked by flags. 'Well, this looks grand,' muttered Imogen. She sat down on the first step and Marie sat next to her. As their breathing steadied, Imogen heard a sound. A sort of snuffling. It was coming from somewhere above their heads.

'Miro,' said Marie, springing to her feet. 'Miro, is that you?' The snuffling stopped. Marie ran up the staircase and Imogen followed. About halfway up, the stairs split in two, looped round and met on the next floor.

The prince was sitting on the top step, with his knees tucked under his chin. His far-apart eyes were puffy and his cheeks looked like dough.

'What do you want?' he said, burying his face in his arms.

Marie approached slowly. 'We've been looking for you,' she said.

'Well, I don't know why. Everyone seems to get on just fine without me.' His voice was thick with snot and tears.

'We don't get on fine without you,' said Marie. 'That's why we've been looking for you.'

'What if I don't want to be found? Ever think of that?'

Imogen hung back. It was awkward seeing Miro like this. She noticed an open doorway behind him and wondered if she could wait through there while he sorted himself out. Miro must have seen her edging towards it. 'Stay away from there,' he snapped, looking at her with watery eyes. 'You're not allowed in.'

Imogen didn't step over the threshold, but she could see into the room. It was a bedroom with ornate furniture and a window overlooking the forests. But, despite the lavish decor, it felt strangely sparse.

Then it clicked. This was the first room she'd seen that didn't contain any of the king's collection. There was just normal bedroom stuff, all covered in a thick layer of dust. A shirt was folded over the arm of a chair. A brush lay on its side, with long hairs trailing from it. A stuffed toy sat on the floor, just a few metres from where Imogen stood. It had a blue mane and an orange face, with a silly smile and buttons for eyes. 'What is this place?' she asked.

'None of your business,' said the prince.

Marie sat down on the step next to Miro. 'Whatever's happened,' she said, 'it can't be that bad.'

'Can't it?' said Miro, lifting his head a little.

'Was your uncle angry about the rings? Is that it? I'm sure Imogen wouldn't mind explaining. She can tell him it wasn't your fault. Can't you, Imogen?'

'It's not about the rings,' said Miro. 'It's about Uncle's visitor: Anneshka Mazanar. She says she's going to be my mother. *He's* going to make her my mother.'

'What? How?'

'They're getting married.'

Miro started crying again and Marie put her arm round his shoulders, but she couldn't quite reach far enough. Imogen watched from the doorway. 'There, there,' said Marie, just like Mum used to when one of them was upset.

'I don't like Anneshka at all,' continued Miro. 'And I don't think she likes me. She's not going to want me around. I'll be banished to my tower forever.'

'Surely she wouldn't do that,' said Marie. 'Surely your uncle has picked her because she's nice.'

'She didn't seem very nice . . .'

Imogen remembered Andel's story and what Drakomor had done to his eye. Maybe Miro's uncle had different ideas about 'nice'. This didn't seem like the time to bring it up . . .

'I think it's normal not to like your stepmum at first,' said Marie, 'but people seem to change their minds – you know, after spending some time together.'

Imogen thought about Mark, Mum's new boyfriend, and she thought that Marie was wrong. Often you knew whether you liked someone at first glance. And often you didn't change your mind. Imogen had known she would hate Mark as soon as she'd heard those stupid squeaky shoes.

'What's a stepmum?' asked the prince.

'A spare parent,' said Marie. 'Sarah at school said she

couldn't stand her stepmum. She said she was going to run away with the circus. Then the stepmum took her to see Cirque du Soleil, with tightrope walkers and everything. Her stepmum was afraid of the clowns too. After that, they got on better.'

Miro blew his nose into a hanky. 'I didn't know this happened to other people.'

'Oh yes,' said Marie. 'All the time.' She thought for a minute. 'But other people aren't the prince of an entire kingdom. That's the only difference.'

The corners of Miro's mouth twitched. 'Yes, I'm the only one of those.'

'Our mum has a boyfriend too, remember?' said Imogen. 'It's basically the same thing.'

'Because a boyfriend is a man you might marry?' said Miro.

'Yes, but it's not quite the same,' said Marie thoughtfully. 'Mum's boyfriends never stay.'

Imogen wondered if Mum had split up with Mark yet. He might be annoying, but the thought of Mum all alone made Imogen feel even more homesick. Mum's words floated through her mind: *It will always be the three of us, Imogen. No matter what.*

'So why were you hiding here?' said Marie. 'Why this staircase?'

'It's not really about the staircase,' said Miro. 'It's about the room. That's my parents' room. My *real* parents.'

'Is that your toy cat on the floor?' said Imogen. 'Why have you left him there?'

'He's a lion and I'm too big for toys ... Besides, even if I did want him, I'm not allowed. No one goes in that room. We're keeping it exactly as it was on the day that my parents died.'

Imogen wasn't sure what to say. Miro wiped his face on his sleeve.

'I suppose you two are keen to get going,' he said. 'We need to ask Lofkinye Lolo if she'll take you up Klenot Mountain.'

'Well,' said Marie, 'when you feel up to it ...'

'I thought so. Let's get it over with.'

Miro stood up and offered Marie his hand. She took it. 'You know, Miro,' she said, 'you could always come with us.'

The thought hung there for a moment, suspended somewhere above the boy's head.

'With you?'

'Up Klenot Mountain and back down again,' said Marie. 'It'll be an adventure ...'

'I won't be much help in the mountains. I don't like the cold.'

'I'm not inviting you to help.'

'Why are you inviting me?' said the prince.

'Because you're our friend, of course.'

Miro looked at the floor and scuffed his feet against the banisters.

'You're inviting me . . . just because . . .'

'Yes.'

'You don't want to make a new pact?'

'No.'

The last of his tears glinted on his eyelashes.

'All right,' he said. 'I'd like that very much.'

CHAPTER 47

B ack in the king's study, the grown-ups' conversation had turned from whispering sweet nothings to something altogether more serious.

'There's no mistaking it,' hissed Anneshka. She was holding a scrap of cloth. It was the remnant that the Royal Guards had delivered, along with the news that the rings had been stolen. 'It's not just *similar*. It's *identical* to what that boy was wearing!'

'There must be other children in Yaroslav wearing tunics cut from this cloth,' said the king.

'And the boy just happens to have stumbled upon the stolen rings!' said Anneshka. 'Do you really believe that?'

The king bowed his head. 'What does it matter?'

'Are you serious?' She took his face in her hands. 'Look at me, Drakomor! Are you really telling me you don't understand what this means? That boy is a liability! He's only small now, but it won't be like that for long. Today it's childish pranks and teaming up with lesni to steal our precious things—'

'We don't know what happened . . .'

'—Give him a few years and it'll be much worse. How is he going to feel about *our* children? *Our* sons? God only knows what he'll do when he's old enough to wear the crown. He'll send me away – you can be sure of that! He'll have me and you and any family we've raised sent across the mountains to perish!'

Now Drakomor was looking at her in horror, his face even paler than usual.

'I'm telling you,' she continued, 'it's me or him.'

The king took the ring off his finger and put it back in the box. 'Your point is well made.' He held out his hand for the ring she was wearing.

'You mean you'll do it?' she said. 'You'll get rid of the boy?'

'I'll have him sent away.'

Anneshka gave a little squeak of joy and bounced into Drakomor's arms.

'But I do mean sent away,' said the king. 'I won't have him harmed.'

'Of course, láska.' She pulled back, removed the ring and handed it to her beloved.

'And I'm not sending him off unaccompanied. I want him taken somewhere safe. If he goes beyond the mountains, he'll need an armed guard and special provisions.'

'Yes, yes.'

The king closed the lid of the little black box.

'I understand completely,' said Anneshka. 'Just leave it with me.'

'And what about the wedding preparations?' said Drakomor. 'We haven't decided how to get rid of the Maudree Král. Should I have the Royal Guards slit his throat after the ceremony?'

'No,' said Anneshka, 'it needs to be more spectacular than that. Something that people will talk about for centuries to come.'

'You think we should use some kind of weapon?'

'Perhaps . . . It would need to be powerful enough to destroy the Maudree Král and any skret he brings with him. It would also have to be beautiful, so that they don't suspect its true purpose. And it has to be assembled with haste.'

'Sounds like quite the challenge,' said Drakomor, stroking his moustache. 'I once knew a lesni who was such a good craftsman that the peasants said he worked miracles. He made a clock – claimed it could read the stars.'

'He sounds perfect!' said Anneshka.

'There's only one problem.' Drakomor looked sheepish. 'He refused to work for me . . . years ago . . . so I took out his eye.'

'Well, that's easy to fix,' said Anneshka. 'Tell him that if he refuses again you'll take the other one.'

CHAPTER 48

Yaroslav's prisoners were kept underground. In this place, there was no difference between day and night. Miro held a torch to light the way and Imogen and Marie followed him down the stone steps.

'Do you think Blazen was telling the truth?' asked Imogen. 'Do you think Lofkinye really is the same woman I saw being attacked by the Royal Guards? I think we saw her feeding the velecours too.'

'No idea,' said Miro. 'So long as she's willing to take us up the mountain, I don't suppose it matters.'

The children climbed down through the castle's foundations. The walls were made of rock and the air smelled like it hadn't been changed for centuries.

'How deep are we going?' asked Marie.

'To the very bottom,' said Miro. 'That's where the worst prisoners are kept – in the Hladomorna Pits.'

'The what pits?'

'Hladomorna. There's one hole per prisoner to stop them sharing dangerous ideas.' Miro sounded proud, as if it had been his invention.

The steps led the children to a sleeping guard. He snored softly. They climbed over his legs to get to another staircase that took them deeper still.

'It might be best if I do the talking,' said Miro. 'When we get there, I mean.'

'Why?' asked Imogen.

'Lesni are disobedient. It's not going to be easy to persuade her to help us, but she might listen to her prince.'

'Who are the lesni?' asked Imogen.

'They're the people who used to live in the forests.'

'Why don't they live there now?' said Marie.

'No one lives in the forests any more. Because of the skret.'

'But why aren't lesni people allowed to hunt rabbits?' asked Imogen. 'I'd be disobedient too if the rules were unfair.'

Miro looked confused and then annoyed. He shook his head quickly as if trying to get rid of the thoughts. 'I don't know. My uncle makes the rules. That's just how it is.'

The stairs took them to a small cave where two guards were playing dice. When they saw Miro, they hid the game, struggled to their feet and bowed.

'Sorry, Your Highness. Didn't know you were planning a visit today.'

'I'm looking for a woman called Lofkinye Lolo,' said the prince. 'Can you tell me which Pit she's in?'

'Down the steps. Fourth on the right.'

'Thank you,' said Miro.

'Will you be wanting any assistance, Your Highness? She's got a bit of a mouth on her.'

'That won't be necessary.'

Imogen couldn't decide whether she was more irritated by Miro's pompous tone, or impressed by his ability to boss grown-ups around.

They walked down the third staircase. It was narrower than the others and the walls were covered in green slime. At the bottom, they counted three doors on the right and went through the fourth. There was a hole cut into the ground. 'This,' said Miro, 'is a Hladomorna Pit. The bars stop visitors falling in and prisoners crawling out.'

The children crouched down and peered in. Imogen recognised the prisoner at once, with her hair twisted into two buns and her determined eyes. But the human firework had lost her spark. Her clothes seemed duller, her hair had been messed up and her brown skin showed bruises.

Imogen didn't understand. All of this for hunting a rabbit?

Miro cleared his throat. 'My name is Prince Miroslav Yaromeer Drahomeer Krishnov, Lord of the—'

'Skip the intro,' said the woman.

'Er ... Are you Lofkinye Lolo, lesni huntress and friend of Blazen Bilbetz?'

'I'm not friends with that pumpkin-brain.'

'Right.' Miro hesitated. 'But you are all the other things?'

The prince held his torch closer to the bars and Lofkinye turned away. 'We've brought you something in case you're hungry,' he said.

'I don't need charity,' replied Lofkinye.

'We're not offering charity,' said Imogen. 'It's actually the other way round. We need your help.'

Lofkinye's shape shifted in the gloom. 'What help can I give anyone while I'm stuck down here?'

'That's just the point,' said Miro. 'We're going to help you escape.'

Lofkinye laughed. The laugh turned into a cough. 'So this is my rescue party?' she said. 'A half-grown prince and a couple of serving brats?'

Imogen and Marie exchanged glances. *Servants?* That was a new one.

'We want you to be our guide,' said Miro. 'We need to leave Yaroslav. Urgently.'

'Ah, so you're running away.'

'No! My uncle's the king. Why would I run away? We

have to talk to the Maudree Král. We need you to take us up Klenot Mountain.'

'*What?*'

'My friends are looking for a door that leads to another world and we think the skret know where it is.'

'I've heard of such things,' said Lofkinye. 'Doors among trees.'

'Really? Great!' said Imogen.

'But I've never seen one for myself.'

'Oh.'

'What food did you bring?'

'Cake,' said Miro.

'You bring a starving woman cake?'

'Why not?'

'Never mind. Just give it here.'

Imogen held a parcel through the bars. When Lofkinye stood up and stretched her arms above her head, she could just about reach it. She ate the cake, then looked directly at Imogen. 'Don't I know you?'

'I was there when you were arrested,' said Imogen.

The huntress scrunched up her eyes and opened them again. 'Oh yes! You're the girl that took the dagger. I didn't think you'd get away ...'

Lofkinye moved back from the hole's opening so the children couldn't see her face.

'This expedition you're talking about,' she said quietly. 'What's in it for me?'

'Your freedom,' said Miro.

'I imagine that's essential if I'm to act as your guide.'

'Yes,' said Imogen, and she scowled at Miro. 'We'll help you escape either way.'

'But I don't have any more money,' said the prince, irritation creeping into his voice.

'I hear the king's quite the collector,' said the woman.

'I suppose I could get you my uncle's miniature Pustiny Jewel Collection,' said Miro. 'That'd be quite easy to smuggle out.'

'What's it worth?'

'I don't know ... thousands of crowns. It's the only one in Yaroslav.'

'Okay,' said Lofkinye. 'It's a deal.' She stretched up again and held out her hand.

Miro turned to Imogen and whispered, 'The word of a lesni is worth less than the fart of a dog. Yeedarsh said so.'

'Don't be so horrible,' hissed Imogen. 'She seems trustworthy to me. Get on with it before she changes her mind.'

Miro reached down and shook Lofkinye's hand.

'And what are you going to do if you find this door?' asked the prisoner.

'Go through it,' said Marie. 'Go home.'

'You're telling me you're from ...?' Lofkinye's voice trailed off. 'Well, you're certainly the craziest people I've met, I'll give you that. It sounds like an interesting expedition. I'm in.'

'Thank you!' cried Marie.

'Yes, thanks, Lofkinye,' said Imogen.

'We'll come for you tomorrow,' said Miro.

'I have nowhere else to be,' said their new guide. 'Do you know what to pack?'

'I was thinking about that,' muttered the prince. 'There are chocolates in the kitchens. I think they're for the wedding, but if I take a few and space them out again the head cook won't notice.'

'If stupidity floated, you'd be up there like a little duck.'

'Huh?'

'We're not taking chocolate,' said the woman. 'Listen carefully. I'll tell you what to bring.'

CHAPTER 49

That evening, Petr Voyák, the Chief of the Royal Guards and the very same man who lost the king's wedding rings, arrived at his quarters. He slipped off his boots and heaved a sigh of relief.

Since that blasted girl had escaped with the rings, every hour of Petr's day had been spent hunting for her. There wasn't a door in the city that he hadn't knocked on. He'd threatened, he'd bribed, he'd pleaded. After nightfall, when it was too dangerous to go outside, he'd busied himself writing Wanted notices.

But not tonight. Tonight Petr was determined to have a break. He poured himself a glass of red wine and checked his black eye in the mirror. It was healing well. The woman who'd given it to him was in the Hladomorna Pits. That ought to knock the fight out of her.

Petr was just applying some mountain-daisy cream to the bruised skin when there was a knock on his door. It opened before he had a chance to say 'come in' and Anneshka Mazanar appeared.

'I do hope I'm not disturbing you,' she said in a honey-coated voice. Her violet eyes flicked from the undrunk wine to his cream-circled black eye.

'No, not at all, m'lady. I was just – I was just cleaning my sword.' He tried his best to look natural.

'It's "Your Highness" now, Voyák. I'm to marry the king. Haven't you heard?'

'Right, m'lady. I mean, yes, Your Highness.'

'May I have a seat?'

Petr scrambled to clear her a space. 'What can I do for you?' he asked, sitting down opposite and wishing he hadn't put so much cream on his face.

'It's not about what you can do for me,' she said. 'I'm here for King Drakomor.'

'Well, as you know, I am the king's most loyal servant,' said the guard.

'That's exactly why I'm talking to you.'

Petr sat up a little straighter.

'You see,' continued Anneshka, 'the task at hand is a rather delicate one. It has to be done by someone the king trusts. Someone who can do the job and keep quiet about it afterwards.'

'Oh yes, m'lady. My lips will be sealed. Whatever it is, you can trust me to be discreet. I'll be the—'

'Of course –' she cut him off – 'the king is still upset about the wedding rings.'

'It won't happen again,' said Petr. 'You can count on me.'

Anneshka's eyes went to the half-open door. 'All right,' she said. 'I'll tell you what you must do.'

Petr nodded.

'The king wishes for Miroslav to be disposed of.'

Petr stopped nodding. 'Disposed of?'

'Yes.'

'Sent away?'

'No.'

'As in . . .' Petr put his hands round his neck.

'He wants the boy killed,' said Anneshka. 'Can you manage that?'

'He wants the boy killed?'

'Isn't that what I just said?'

'Yes, m'lady.'

Now it was Petr's turn to look at the door. He got up, peeped round it, then pulled it shut. He turned back to his visitor. 'But . . . he's just a child . . . I've known him since he was a babe.'

'I don't see what that's got to do with anything.'

'Why would the king want his own nephew dead?'

'Are you paid to ask questions, Voyák?'

'No, m'lady.'

'Then why are you doing it?'

'I – I'm not in the business of killing children. It's

supposed to be enemy soldiers and skret and the like. That's what I'm trained to kill.'

'I thought you might say that,' sneered Anneshka, standing up to leave. 'From what I hear, you allowed a child to run off with our wedding rings, without so much as giving chase.'

'Jan got stuck in an alleyway and—'

'—I must say I had no idea you had such a soft spot for children. What else have you got a soft spot for?'

'It's just—'

'It was a rhetorical question, Voyák. You're not supposed to answer.'

His throat was dry. 'Sorry, m'lady.'

'You will be,' she said. 'If you're so full of soft spots, I'm not sure you're the right man to be heading up *my* Royal Guards. Perhaps you should step down. Perhaps you should take a trip beyond the mountains.'

Anneshka moved towards the door, but Petr leaped in front of her. 'Please,' he said. 'Don't send me away.' There was sweat above his lip. Why was there always sweat above his lip? 'I'll do it. I'll do whatever the king commands.'

'Good,' she said. 'It needs doing tomorrow night.'

'Yes, m'lady,' said Petr. 'But I'll need another pair of hands.'

'Is there someone that can be trusted?'

'My brother, Jan . . . He won't like it either, but I'll tell him he can be my deputy if he helps.'

'I'll leave that to you,' she said. 'Just don't tell anyone else.'

'Very well, m'lady . . . Also, what should we do with the . . . how should we dispose of . . .'

'The body? The king doesn't much care what you do with the body,' said Anneshka. 'The main thing is to bury it deep. The story will be that the boy has been sent away. I'll say he's staying beyond the mountains, with his mother's relatives.'

'Right. I suppose you'll be wanting some kind of evidence that the deed has been done?'

Anneshka thought for a moment. 'You mean like the boy's heart in a box?'

Petr felt the blood drain from his face. Surely she wasn't going to ask him to . . .

'No, I won't be needing anything like that,' she said. 'How would I know it belonged to the boy? It could just as easily be a pig's!' She laughed, but Petr couldn't bring himself to join in.

'Besides, I have my own ways of knowing if people are telling the truth,' whispered Anneshka, wrinkling her pretty little nose. 'If you get close enough, you can almost smell it.'

Petr swallowed.

'And Voyák . . .'

'Yes, m'lady?'

'It's "Your Highness".'

CHAPTER 50

The night before they left for the mountains, the children didn't sleep well.

Every time Imogen was about to drift off, things moved in the corners of her mind: her worry creatures would not rest. She closed her eyes and they stirred behind curtains and made the drawers rattle. *Let me out, let me out,* whispered a thousand tiny voices. *You can't go to the mountains. You'll get yourself killed and sliced up. You'll get lost. You'll get eaten. You'll never make it home.*

Left to their own devices, the worry creatures would break free. They'd clutch at her stomach with their bony fingers until she felt sick. They'd sit on her chest so she struggled to breathe. They'd squeeze their ugly little bodies round her heart until—

Imogen imagined grabbing the worry creatures by the throat and stuffing them back where they belonged. Slam the drawers shut. Close the curtains. Give them all a good kicking.

She tried to think of something else. Something cheerful. She tried to think about being in bed with her mum, with books and fairy lights and a pinkish glow. The worry creatures were still for a minute – two at most – then they started to fidget and whisper and the whole thing began again.

Miro's worry creatures were different. They hid from him. They left him behind. They were grown-ups closing the door in his face. They were shadows of little girls running between trees. A shoe disappearing behind a trunk. An echo of laughter. Miro would turn on the spot and call, 'Wait!', but the ghosts wouldn't wait and soon it was just him and a moon that took up half the sky.

Outside, the skret howled.

Finally, morning came and the clock struck seven. A pair of jewelled planets flew in circles round the nine before the hatch popped open. 'What will it be this time?' asked Miro, sitting up at the bottom of the bed.

A tiny carving of a boy trotted out of the clock's hatch. He was wearing a miniature crown. 'Oh look, it's a prince like me!'

The little prince started running on the spot. His arms and legs swung on their hinges. Suddenly the running stopped. The figure moved back towards the hatch, but this time it was as though he was being dragged through it, pulled against his will. His tiny hands held on to the edges of the open door, fighting an invisible force. He let go. The hatch slammed shut. The prince was trapped inside the clock.

'That's weird,' said Marie. 'None of the others did that.'

Imogen looked at Miro. He had turned pale. 'Are you okay?' she asked.

'We need to pack,' said the prince.

Lofkinye had given them a long list of things to bring with them. 'I'll sort out the clothes,' said Imogen. 'Marie, you fetch the food. The cook loves you. She'll let you have whatever you ask for.'

'What about Miro?' said Marie. 'What's he going to get?'

'Weapons,' said Miro. 'I'll get the weapons.'

CHAPTER 51

Imogen was the first to return to the room at the top of the second tallest tower. She'd brought animal skins to sleep on and wear. Marie arrived next, dragging a sack through the door and dumping it by the bed.

'Here, try this on for size,' said Imogen, throwing her sister a coat. Marie pulled it on. The hood flopped over her face, the sleeves covered her fingers and the hem finished by her ankles. Imogen smothered a laugh.

'It's too big!' said Marie.

'It was the smallest one I could find.'

'And it smells funny.'

'It's made from a dead animal. What do you expect?'

'Urgh!' Marie tossed the coat aside. 'That's disgusting.'

'What did you manage to get?' asked Imogen, opening Marie's sack.

'I'll show you.' Marie pulled out a bag of things that looked like shrivelled ears. 'Dried apples and mushrooms.' She tossed the bag aside and pulled out another. 'Honey oatcakes. Bet they'll taste good.' She opened a third bag.

'Venison pies. Smell them. Mmmm, tasty. Oh yes, and a load of dry bread.'

'Dry bread? I don't fancy that,' said Imogen.

'It's twice-baked, like Lofkinye wanted. Cook was asking a lot of questions.'

'What did you say?'

'That we were preparing a special dinner for Miro.'

'Did she buy it?' asked Imogen.

'Not sure,' said Marie. 'She said he never used to like mushrooms.'

Miro burst into the room with a manic look on his face. 'Guess what!' he cried. 'I've raided the armoury!'

He knelt on the floor and unrolled a long sheet of leather. Inside were blades of all shapes and sizes. 'Uncle would be furious if he knew . . .'

'I like that one,' said Imogen, pointing to a short sword with a jewel-encrusted handle.

'I want the little one,' said Marie.

Miro handed the girls the blades they'd asked for. 'They aren't full-sized,' he said, 'but they're sharp.'

'What about the bow for Lofkinye?' said Imogen.

'Got that too.' Miro finished unrolling the sheet of leather, revealing an unstrung bow, a case and a quiverful of arrows.

'Okay,' said Imogen. 'What's left on the list?'

'Rope and candles and a tinderbox,' said Marie.

'Don't you need to get Lofkinye's payment?' said Imogen. 'She wanted something from the king's collection.'

'She can have it after the expedition,' said Miro.

'I'm not sure she'll be happy with that.'

'Well, she'll have to be,' said the prince. 'I don't trust her. She needs an incentive not to dump us on the side of the mountain. Besides, it'd just be more to carry.'

'I'll leave you to explain that to Lofkinye,' said Imogen, narrowing her eyes. 'But, if you ask me, we shouldn't go upsetting our guide before we've even left the castle. We've got bigger challenges ahead than your *trust issues*.'

Imogen ran her finger over the jewels in the hilt of her sword. It felt good to be armed. The stones were smooth. The blade was anything but.

She had a feeling she was going need it.

CHAPTER 52

Petr picked a small church in a quiet corner of Yaroslav. While the cemetery's earth was full of dead humans, the church walls were topped with the skulls of skret.

As Petr had predicted, his brother hadn't been happy about Anneshka's order to kill the boy, but Jan wouldn't leave Petr to do the deed alone. He was a good brother. Besides, Jan liked the sound of *Deputy Captain Jan Voyák*. He said it had 'a nice ring to it'.

Petr threw Jan a spade. 'Here,' he said, 'the priest said we could put him under this old tree so long as we mind the roots.'

'What did you tell the priest?' said Jan.

'That a young boy is very ill,' said Petr, 'and likely to die this evening and his parents can't afford a funeral.'

'Didn't he ask why we were doing the digging?'

'It's not *so* unusual for the king's men to lend the poor a helping hand,' said Petr.

Jan snorted. 'If you say so.'

Very few mourners visited the graveyard that

afternoon and those that did paid little attention to the Royal Guards. They were too busy thinking about the dead to worry about the living.

When the grave was half finished, the priest came out and offered the brothers a shot of slivovitsa to 'reward them for their charitable work'.

The guards knocked back the firewater. 'Thank you,' said Petr, not looking the priest in the eye.

The sun was just beginning to set when the brothers threw down their spades. 'Reckon that's deep enough?' asked Jan, standing back to inspect his work.

'I think so,' said Petr, jumping into the hole. The grass came up to his forehead. 'Yes, that'll do. Give me a hand.' Jan pulled his brother out of the grave.

They went into the church and said a quick prayer. Jan gave the priest a coin. 'Would you include the boy's name in the mass?'

'Of course,' said the priest. 'What's the child called?'

'Miroslav,' said Jan.

'Second name?' asked the priest.

'Just Miroslav,' said Petr, eyeballing his brother.

PART 3

CHAPTER 53

'Come on, you must have rucksacks,' said Imogen. 'They're bags with pockets and zips.'

'What's wrong with packs?' said Miro, pointing at four wooden frames with leather straps that he'd dumped on the floor. 'They're easy to use.' He rolled up a fur coat. 'You just tie things on.'

'Easy for you to say,' said Imogen. 'I'm not a Brownie. I haven't got a knots badge.'

'What's a knots badge?' said Miro.

'Never mind.'

An hour later, everything was secured to the packs. Food was stuffed into waxy fabric bags. Water carriers were sealed and strapped on the side.

'We ought to keep our weapons handy,' said Miro. Imogen wrapped a belt round her waist and slid her sword into place.

She lifted the smallest pack on to Marie's shoulders. Marie stumbled backwards. 'It feels like I'm carrying a hippo!'

'You'll get used to it,' said Imogen, pulling on her own pack. The sisters faced each other.

'We look like we're going on a very long journey,' said Marie.

'We are,' said Imogen. 'We're going home.'

'Home ... yes. We're going to see Mum!'

'And Grandma. Don't forget about her.'

Marie pressed her lips together. 'Imogen, it is going to be okay ... isn't it? We are going to find the door in the tree?'

'Of course,' said Imogen, sounding more certain than she was. She felt nervy – as if the worry creatures had got hold of her insides and were twisting them like a dishcloth.

'We're not going to get killed by skret?' said Marie.

'No,' said Imogen, 'we're not.'

Marie looked reassured. Imogen wished someone would reassure *her*.

Marie waved goodbye to the room at the top of the second tallest tower and started walking down the spiral staircase. Miro was still plumping the cushions on the four-poster bed. 'Come on, Miro,' said Imogen. 'It's time to go.'

'I want it to look nice for my return,' said the prince.

'It does look nice,' said Imogen.

'This cushion always gets a bit—'

'It's fine.'

'I hope someone brings wood for the fire.'

'Miro!'

'Oh, all right. I'm ready.'

Miro and Imogen took a final look at the room. The sun was setting and they'd lit the candles so the grown-ups would think they were there after dark.

The clock was the only thing ruining the scene. There was something unrelenting about the way it ticked. It was a little too loud. A little too fast.

Tick-tock, tick-tock, don't stop, tick-tock.

Marie called from somewhere down the staircase. 'Imogen! Miro! What are you doing?'

'We're coming,' they said and they closed the door behind them.

Imogen could still hear the clock ticking as she climbed down the stairs.

CHAPTER 54

Petr surveyed the weapons in the castle's armoury. There were spiked clubs, war hammers, winged spears and more.

'Some of the small swords are out,' said Jan.

'Must be on loan to the new recruits,' said Petr. 'So . . . what should we take?'

'I dunno. What do you usually take to kill a twelve-year-old?'

'Something quick and quiet. Nothing too fancy.'

'That'll be the Vrach,' said Jan, removing a double-edged sword from the rack. Petr picked a weapon too and the brothers set about sharpening their blades in silence.

When they were done, they began their walk across the castle to the prince's tower. They took a meandering route, avoiding the places where the other Royal Guards would be stationed. Petr had no desire to answer his men's questions about what he was up to, armed to the teeth and off duty.

The brothers crossed a courtyard from which the light

of the second tallest tower was visible. 'Do you see that?' said Petr.

'Candles are lit,' said Jan. 'Boy must be home.'

Something landed on Petr's bald patch. 'What was that?' he cried, smacking his head. In the palm of his hand there was a squished moth with pale green wings.

When the men reached the bottom of the prince's staircase, they paused. Petr drew his sword and was surprised to see that the hand holding it trembled. He took a deep breath.

'It's all right,' whispered Jan. 'The boy's probably asleep. Won't even know what's happening till it's too late.'

'What if he screams?' said Petr.

'It's a long way up . . . a quick cushion to the face and no one will hear.'

Petr grimaced. 'Let's get this over with.'

CHAPTER 55

Imogen and Miro left Marie at the top of the steps that led down to the Hladomorna Pits. She was in charge of the packs. They were in charge of rescuing their guide, Lofkinye Lolo.

The first guard was asleep again. Miro removed the keys from the man's pocket with expert skill. 'Have you done that before?' hissed Imogen, trying not to look impressed.

'Going places you shouldn't is one of the best games you can play on your own,' said Miro.

They tiptoed down the staircase, but the next guard was awake. 'What can I do for you, Your Highness?' he said, getting to his feet.

'Ah, Vlado,' said Miro. 'My visitor is curious about the Hladomorna Pits. We'd like a tour.'

'Of course,' said the guard, without hesitation. He'd clearly had stranger requests.

The children followed the guard down the staircase with the slimy green walls. 'We're pretty full at the moment,' said the man in a jolly voice. 'The king wants the city cleaned up before the wedding and where do you think all that dirt goes?'

'The Hladomorna Pits,' said Imogen, keen to keep him talking.

'Got it in one, miss.'

The guard walked into the first cell on the left and Miro slammed the door shut behind him.

'Imogen, the bar!' cried the prince. She grabbed a plank of wood and slotted it across the door, securing it so the man couldn't get out.

The guard didn't even resist. 'Is everything all right, Your Highness?' he asked from inside the cell. Miro didn't reply.

He and Imogen hurtled along the corridor into Lofkinye's cell. They crouched down at the edge of the Pit. 'Lofkinye,' said Imogen. 'Are you ready?'

The human firework's face appeared in the darkness. 'As ever,' she said.

Miro fumbled with the lock that held the bars across the Pit. He tried all the keys until one of them worked and the lock sprang open. It took both children to pull the bars back. Imogen tied one end of the rope to the door and lowered the other end into the hole. 'You can come out now!' she called.

Lofkinye climbed up the rope with ease. 'You were serious, then,' she said. 'I had my doubts.'

'I always keep my promises,' said Miro, winding the rope round his shoulder.

Banging and shouting echoed down the corridor. 'What's that?' asked the huntress.

'Don't worry,' said Miro. 'The other guards will find him in the morning.'

'You've locked up the guard,' said Lofkinye, suddenly understanding. 'Did he see your face?'

'Yes . . .'

'Your name will be mud.'

'Uncle will get over it . . . in a few weeks.'

'You have a higher opinion of the king than most.'

'Come on,' said Imogen. 'Let's get out of here.'

They ran up the slimy green staircase, tiptoed round the sleeping guard and climbed up the final set of steps. 'You did it!' cried Marie. 'You freed Lofkinye!'

'We did,' said Imogen. 'Now what?'

The girls looked at Miro. Miro looked at Lofkinye. 'I don't know why you're looking at me,' she said. 'I said I'd guide you up Klenot Mountain, not out of your own house.'

'You mean you don't have a plan?' said Miro.

'How was I supposed to come up with a plan from the bottom of a Hladomorna Pit?'

'You had plenty of time to think.'

'Think? Think! There's more to escape plans than pure imagination.'

'Can we borrow some horses?' asked Imogen.

'The stablemaster would catch us,' said Miro. 'But we can't just walk through the city at this time of night. It'll be crawling with skret.'

'I don't like horses,' said Marie.

'I don't like skret,' said Miro.

'We'll have to sprout wings,' said Imogen, making a chicken movement with her arms.

Lofkinye held up her hand for quiet. 'That's exactly what we'll do,' she said.

'Huh?'

'We'll take the giant birds.'

'I don't understand,' said Marie. 'What giant birds?'

'The king keeps them in his garden,' said Lofkinye. 'Surely you've heard of the velecours?'

'Oh, *them*,' said Marie. 'Yes. Sometimes we race on them. They go fast. It's scary.'

'Perfect,' said Lofkinye. 'And how long has it been since the last velecour delivery?'

'I don't know,' said Miro. 'Probably a few days.'

'We could be too late,' said the huntress.

'Too late for what?' said Miro.

'Have their wings been clipped?'

255

'I doubt it. Everyone's been so busy getting ready for the wedding ...'

'That's perfect too. Lead the way, little prince. Tonight we leave by velecour.'

CHAPTER 56

The children and Lofkinye walked through the castle towards the velecour stables. They crossed a hall where the king kept his collection of statues, passing between stone knights and lovers and other people's gods.

'That one's my father,' said Miro, pointing to the statue of a stern-looking man with wide-set eyes and an angular face.

'He has your eyes,' said Marie.

'That's what Uncle says!' said Miro.

'Very nice,' said Lofkinye. 'Keep walking.'

Imogen tucked her thumbs under the straps of her pack. She wondered if the velecours would be fast enough to outrun skret. The skret might be small, but she'd seen how quickly they could climb houses and disappear over rooftops.

She wanted to ask their newly acquired guide, but she was afraid of looking stupid so she kept her mouth shut. Miro didn't have any such concerns. 'Velecours aren't like ponies,' he said. 'You can't control which way they go. You do know that, don't you?'

'Hush,' said Lofkinye. She grabbed Miro's shoulder. 'Did you hear that?'

'Hear what?'

There were voices. Grown-up voices. Imogen turned to see two men enter the hall. One was fat and the other was thin, with a black eye and very little hair. They were dressed like Royal Guards, but they weren't wearing helmets and their swords were drawn.

Dozens of statues stood between the guards and the children.

'Your Highness,' said the fat man. 'We were looking for you.'

Imogen had seen that red face before – all scrunched up and stuck down an alley. Those were the guards who'd attacked Lofkinye.

'They're bad men,' Imogen whispered to Miro.

'No, they're not,' he whispered back. 'I know them. They're called Jan and Petr. They work for my uncle.'

Miro turned to the guards. 'What do you want?' he said. 'I'm busy.' It was an absurd response.

'We want you,' said the fat guard. He took a few steps towards the children.

'Stay where you are!' shouted Lofkinye.

'That lesni poacher is a wanted woman,' said the same guard. 'Does your uncle know you're with her?'

Miro looked at Imogen. She nodded. 'Yes,' said Miro. 'Yes, he does.'

'Are you sure?' The guards took another step closer.

'I said stay where you are!' cried Lofkinye.

'It's your uncle who sent us,' said the guard with the black eye.

'We can't fight them,' muttered Lofkinye, peering at the men between the statues. 'They're too well armed. I haven't even strung my bow.'

'My uncle sent them,' whispered Miro. 'He wants to see me.'

The thin man with the black eye lowered his sword and extended his hand. 'Come with us, Miroslav.'

'But your uncle never wants to see you,' whispered Imogen. 'Why now? What's he after?'

Miro turned back to the guards. 'What does my uncle want?'

'He wants to talk to you,' said the fat guard. 'Man to man.'

Miro hesitated. The guards hesitated too. For a moment, they were all statues.

Miro opened his mouth, but he was interrupted by the first chime of the evening bells.

The spell was broken. The men rushed forward. Lofkinye rushed back. The girls followed, pulling Miro with them.

The children and the huntress hurtled out of the hall of statues and down a corridor, packs jangling. 'We need to get to those velecours!' cried Lofkinye. 'Which way?'

'Left,' said Miro. 'Turn left!'

They veered to the left, sprinting through a maze of walkways. Behind, the men were shouting at them to stop.

'In here!' cried Miro, taking a sharp right. He opened a door into an unlit room and the girls and their guide rushed through. Miro followed and pushed the door shut, sealing them in the dark.

It smelled like straw, and Imogen could hear Marie panting nearby. 'Are you okay?' she whispered.

'I think so.'

Something rattled. 'What was that?' said Imogen.

'Me,' said Miro. 'I'm trying to unbolt the doors to the garden.'

Something soft brushed against Imogen's hand. 'Marie, was that you?'

'Was what me?'

'There's something in here.'

'The velecours,' said Miro. 'This is where we keep them when they first arrive from the forests – before they've been broken in and had their wings clipped. Can you give me a hand with these bolts?'

Imogen followed his voice and felt for the garden doors.

The guards were talking in the corridor. 'Where have the little twerps gone now?'

'They can't have got far.'

'It's all right,' whispered Miro. 'I dropped the latch when we came in. They won't be able to follow.'

Imogen's fingers found the bolts at the bottom of the garden doors. She tried to wiggle them free without making any noise. All around, the velecours began to fuss.

'That's strange,' said one of the guards. 'This door doesn't open.'

'Here, let me try,' said the other.

The velecours were getting worked up. Lofkinye made clucking noises and it seemed to calm them – until a heavy thud set them off. The birds squawked and one bumped into Imogen, nearly knocking her off her feet.

'We've got to get these bolts open,' said Miro. 'It's our only way out.' But the bolt Imogen was trying to undo wouldn't budge.

There was another thud and Marie whimpered. The guards were kicking the door down.

CHAPTER 57

Imogen's bolt slid free. Miro must have unlocked his too because the garden doors swung open. Moonlight poured in. Velecours stampeded out. Imogen stood aside to avoid getting trampled.

When the last velecour had left the stable, Imogen looked around for Marie. She found her on her back, covered in straw. 'I can't get up,' cried Marie. 'My pack's too heavy!'

Imogen helped her to her feet. 'Marie, you need to grab a bird and climb on. Can you manage that?'

Marie looked unsure.

'Can you *try?*' pleaded Imogen.

Marie nodded.

'Okay. Good enough.'

The girls ran out into the moonlit garden. Behind them, the door between the stables and the castle was about to give way. *Thud, thud, thud.* The guards were smashing through.

Ahead, the velecours ran across flower beds, squawking with delight. One tore through the shrubbery. A couple more disappeared into the rose garden.

Lofkinye caught a tall bird by the neck, swinging herself on to its back. Imogen cornered a smaller one by the fountain. It was drinking, but when it saw Imogen approach it clucked and fluffed up its feathers as if preparing for a fight. Imogen lunged at the bird as quickly as she could with her heavy pack and missed. She went for it again. This time she grabbed handfuls of feathers and scrambled on to the velecour's back, narrowly avoiding a peck on the head. Holding on to its neck, she tucked her legs behind the wings, just like she'd done when she was racing her sister.

The bird screeched and ran in a circle, giving Imogen a full view of the garden. She couldn't see Miro, but back near the castle Marie was struggling to mount the smallest of the birds. The guards were racing towards her, swords glinting.

'Marie!' shrieked Imogen.

Her bird bolted to the right. She tried to make it go back, but it wouldn't. The bird ran in a wobbly figure of eight and, when it faced the castle again, Imogen saw Lofkinye jump down from her velecour and lift Marie up. Surely the guards were going to get them. Surely there wasn't enough time, but Imogen was powerless to help.

Her bird squeezed its wings, as if trying to crush her legs, then it started running – running at the hedge. It extended its wings and beat them up and down. The hedge was too close. Imogen could feel the bird's muscles straining to be airborne. Just when she thought it was too late, just when she thought they'd crash, Imogen was lifted up. Her belly did a flip. The top of the hedge kissed the soles of her boots. She was flying.

Lofkinye, Miro and Marie were flying too. Imogen leaned forward and held on to her velecour's neck. Below, she could just about see the outlines of the guards as they slashed at the air above their heads. The birds were out of reach. The men howled with rage.

The velecours lifted the children and the huntress higher. Imogen looked down again and she saw the silhouette of the castle falling away. The whole earth was sinking and she was rising up, gliding on currents of air.

'Thank you,' she whispered into the hole that served the velecour as an ear.

The night air was cool, but the bird's body was warm and the glossy feathers were as soft as could be. Imogen was surprised to discover that flying was not that scary, once you got used to it. She sat back, letting go of the velecour's neck. It clucked appreciatively. Its wing movements were slow and confident and it didn't seem to mind having a passenger any more.

How amazing to think that a creature that was so frantic and ungainly on the ground could be so at ease in the sky.

Soon they were flying with the moon. The birds pulled into a V-shape formation, with Lofkinye's bird taking the lead. Imogen looked to her right. Marie was pale and her eyes were wide.

'Are you okay?' shouted Imogen. Marie nodded in a mechanical sort of way.

Miro flew behind the girls, followed by a couple of riderless birds. He was beyond pale. He was green. Imogen didn't ask him if he was all right. *If he's coming along on our adventure*, she thought, *he'd better be able to look after himself.*

'Where are we going?' cried Miro.

'Wherever the birds want to go,' replied Lofkinye. 'They know what they're doing. The forests are their home and free things always return home.'

Miro shouted something incoherent over the roar of the wind. Perhaps he didn't like the bird being in control. Perhaps, thought Imogen, it was because he was leaving his home behind. For a fleeting moment, she felt sorry for him.

Some of the stars were so excited to see the children escape that they shot across the sky, leaving glowing arcs in their wake. The trails burned bright above the snow-capped mountains.

'Look,' cried Imogen, 'shooting stars!'

'I'm not looking at anything!' shouted Miro. 'Until we land, I'm keeping my eyes shut!'

'But you're missing so much!' cried Imogen.

'That's fine by me . . .' said the prince.

CHAPTER 58

The velecours flew on, carrying their riders towards the Kolsaney Forests. Imogen's hands and face went numb. She wished she'd worn her fur coat instead of tying it to her pack. Miro shouted complaints about the wind and the cold and the height at which they flew.

'I thought you had your eyes closed!' said Imogen.

'I'm trying,' he called back. 'But it's scary when you *can't* see too.'

Marie was tight-lipped, but shivering.

'How much further?' called Imogen.

'Ask the velecours,' replied Lofkinye, without turning round.

Below, the meadows turned to forest. From this great height, the treetops looked soft, as if the canopy was cushioned. Imogen knew that this wasn't the case. She knew that if she slipped sideways she'd fall to her death. She stroked her bird's feathers as if it was the one needing reassurance.

'*Imoooogeeeeen!*' called Marie as her bird folded back its wings and accelerated towards the forest. Imogen didn't have time to respond before her bird did the same. The treetops flew closer and Imogen squeezed the bird with her knees. Her hair whipped back from her face and she pressed her body as close to the velecour as she could.

Somewhere behind, Miro was screaming shamelessly.

The forest canopy separated out into individual trees that whizzed by. If she'd wanted to, Imogen could have touched the tips of the highest branches with her boots. Her velecour extended its wings and her descent slowed as if a parachute had been released. The bird circled down into a clearing, clucking as it landed.

Imogen dismounted with shaky legs. She patted her velecour on its side. A few metres away, Lofkinye jumped off her bird and sank to her knees, turning her face to the sky.

'Everything all right?' asked Imogen.

'It's more than all right,' said Lofkinye. 'It's home.'

Miro slid off his bird like a seasick sailor and collapsed on the ground. 'I don't feel well,' he bleated.

'That was the fun bit,' said Lofkinye.

'I'm going to vomit,' said the prince.

Imogen felt a bit queasy herself. She helped Marie off her bird, and Marie smiled tentatively. Imogen was surprised – she'd thought her sister would be more shaken up.

Miro retched but nothing came out. 'I don't travel well,' he said.

'Now you tell us,' said Lofkinye, helping him to his feet.

Marie and Imogen exchanged a look.

The velecours were already scattering among the trees. They blended in surprisingly well, considering their colourful plumage, and their large feet made no sound on the mossy forest floor. Imogen watched the last one disappear into the gloom.

'Did you bring everything I told you to?' asked Lofkinye, rifling through her pack.

'I think so,' said Marie.

Lofkinye put on her fur coat and the children did the same. Then the huntress strung her bow. 'You never know what's waiting among the trees at night,' she said.

When they were all wrapped up, Lofkinye marched into the forest and the children followed. 'Where are we going?' asked Miro.

'A safe place,' said their guide.

Under the forest canopy, it was darker than it had been in the clearing. Very little moonlight made it through the branches, which were knitted together like badly made blankets.

Every so often, Imogen would catch a glimpse of movement or feel eyes watching her and her hand would go to her sword. She was half expecting to see her moth, half expecting to meet a skret, but the 'eyes' in the dark always turned out to be nothing more than a strange patch of bark and the movement was just falling leaves.

They had been walking for about an hour when Marie gave a little squeak.

'What is it?' said Imogen.

'I trod on something!' They all gathered round to see the tiny skeleton at Marie's feet. Lofkinye picked up the skull. 'What is it?' asked Marie, her voice full of fear.

'It *was* a bird,' said Lofkinye.

'Why is it here? Why is it dead?'

'It's hard to say for certain,' said their guide, tossing the skull over her shoulder, 'but this won't be the last skeleton we find. The forests contain more dead things than living. It's getting worse.'

'What is?' said Imogen.

'The Žal. Everything's affected. Even the trees.'

Imogen looked up at the trees. They looked okay to her.

'The Žal? What nonsense,' said Miro, with an air of great authority. 'It's just autumn. Things always die in autumn.'

'Do they now?' said Lofkinye, looking at him with a half-smile that was not altogether friendly. 'Well, if the little prince says so, it must be true.'

Imogen wanted to ask more about the Žal, but Lofkinye turned away and started walking again.

'I hate being called that,' muttered Miro to the girls.

'What?' said Imogen.

'Little prince.'

'But you are a prince.'

'I'm not little.'

'There's nothing wrong with being small,' said Marie.

'Keep up,' called Lofkinye. 'There are things living among the trees that love the taste of little prince.'

CHAPTER 59

Lofkinye didn't stop walking until they were at the foot of an enormous tree. Imogen wasn't sure if it was bigger than the one she'd found in the Haberdash Gardens. It was hard to tell in the dark.

'This is our safe place,' said Lofkinye. The children looked around. All Imogen could see was a fern-covered floor and endless trees.

'What's so safe about it?' asked Miro.

'Pass me the rope and I'll show you.'

Imogen untied a rope from Miro's pack and handed it to Lofkinye. Lofkinye knotted the end and swung it like a lasso, releasing it above her head.

'You'd be amazed,' said Lofkinye, 'how many people forget to look up.'

'Wow,' said Marie, looking up. Imogen did the same.

At the top of the big tree, perched among the forest canopy, was a tree house. It was made entirely of wood, just like a garden shed. But, unlike a garden shed, it was built around the tree. The trunk went through the middle and branches stuck out through the walls.

Beneath the floorboards there was a cone-shaped structure. It looked like one of those bird feeders – the ones designed to keep squirrels off. 'What's that?' asked Imogen. 'Squirrel protection?'

Lofkinye laughed. 'Bear protection,' she said. 'The bears of the Kolsaney Forests aren't great climbers, but a sloping base stops them from even trying. They can't get a grip.'

Lofkinye's rope had caught on a branch just below the tree house. She clapped her hands. 'Right,' she said, 'who's going up first?' No one volunteered. 'Little prince. You show us how it's done.' There was that smile again. 'You can take off your pack.'

'You want me to go up that rope?' said Miro.

'Yep.'

'All the way?'

'Yep.'

Miro hesitated. 'Go on, Miro,' said Marie with genuine enthusiasm. 'You can do it.'

Miro looked doubtful. 'I wouldn't hang around,' said Lofkinye. 'The sooner we get up there, the better.'

Miro took off his pack and tugged on the rope, checking it would take his weight. Then he grabbed it with both hands and started to climb. He got a metre or so up before sliding back down. 'Argh! My fingers!'

He tried again, moving his hands more slowly. His legs were dangling near the girls' faces when his arms began to shake. 'I can't do it!' he cried as he slid to the ground. 'It's impossible.'

The girls looked at Lofkinye, concerned. 'He's not doing it right,' said the huntress.

'Not doing it right?' said Miro, exasperated. 'There's no other way! I was holding on like *this* and pulling myself up like *this*. That's how you climb a rope. That's how everyone climbs a rope.'

'Keep talking,' said Lofkinye. 'Something might occur to you eventually.'

Miro scowled. Lofkinye turned to Marie. 'You – small one. Take off your pack.' Imogen wasn't sure how she felt about Lofkinye bossing her sister around, but Marie didn't seem to mind. 'Now hold on to the rope with your hands above your head.' When Marie had done that, Lofkinye took the end of the rope and passed it between Marie's legs, looping it under one foot and over the other.

'Very good,' said Lofkinye. 'You've made a lock.'

'I have?'

'Now pull your knees up – yes, that's it – and push down hard on the rope with that foot.' Lofkinye stood back. Marie repeated the action.

Imogen watched with her hands out in case Marie fell.

But Marie didn't fall. She was above their heads in a matter of seconds.

'Don't forget to squeeze your feet together,' said Lofkinye. 'You need to keep the rope between them. And, if you get scared, just take three deep breaths. You can't do anything if you don't breathe.'

'It's working!' cried Marie.

'That's great. Keep going. You need to get to that branch at the top.'

Imogen thought it was irresponsible of Lofkinye to send the smallest and weakest up first. It was only a matter of time before Marie freaked out. Then what would they do?

'Are you okay?' shouted Imogen. 'You don't have to go all the way if you don't want to. You can come back down.'

'I'm at the top,' said Marie, surprising Imogen for a second time since they'd left the castle. 'What now?'

'Climb on to the branch,' said Lofkinye. 'You should be able to crawl along it and into the house.'

Marie struggled for a moment, making the rope wiggle, but she managed to grab hold of the tree. The next time Imogen looked up, her sister was sitting on the branch.

'I did it!' cried Marie. Lofkinye clapped her hands. Imogen and Miro watched in silence.

'Right,' said the huntress. 'Who's next?'

Imogen turned to Miro, but he was looking at the ground. 'Me, I suppose,' she said.

CHAPTER 60

The tree house was a complete home. It had a stove for cooking, bunk beds and a row of well-stocked bookshelves. Rag rugs were scattered across the floor and there were paintings on the walls.

Imogen looked closely at the painting by the stove. It was of a woman in a leaf-green dress. She had her arm round a golden-skinned boy.

'Who are they?' said Imogen.

'The people that used to live here,' said Lofkinye.

'Will they mind us staying in their house?'

'They won't mind, so long as we're careful.'

'They left because of the skret?' asked Marie.

Lofkinye was going through the packs. 'Yes, but that's a story for another day,' she said. 'Come and help me find firelighters.'

She lit the stove and heat filled the tree house, making the wood creak. Imogen pulled a patchwork blanket from the bunk bed and wrapped herself in it, sitting close to the flames. She let Marie snuggle under the blanket too.

'Won't the skret see the smoke?' said Marie.

Lofkinye shook her head. 'I think we'll be okay up here. They won't see it from the ground and we're far enough from Klenot Mountain to go unnoticed.'

'The peasants in Yaroslav never light their fires at night,' said Miro. 'They say it attracts monsters.'

'Trust me, little prince,' said Lofkinye. 'I know what I'm doing.'

They had pies for dinner. Marie devoured hers fast – like she was scared it would sprout legs and escape.

'What's for pudding?' asked Miro, when he'd finished.

'Pudding?' smirked Imogen. 'You do realise we've left the castle?'

'And it's time for bed,' added Lofkinye.

'I can't go to sleep yet,' said Marie. 'I never go to sleep without a story.'

Normally, Imogen would have told her not to talk such rubbish, but she quite fancied a story as well. She looked at the huntress, expecting her to say that she 'wasn't here to tell stories', but it turned out that Lofkinye did tell stories.

'The skret aren't the only dangerous creatures in the Kolsaney Forests,' said Lofkinye. 'There are bears too. Whether you're stargazing, hunting or asleep in your tree, the bear continues about her business. Her shaggy head turns at the slightest sound. Her great paws move slowly, purposefully.

'She doesn't care where you're from, who your parents are or whether you're considered a very important person. You all taste like crackling to her.'

'Hang on a minute,' said Miro. 'Bears don't eat people.'

'Yes,' said Imogen. 'I met Yeedarsh's bear and she was quite friendly.'

Lofkinye made a scoffing sound. 'A tame bear and a free bear are not the same thing. It's true that people are not a bear's favourite food. Most would much rather have honey, fish or berries to eat. But, if you surprise a bear when she thinks she's alone, she'll make short work of you.

'Once a bear killed a child. He was a sleepwalker – left his tree in the moonlight with nothing but his teddy. The next day they couldn't find the child or the stuffed toy. They searched high and low. They climbed every tree and crossed every lake. The boy was never found. That was years ago, but, from time to time, people still see her – a big female bear carrying a teddy on her back.'

'I don't believe you . . .' said Miro.

'That doesn't matter,' said Lofkinye. 'The story stays the same whether you believe in it or not.'

'So the bear eats the child and steals his toy?' said Marie, putting her head on one side. 'It's a strange bedtime story

... Mum normally tells us something nice before we go to sleep. She says it's important to think positive thoughts.'

Lofkinye shrugged. 'My mother never said that.'

The stove continued to crackle, the tree house continued to creak and Marie cuddled up closer to Imogen under the patchwork quilt. Imogen didn't stop her.

CHAPTER 61

The morning after the children's escape, Jan and Petr sat in a quiet corner of the Hounyarch. The barmaid was half-heartedly cleaning glasses and wholeheartedly trying to eavesdrop on their conversation.

'I told you killing the prince was a bad idea,' said Jan. 'What fools we must have looked in the gardens ... chasing little people on big chickens.'

'Keep your voice down,' said Petr. He drained his glass and shot a look at the barmaid that said *mind your own business*.

She walked over, bottle of brandy in hand. 'Can I tempt you to another?'

'No,' said Petr, irritated, but Jan held out his glass. The barmaid poured the brandy and lingered. Petr stared her down until she left.

'You weren't the only one to be outsmarted by the prince,' said Jan, draining his glass in one gulp. 'Vlado was on duty in the Hladomorna Pits last night. Apparently, Prince Miroslav locked him in a cell before he set the woman free.

Poor Vlado was there for hours before anyone found him.'

'Why would the prince want to free a lesni poacher?' said Petr.

'Beats me,' said Jan. 'The boy's obviously a wrong'un.'

'Well, I'm telling Anneshka today,' said Petr in a low voice. 'And I'm telling her the truth.'

'That you never signed up to slit little boys' throats?' said Jan.

'No, not that truth. I'm going to tell her that the lesni woman helped the boy escape. It was *her* fault he got away. Not mine.'

The brothers sipped their brandy in silence. When Jan had finished, he signalled to the barmaid. She sidled over. 'What's going on here, then?' she asked.

'Another,' said Jan. 'Same as before.'

The barmaid poured the brandy. 'Are we celebrating something?' she said.

'Yeah,' said Petr, not looking at her. 'The royal wedding.'

'Bit early for that, isn't it?'

'Bit early for you to be asking so many questions, I'd say.'

The barmaid left, pouting.

'On your health,' said Petr, touching glasses with his brother.

'No, on yours,' said Jan. 'You're going to need all the luck you can get. Anneshka Mazanar doesn't strike me as the forgiving type.'

'I think you're right there,' said Petr darkly. 'The sooner this is all over, the better.'

CHAPTER 62

I mogen slept well in the tree house. At first light, she clambered down from the bunk bed and looked out through a window.

The roof of the forest spread out before her. The trees were all different shapes, all fighting for a bit of sun. Most of the leaves had turned for autumn and the canopy was yellow and red.

In the distance, beyond the forests and beyond the meadows, lay Yaroslav. The castle's pointy towers rose high above the city walls.

Imogen ate oatcakes for breakfast and helped Lofkinye tidy the tree house, putting everything back where it had been when they first arrived. In a matter of minutes, they were on their way again, following a narrow track between the trees.

'How far into the forest are we now?' asked Miro, when they had been walking for a few hours.

'Not far,' said Lofkinye. 'But further than any of your město hunters go.'

'How long until we're there?' said the prince.

'Three days if we're quick.'

'Three *days?*' Miro looked horrified. Imogen was surprised too, but she tried to hide it.

'I'm not sure if I can walk for three days,' said Marie.

'Without work, there are no pastries,' said Lofkinye.

'How come there are skret in Yaroslav every night if it takes three days to get there?' asked Marie.

'They move in packs,' said Lofkinye. 'While one lot are crawling over the city, another pack is preparing for the journey and yet another is halfway to Yaroslav. There are always skret in the forests.'

'Why do they only come at night?' said Imogen.

'Their skin's very sensitive to the sun,' explained Lofkinye as if it was the most natural thing in the world.

Imogen looked at the trees either side of the track. She couldn't see any skret hiding among the trunks, but she felt nervous all the same.

Some of the trees were tall and straight. Others were so bent that they seemed to crawl with their knobbly knees on the ground. There were gnarly bits on their branches, like the swollen joints of Grandma's fingers, and their leaves were covered in black spots.

Imogen wondered if this was what Lofkinye had been telling them about last night. 'Lofkinye,' she said, 'that thing you mentioned yesterday, the thing that's killing the forests, what was it called again?'

'The Žal.'

'Is that what's making the leaves spotty?'

'I think so, yes,' said the huntress. 'The Žal is the mountain's sadness. It's dying of heartache and, when the mountain is sick, everything around it sickens too – the trees don't grow properly, the animals die.'

'I don't understand,' said Marie.

'It's just a lesni story,' muttered Miro, so only Imogen could hear. 'Mountains don't have hearts. They can't die of heartache.'

'You haven't heard how the mountain lost its heart?' said Lofkinye.

'No,' said Imogen and Marie at once.

Lofkinye looked strangely serious. 'All right. I'll tell you tonight.'

The travellers stopped walking to have lunch. They ate by a small stream and Lofkinye splashed water on her hands and face, washing off the dirt from the Hladomorna Pits.

After lunch, Imogen's shoulders started to feel sore. She kept shifting the straps of her pack around, but they soon started rubbing again.

Marie struggled with the weight of her load and, as the afternoon wore on, Lofkinye carried more and more of

Marie's things. Imogen watched with narrowed eyes. Why did Marie always have to be such a baby?

'I hate being among all these trees,' said Miro. 'It makes me feel hemmed in.'

'People are supposed to live in the gaps between trees,' said Lofkinye.

'Lesni people, perhaps, but not me.'

'And where should you be, little prince? On top of a mountain?'

'In my castle.'

'No one forced you to come,' muttered Imogen.

'Your castle,' said Lofkinye. 'I'm not sure how easy it will be for you to return there.'

'What do you mean?' said Miro.

'You've been seen helping a wanted woman escape. You locked a guard in a cell. You released a flock of velecours. Your uncle is unlikely to be pleased.'

'Oh, he'll be fine.'

'What about the men who were chasing us?'

'The Voyák brothers? I've known them for years.'

'Why did they have their swords drawn?' asked Lofkinye.

'You don't understand,' said Miro, his voice rising. 'None of you understand. Uncle and I have fallen out before. It always comes right in the end.'

They plodded on in silence.

Lofkinye walked at the front since she knew the way. Miro went second since he would have liked to be first, but didn't know the way. Marie came third since Imogen said she was too small to go last. Imogen brought up the rear.

At dusk, Imogen's worry creatures began to reappear. It was strange. She didn't feel particularly anxious, but there they were, rustling in the leaves a few metres behind her. She closed her eyes for a second, trying to imagine the worry creatures being swept away. It didn't help. She touched the hilt of her sword. A twig snapped behind a tree.

'Go away!' she said, louder than she'd intended.

Marie turned round. 'Not you,' said Imogen, but then she saw the look on Marie's face. Her eyes were big and fearful. 'What is it?' said Imogen. 'What's wrong?' She turned. It wasn't her imaginary worry creatures at all.

There, in the low forest light, was a skret.

CHAPTER 63

The skret was built like a human, but it was smaller and stronger than an adult, with pale grey skin and luminous eyes. The monster crouched down, just a few paces away from where Imogen stood. Spikes ran along its spine and every muscle was tensed.

Imogen backed away, holding her arm out in front of Marie. 'Imogen,' whispered Marie. 'Is that what I think it is?'

The skret growled, revealing triangular teeth.

'It's all right, Marie,' said Imogen. 'I'm sure it's more afraid of us . . .' Her voice trailed off.

The skret advanced on all fours. An arrow whizzed past Imogen's neck, landing near the skret's claws.

'Stay where you are,' said Lofkinye. The monster looked at her bow and arrow. She was ready to shoot again. 'I don't want to hurt you,' she said.

The skret narrowed its eyes. And then, much to Imogen's surprise, it spoke.

'What *do* you want?' it said. Its voice was a series of

snarls, creaks and hisses, strung together to form words. It made Imogen's hair stand on end.

Lofkinye hesitated before she replied. 'We're on our way to Klenot Mountain. We need advice from the Maudree Král.' She sounded calm.

The skret pulled back its lips and screeched, rocking on its haunches. It was laughing. 'The Král does not help humans. Not any more. Not after what you did.' It raised a hand with meat-cleaver claws, and gestured at the children. 'He'll drain your blood and slice up your flesh.'

'What?' said Marie. 'That's horrible!'

'Smallest first,' said the skret, turning its piranha eyes on her.

'Tell the Král that we're coming,' said Lofkinye, still calm. 'Tell him we expect a warm welcome.'

'He'll hollow you out,' said the skret. 'He'll send your empty skins back home.'

'I feel a bit funny,' muttered Miro.

'If he cooperates, we'll make it worth his while,' said Lofkinye.

'What could a pack of pups and a lone woman give the Král? You have nothing. You *are* nothing.'

Lofkinye strode forward, keeping her bow drawn. She didn't stop until the arrow was a hand's length from the skret's skull. The monster's eyes followed the point, crossing slightly.

'Do not talk to me like that,' she said. 'My name is Lofkinye Lolo. I belong to the lesni people and we belong to these forests. I am not "nothing".' Her voice had lost its calm.

Imogen covered Marie's eyes and looked away. She didn't want to see the skret die, even if it was a monster.

When the skret replied, it did so quietly and slowly, with a voice full of malice. 'You are all traitors. You shall be treated as such.'

When Imogen looked back, the skret had gone and Lofkinye's arrow was pointing at thin air.

Marie ran towards Lofkinye and wrapped her arms round her middle. Lofkinye dropped her weapon. She had a strange look on her face, as though she had slipped out of time with the rest of them. It only lasted a second.

'Right,' she said. 'At least the Maudree Král can't say we arrived unannounced.'

'We're all going to die,' said Miro mournfully.

CHAPTER 64

The second tree house that the children and their guide stayed in was smaller than the first. Most of the space was taken up by a double bed.

'Who used to live here?' asked Marie.

'A woodcutter and his wife,' said Lofkinye. She hung the packs on hooks by the door and lit the stub of a candle. In the flickering light, Imogen saw that the walls of the tree house were lined with shelves. These held everything from pots and pans to glass beads and axes.

The children sat on the tiny patch of floor and removed their boots. Imogen's feet felt fuzzy and her shoulders were sore. In that moment, it was hard not to think of the things she'd left behind – her mum's cooking and warm bubbly baths. She wouldn't admit it, but she missed her home comforts just as much as Miro missed the castle.

'Lofkinye, thank you for saving us from the skret,' said Miro. He seemed to be struggling to find the right words.

'That's no problem, little prince. I wouldn't be much of a guide if I let you get sliced and diced.'

'No, but still. You were fast. You were . . . good.'

Lofkinye nodded, accepting the compliment.

They ate a dinner of cold venison pie and dried apples. Then the weary travellers crawled into bed, arranging themselves top to tail. Imogen tucked the blanket up round her neck. Her tired limbs sank into the mattress.

The wind outside was picking up, making the tree house groan like a ship in a storm. 'Don't worry,' said Lofkinye. 'These houses have withstood far worse.'

The howling of the wind was soon joined by the cries of the skret. Imogen wriggled deeper under the blankets, glad that the tree house was so high up.

'So you've seen your first skret in these forests,' said Lofkinye. 'What do you think? Still want to meet the Maudree Král?'

'Not really,' said Marie. There was a long pause.

'Shall we go back?' said Miro.

'We can't,' said Imogen. 'This is our only chance of getting home.'

Marie turned to Lofkinye. 'Isn't there someone else we can ask about the door in the tree?'

'If I had any better ideas, I would have mentioned them already,' said the huntress. 'Besides, I've heard the skret talk of these doors before – back in the old days, when relations between people and skret were a little less frosty.'

'I can't imagine being friends with those monsters,' said Marie. 'Things must have been very different back then.'

'Oh yes, very different,' said Lofkinye.

'But why?' said Imogen. 'What changed?'

Lofkinye pulled the candle close so it illuminated the bottom half of her face. 'Well, I suppose I did promise to tell you how the mountain lost its heart. Though, in order for you to understand that, I'm going to have to go back further.'

Imogen could feel Marie's body heat next to her and she was grateful for the warmth. For a split second, she felt as if she was back home, tucked into her mum's big bed.

'It's quite a long story,' warned Lofkinye.

'Those are just the kind we like,' said Marie.

'I'm not listening,' said Miro, turning from grateful to grumpy in an instant. 'I already know this one.'

'Not like this you don't,' said Lofkinye, and she blew out the candle.

CHAPTER 65

Lofkinye unwrapped her story in the dark. She'd been carrying the first part of it since she was a child. Sometimes she could feel its weight in her pocket, like a stone worn smooth by the touch of her fingers. It had been a long time since anyone had asked her to take it out.

Many of the lesni people carried similar stories. Some of the older generation carried so many that you could almost see the stones in their pockets, dragging them down. They kept their secrets to themselves. But the children had asked for a story and those first familiar words were already there, right on the tip of Lofkinye's tongue . . .

'Many hundreds of years ago, the lesni were the only people in these parts. We lived in the forests. The skret lived in the mountains and the valley was empty. No fields, no stone walls, no castle and no město.'

'What's město?' said Imogen.

'It's a stupid lesni word,' said Miro. 'It's what they call the people of Yaroslav.'

'I thought you weren't listening,' said Lofkinye.

'Well, I am and your story makes no sense.'

'Hush!' said the girls in unison.

Lofkinye cleared her throat. 'It was our world, the forests. Our place. There had been travellers from beyond the mountains before and some had stayed and built their houses among the trees. Others came and went. But the město were different. When they first arrived, they imagined that the valley and all that surrounded it was theirs. They had no idea that the lesni even existed.'

'This is ridiculous!' cried Miro. 'How does she know? She wasn't alive back then.'

'True,' said Lofkinye. 'This happened a long time ago, but the story has been passed down. The město arrived in the valley on horseback. They came from beyond the mountains and they'd been travelling for years.'

'My father's family has always lived in Yaroslav!' cried Miro. 'We were here long before any— Ow! Who kicked me?'

'As I was saying,' continued Lofkinye, 'your father's ancestors were hungry. They were weary. They were half frozen and they hadn't got anywhere to call home. When they saw this great green valley, surrounded by luscious forests and protective peaks, they thought they'd found paradise. The only thing was they didn't realise that paradise already belonged to someone else.'

Miro huffed and puffed, but he kept his mouth shut.

'When the lesni heard the město horses approach, they dissolved into the forests, but they didn't go far. They hid, watching the people on horseback.

'The město stopped in front of the first line of trees. It didn't matter how hard they squinted into the forest depths, they couldn't see lesni people looking back out.

'The newcomers set up camp at the bottom of the valley and the lesni continued to watch and wonder what to do. Some of the elders wanted to fight – send the město back where they came from. They spent many days discussing their options. Meanwhile, the greedy město continued to chop wood and cut stone and eat the fish from the river.'

'So what did the lesni people do?' asked Marie.

'It wasn't the lesni who had the idea. It was the old ruler of the skret: the Maudree Král. She wasn't much to look at. Her skin was covered in warts and her claws were yellow with age, but they say that Král was wise – wiser than all the other Králs put together.'

'The Král is not a woman,' said Miro.

'He might be male now,' said Lofkinye, 'but centuries ago it was different . . . The Král arrived at the elders' tree house. She told them that, together, they could easily overpower the newcomers. The battle would be over in a day and the město would be sent packing.

'But the skret had no use for that swampy land at the base of the valley. They preferred their mountain caves. And the Král suspected that the lesni felt the same way about their treetop homes. There was no use fighting for land they didn't want. So the Král suggested that, as long as the město paid for the wood and the stone that they needed, why not let them stay? The lesni elders agreed.

'A welcome party went down to talk to the newcomers. At first, the město were reluctant to enter into any agreements. After all, they'd been getting what they needed for free. But the Maudree Král had thought of all that. She'd come with a box of precious stones. These stones were quite unlike any rocks the město had seen before. They sparkled as brightly as newly formed stars. The Král let the město keep one stone as a goodwill gesture. The rest would have to be bought.

'That is how the město got their home and that is where the old tale ends. But I have my own chapter to add: the story of how the mountain lost its heart.'

Miro groaned. Lofkinye ignored him.

'For generations, there was peace. Just like before, merchants and travellers continued to come from beyond the mountains. They arrived every summer. Some stayed in the city, with the město, and some stayed in the forests, with the lesni. But most moved on once they'd rested their legs and sold their wares.

'The město traded wool and crops. The lesni traded wood and the things they made with it. The skret traded rocks, but there was one stone they would never sell. You might have heard of it before: the Sertze Hora.'

'There's no such thing,' said Miro.

'The Sertze Hora is a beautiful stone,' said Lofkinye, 'but it's more than just a pretty object. Millions of years ago, it fell from the skies. It was a gift from the stars, and the mountains sprang up to protect it.'

'The Sertze Hora is a myth,' said Miro.

'When the mountain's heart is where it belongs,' continued Lofkinye, 'everything around here flourishes. The forests are full of life, the rivers are full of fish and the sky is full of birds. When it's not . . . well, we have the Žal. And where do you think Klenot Mountain's heart belongs?'

'In the mountain?' said Marie.

'Correct,' said Lofkinye. 'And that is where it has always been. So imagine my surprise when, centuries after my ancestors decided to let the město stay, I saw a thief sneaking through the forests with the Sertze Hora clutched to his chest.'

'Who was it?' cried Imogen. 'Who took the mountain's heart?'

'King Drakomor,' said Lofkinye. 'King Drakomor took

the mountain's heart. He had it wrapped up in his cloak, but you don't mistake a parcel like that. It made the forests thud. It made the tree houses shake. It wasn't supposed to be there.'

'What you're saying is treason,' said Miro.

'No,' said Lofkinye. 'What your uncle *did* was treason. He betrayed us all – město, lesni and skret. Ever since he took the heart from the mountain, things have been dying. The Žal is down to him.'

'Lies!' shouted Miro, wriggling around in the bed. 'Uncle says lesni do nothing but lie!'

'Miro!' cried Imogen. 'Lofkinye's helping us and you haven't even paid her like you promised. *You're* the only person in this bed telling lies. And stop moving. You're messing up the covers.'

'She calls my uncle a thief when she steals rabbits?' cried Miro. 'These forests don't belong to her and neither do the animals in them! It all belongs to me!'

Marie gasped. Imogen couldn't believe her ears.

'Call me a liar or a thief once more and you'll spend the night outside,' threatened Lofkinye.

'I'm going to sleep anyway,' snarled Miro.

They waited for the prince to stop squirming and for his breathing to slow.

'But haven't the skret been able to get the mountain's heart back?' whispered Marie.

'Why do you think they attack Yaroslav every night?' said Lofkinye. 'That's what it's all about. That's why I lost my home too.

'The current Maudree Král seems to think all humans are the same – lesni and město. As soon as he realised the Sertze Hora was missing, he sent skret into the forests, raiding our tree houses, killing our children. The lesni were forced to leave and seek the shelter of Yaroslav's walls.

'People have stopped visiting from beyond the mountains too. It used to be dangerous to cross in the winter. Now, with the skret as they are, it's dangerous to cross all year round.'

'And it's all because of King Drakomor?' asked Marie.

'Yes,' said Lofkinye.

Imogen thought back to Andel, the clockmaker. So much had happened since she'd met him that she'd almost forgotten his tale. 'Stealing isn't the only thing Drakomor's done wrong,' she declared. 'I met a man who said the Royal Guards gouged out his eye.'

'None of this is true!' cried Miro.

'You said you were going to sleep,' snapped Imogen.

'I command this story to stop.'

'You're in luck, little prince,' said Lofkinye. 'It's over.'

'It's a terrible story!' cried Miro. 'I hate it. I hate you.'

'Hate all you like, but it won't change the facts,' said the huntress.

'I'll tell you the facts.' There was more wriggling as Miro sat himself up in the bed. 'There *is* no Sertze Hora. The lesni moved to Yaroslav because they were too lazy to make things from the trees and they had nothing left to trade. You were little more than beggars. My uncle says he did you a great kindness allowing you into our city.'

'Is that so?' said Lofkinye. There was a dangerous edge to her voice.

But Miro wasn't listening. 'The skret attack Yaroslav every night because they're monsters and that's what monsters do. The lesni tell stories because they're liars and if you say one more thing about my uncle I'll have you all sent to the Hladomorna Pits.' Miro's voice wobbled.

There was silence in the bed. Imogen wondered if Lofkinye was going to throw the prince out of the tree house.

If she holds his legs, thought Imogen, *I'll take his arms.*

But Lofkinye didn't touch Miro. When she finally spoke she did so slowly and carefully, as if each word was barbed. 'You talk about the lesni as if we're a different species,' she said. 'And so be it. I don't need acceptance from bigots like you.'

Miro sniffed. Was he crying?

'You've spent too long in that castle, little prince,' continued the huntress. 'Your thoughts are as mean and as dark as the Pits you're so fond of. Be careful, or your hate will swallow you whole . . . But in spite of all that, I'll offer you a new trade. You've already agreed to pay for my services. You've already sworn to give me something from your uncle's collection.'

'So what?' snivelled Miro.

'So I don't want the Pustiny Jewels. I want the Sertze Hora instead.'

'Ha! You can have it. A sackful of air.'

'If it doesn't exist, as you claim, then I'll happily accept a sackful of air. But if there is such a stone, and if your uncle just happens to have it, you must give it to me.'

'That's the stupidest trade I've ever heard,' said Miro.

There was a flurry of skret cries from the forests below. Lofkinye lowered her voice. 'So, do we have a deal?'

'I said yes, didn't I?'

'Do you promise?'

'Do you doubt the word of a prince?'

'There's more honour in my toenail clippings,' muttered Lofkinye.

The skret cries moved further away.

'Lofkinye,' said Marie, after a little pause, 'do you think the skret we met earlier was telling the truth? Do you think the Maudree Král will drain our blood and slice up our flesh?'

'No, I don't,' said the huntress. 'The skret are not nearly so violent as they like to pretend. It's the monsters dressed as kings that you've *really* got to watch out for. Not the creatures with claws and sharp teeth.'

Meanwhile, back in the castle, Miro's clock continued to tick. Even though the children weren't there to see it happen, the hatch opened and a little man marched out.

He was dressed in the uniform of the Royal Guards, with a sword at his side and a plumed helmet on his head. His arms swung in time with the clock.

The figure gave a salute and promptly sank to his knees. Then he collapsed altogether. The body was drawn back into the hatch and the clock ticked on.

CHAPTER 66

It was Jan who discovered his brother's body, all stiff and pale in the morning light. He sat on the floor and sobbed like a child. If only he'd gone with Petr to tell Anneshka about the prince's escape. He shouldn't have let Petr go alone.

Jan didn't know how long he'd been crying when Anneshka walked in. He saw her jewelled slippers first. 'I'm sorry for your loss,' was all that she said.

Jan clenched his jaw and got to his feet. He looked at her with pure hatred. He knew what she'd done. Men like Petr didn't just die. This was revenge. This was because Petr hadn't killed the boy.

'What do you want?' he said, wiping the tears from his face.

'He'll need burying,' said Anneshka. 'And I believe you've already dug the grave.'

It took Jan a moment to realise what she meant. 'That grave's not big enough,' he said, not bothering to disguise his disgust. 'It was intended for a child.'

'So make it bigger.'

Jan wanted to hurt her. He wanted to squeeze the air out of her lungs, make her pay for what she'd done . . . But it would be suicide. She was protected by the king. Instead, Jan watched the pulse beating on the side of her neck. He focused all of his energy on it – willing it to stop.

'I know this was you,' he said. 'I know about the boy.'

'Know what about the boy?' She spoke with a smile in her voice as if she was asking about the weather.

'I know you wanted him dead and I know that he got away.'

Anneshka laughed. 'What nonsense, Voyák! The boy has been taken beyond the mountains. That's what the king commanded . . . Speaking of the king, he'd like to offer you his congratulations.'

'What for?'

'For your promotion to Chief of the Royal Guards.'

'I don't want the job.'

'It's not an offer. It's a command.'

'Why me? I've no experience leading men.'

'Because I think you understand better than most.'

'Understand what?'

'The price of failure.'

And, with that, Anneshka left the room.

CHAPTER 67

I mogen felt stiffer getting out of bed than she had done getting into it. 'Once we're home, I'm never going walking again,' she proclaimed. Her whole body felt tight as though her muscles had shrunk while she'd slept.

After breakfast, Lofkinye and the children climbed down the rope and began their second day of hiking. It was raining and the trees protected them from the worst of the weather, but, every so often, droplets came tumbling from the canopy, drenching an unhappy hiker.

When this happened to Miro, he yelled and drew his sword, brandishing it at the nearest tree. 'That's the first sound you've made all day,' said Imogen.

Miro scowled and put his sword away. He was still sulking about his argument with Lofkinye, although Imogen thought he'd got off rather lightly.

The path grew steeper so that walking, even at a steady pace, was hard work. To make matters worse, the fur coats absorbed the rain, becoming smelly and heavy.

The children and the huntress walked round lakes

that were so blue and so oval that Lofkinye called them 'eyes'. Imogen paused and looked into the water. The rain disturbed the surface, but it was the closest thing she'd seen to a mirror for days.

She was surprised to see a wildling looking back. Her short hair stuck up in tufts and her freckled face was dark with grime, making her eyes appear strangely bright. The soggy fur coat lent her a half-child, half-animal look.

Marie stopped next to her. 'What are you looking at?' she asked.

Imogen laughed at her sister's reflection. 'Mum won't recognise us,' she said. 'You finally look like the baby wolf. You know, the one you're always asking to be.' Marie put her head back and howled.

They stopped for lunch and Miro refused to sit with the girls and their guide. Instead, he sat on a rock by the lake.

'Perhaps a venison pie will cheer him up,' said Marie. She walked over, but he knocked her hand away, sending the pie tumbling into the lake.

'Hey!' shouted Imogen, rushing to Marie's side. 'That was the last one!'

'I don't care!' the prince shouted back.

Imogen gave him a shove and he almost followed the pie into the water. 'You should go back to the castle if you can't be nice,' she yelled.

Miro opened his mouth to protest, but Imogen's fists were raised and ready for the fight. He glanced at Marie. Even she looked annoyed. Miro closed his mouth and turned away.

The afternoon continued in much the same manner as the morning. The rain continued to fall and Miro continued to sulk.

'Out of interest,' said Lofkinye, 'whose idea was it to bring the little prince on this expedition?'

'He wanted to come,' said Imogen.

'And he's our friend,' said Marie. 'He's helping us get home.'

'Funny sort of friend,' said Lofkinye.

Imogen watched her boots as she walked, trying to think of something other than her aching shoulders and legs. The forest floor was changing. Rocks poked up through the mossy ground, like bald heads. Imogen imagined they were gnomes coming to the surface for air.

When she looked up, she noticed that some of the trees were dead and others had black spots on their leaves. She plucked a diseased leaf and checked that Miro was out of earshot. 'Hey, Lofkinye,' she said. 'Are you sure the Žal is happening because the mountain's heart was stolen?'

Lofkinye nodded.

'And you're sure it was taken by Miro's uncle?'

'I saw him riding through the forest with my own eyes,' said Lofkinye. 'I felt the Sertze Hora with my own heart.'

The sisters looked back at Miro, who was struggling on a slippery patch of rock. 'Should we wait for him?' said Marie.

'No way,' said Imogen. 'He's perfectly capable of catching up if he wants to.'

'I think he's upset about Lofkinye's story.'

'Well, he'll just have to get over it.'

'But imagine,' said Marie, 'if the skret and the people were at war and the animals were dying – all because of something our mum had done. How would you feel?'

'I'd be upset,' said Imogen, 'but it's not his mum. It's his uncle. And our mum would never do that.'

'No,' said Marie, 'I suppose not.'

Imogen felt a pang of homesickness. Her mum certainly didn't agree with stealing. When Imogen was younger, she'd taken sweets from the corner shop, stuffing them into her socks so her ankles bulged.

Mum had made her take them back and say sorry. Then she'd given her money to buy eggs and flour. They'd spent the rest of the afternoon baking.

Imogen salivated just thinking about it. That cake had been even nicer than sweets – sticky, with a taste like burnt caramel.

Mum always knew what was right and what was wrong.

Imogen couldn't imagine having no parents or an uncle like King Drakomor.

By the end of the day, they were out of the forest and walking along a mountain path that climbed steadily, taking the travellers above the treetops. The rain stopped and they were treated to a spectacular view. The sun broke on the horizon, spilling like a runny yolk.

'How far is it to the next tree house?' asked Marie, leaning against Lofkinye and using a baby voice that Imogen hated.

'There are no more tree houses,' said Lofkinye. 'We're in the mountains now so we'll have to make do with a cave. We'll know we're close when we see a lightning-struck tree.'

Marie glanced over her shoulder.

'It's not here, silly,' said Imogen.

'I'm not looking for the tree. I'm looking for Miro. I thought he would have caught up by now.'

'Oh, he's just dragging his feet,' said Imogen. 'He'll be here any minute.'

The sun finished setting and a half-moon took its place. The forest was still. No squawks or squeaks. Just the hush of a land in decline.

There was still no sign of Miro. 'Come on,' said Lofkinye. 'We'd better go and get him.' They picked their way back down the mountain path.

'Bet this is just what he wants,' said Imogen. 'Bet he's sulking round the corner.' But, when they turned the corner, Miro wasn't there. The path went up and down and round another bend. They turned a third corner and the prince's pack and coat were splayed out on the earth, next to a boulder.

Miro was nowhere to be seen.

CHAPTER 68

Lofkinye sprinted over to the abandoned things. 'Little prince!' she gasped, picking up the coat.

'Where is he?' cried Marie, panic-stricken.

Lofkinye dropped everything apart from her bow and arrow. 'There's no point in you wasting your energy,' she said. 'Take off your packs, unsheathe your swords and stay here. I'm going to check further down the mountain.' She disappeared into the darkness.

The girls stood back to back. 'Can you see anything your side?' said Marie.

'No,' said Imogen. 'Just rocks. What about you?'

'Just trees.'

They waited in silence, alert to the smallest of movements and the softest of sounds.

Marie was the first to break. 'I don't understand,' she said. 'I'm sure Miro wasn't that far behind.'

'I do,' said Imogen. 'He's run away. He couldn't hack it.'

'He wouldn't ...'

'He would. He's been sulking all day. I bet he thought

it'd be easier than this. Bet he thought we'd carry him.'

'But why did he leave his pack?' said Marie.

'Perhaps he reckons he'll be quicker without it.'

'You always think the worst of him. He's not such a coward as you say.'

'Urgh!' cried Imogen. 'You're so naive!'

'What's *nigh-eve*?'

'Stupid.'

'Oh yeah?' Marie jabbed her elbow into Imogen's back. 'Lofkinye says I'm the smartest child she's met.'

Imogen gave Marie a shove in return. 'I don't give a stuff what Lofkinye says. I'm sick of watching you suck up to her.' Imogen put on a simpering voice. 'Ooh, Lofkinye, I'm too small to carry my own stuff. Ooh, Lofkinye, look at these berries I picked.'

'I don't do that.'

'She's not Mum, you know.'

'I know!' yelled Marie.

'Or your sister.'

'Imogen, shut up! Something's moving.'

Imogen whirled round. Dry leaves rustled. The girls held up their swords.

Something ran out from behind a rock. It was a mouse.

Imogen laughed harder than she'd laughed in a long time and Marie laughed too. When they'd finished, they had tears in their eyes. They looked at each other, suddenly awkward.

'You don't have to worry, you know,' said Marie.

'About what?'

'About what you just said. About Lofkinye. I know she's not my sister.'

'Oh, that,' said Imogen, embarrassed. That wasn't what she'd meant. Or at least it wasn't what she thought she'd meant. 'I shouldn't have said that. You're not a suck-up. Well, you are, but it doesn't matter.'

'You're my only sister,' said Marie. 'Whether I like it or not.'

Imogen snorted and looked away. 'Well . . . thanks.'

How had Marie done that? She'd turned things on their heads. She'd made Imogen feel like *she* was the younger one. Imogen tried to think of something to say to reverse their roles, but there was no time.

'I've come across twenty-stone pigs that make less noise than you,' said Lofkinye, running up the path. 'I could hear your bickering halfway down the mountain.'

'Sorry,' said Marie, shrinking.

'No sign of Miro?' said Imogen.

Lofkinye shook her head. She started grubbing about in the dirt. 'There's blood,' she said. 'It's hard to see in this light, but I'm pretty sure that's blood.'

Imogen crouched down too. Sure enough, there were

three red droplets, not far from the abandoned pack. 'And there,' said Lofkinye, pointing at the earth near Marie's feet. 'Skret prints.'

'Are you sure?' said Imogen. 'It couldn't be a wolf or a deer?'

'I'm sure. He's been taken by skret.'

'Oh!' wailed Marie. 'I hope he's all right! What are we going to do?'

'There's only one thing we can do tonight,' said Lofkinye. 'Find our cave.'

Meanwhile, back in Castle Yaroslav, the door in Miro's clock opened up. This time, the figure that crept out was shaped like a skret.

Its circular eyes and triangular teeth were cut with the finest precision. It carried a long pole across its shoulder with a sack tied to the end. The skret was still, but the sack wriggled and writhed. After a few seconds, the monster went back inside the clock.

CHAPTER 69

Miro didn't see the skret coming. They jumped on him from higher ground, pushing him face down into the earth. They ripped off his pack. Then they removed his coat, shaking it from him as though shelling a nut. Miro reached for his sword, but it was too far away.

'Get off me!' he shouted. 'Don't you know who I am?'

A mouthful of jagged teeth appeared next to his face. 'Stop talking or we'll cut out your tongue.'

'Let's slice it and dice it,' said a voice like a crackling fire.

'No, it could be a spy. Ask it what it's doing here first.'

The skret rolled Miro over so he could see their gruesome faces, pale grey in the moonlight with lopsided grins and crushed noses. He tried to get up, but they kicked him in the stomach. He groaned and curled into a ball.

'Oi, human! What you doing so far from home?'

'Yeah,' said the voice like fire, 'this is our neck of the woods.'

The kick had pushed all the air out of Miro and he couldn't reply.

'It's too small to be a soldier.'

'It's too big for an abandoned babe.'

'Who cares why it's here. Let's cut it up.'

The skret with the voice like fire bent down and grabbed Miro's hair, pulling back his head and touching his exposed neck with sharp claws. 'Let's just slit its throat and go home.'

Suddenly Miro could breathe. 'I'm Prince Miroslav,' he gasped. 'My uncle is the king.'

The skret's luminous eyes locked on his face. 'The king?'

'Yes, my uncle is King Drakomor. Don't hurt me.' There was a pleading note in his voice.

'Your uncle is no king here,' said the skret with a voice like fire, raising a clawed hand to strike.

'Wait!' said another skret. 'Didn't you hear? It said it's a prince! It could be useful.'

'*If* it's telling the truth,' said the voice like fire.

'I am telling the truth!' cried Miro.

The monster leaned in and Miro could smell its rancid breath. 'You'd better be,' the skret hissed, and he sliced his claw across Miro's cheek. The pain was sharp. Miro lashed out, but the other skret were on him, holding him down by his ankles and wrists. They were so strong that he didn't stand a chance.

Miro shouted for Imogen and Marie. He shouted for his uncle. He shouted until the skret gagged him and he could shout no more. They bound his hands and feet and, within a matter of seconds, Miro was as helpless as a pig trussed up for market. The skret shoved him into a sack. He closed his eyes and tried not to panic.

The sack was lifted up. It must have been attached to something because Miro could feel himself swinging backwards and forwards. Perhaps this was the bit where he got rescued? He waited, unable to speak, unable to move, but no rescue came.

Why hadn't Imogen and Marie turned back when he'd cried out? Were they too afraid? Or was it that they didn't care? He remembered their faces, looking over their shoulders as they walked ahead. They'd believed the story about his uncle. They weren't the friends they pretended to be.

As for Lofkinye . . . she was a typical lesni. She cared more for trees than for people like him. She'd be glad he was gone.

The cut on Miro's face throbbed and he wished the skret would remove the gag. He tried to distract himself. He thought of his parents as blood trickled down his cheek. He closed his eyes and he could see his mother's hands and the outline of her hair, but the features . . . the features were fading. He scrunched his eyes tighter, willing his imagined mother to smile, but the more he forced it, the further away she seemed until she was just a woman-shaped blur on the inside of his eyelids. Miro opened his eyes. He was determined not to cry.

The skret were grunting and panting all around him and the swinging motion of the sack made Miro feel sick. When the temperature changed, he thought he was imagining it. This was what happened before you froze to death: you felt warm. An old tutor had told him that.

But it wasn't just the temperature that was different. It was the light too. Through the loose weave of the sack, there was an orange glow.

The sack hit the ground and Miro was shaken out. 'Welcome to Klenot Mountain,' sneered the skret with the voice like fire. Miro wriggled in his ties, desperate to get a better look at his surroundings. He was in a cave – that much he could tell – and it was warm. He hadn't expected the skret caves to be warm.

His kidnappers left him tied up on the ground and Miro twisted to look up. The cave was big – bigger than the feasting hall in Castle Yaroslav – bigger than the inside of the cathedral. The ceiling was supported by pillars carved into smooth, organic shapes, like the stems of enormous flowers. It was beautiful. Miro hadn't expected the skret caves to be beautiful.

A few minutes later, a skret returned, removed the gag and cut Miro loose. Miro moved slowly, rubbing his wrists and ankles. His whole body ached from soon-to-be bruises, but the cut on his face was the worst. He touched his cheek. It was sticky from half-dried blood and new stuff was still flowing. It made him feel funny.

The skret gestured at him to follow. 'That's right,' said the monster, 'nice and quiet for the Maudree Král. He doesn't like squealers. Doesn't like 'em too fighty.'

Miro followed the skret towards the centre of the cave where a giant fire blazed. The fire had turned the nearby pillars black and the air roared as it rushed to feed the flames. Miro's blood roared in his ears too.

He saw a figure inside the fire. It didn't move, didn't seem to be in pain. The skret led him round the fire pit and he saw that the figure was not inside the inferno, but behind it, sitting on a throne. It wasn't anything like his uncle's throne. It was carved into the rock, with a seam of gold running through the middle, but it was a throne nonetheless.

So, thought Miro, *this is the famous Maudree Král.* His uncle would never believe that he'd got this far. From a distance, the Král looked much the same as any other skret: grey skin, long arms, hooked claws. But, as Miro drew closer, he saw that the skret king's talons were tipped with gold and he wore a crown on his hairless head. A drop of blood ran along Miro's jaw and hung on the end of his chin. He brushed it away.

The Maudree Král tapped his claws on the throne.

Miro looked to his left. The skret that had captured him stood a little distance away. There were more skret to his right. At his back, the fire roared on.

'My name is Prince Miroslav Yaromeer Drahomeer Krishnov, Lord of the City of Yaroslav, Overseer of the Mountain Realms and Guardian of the Kolsaney Forests.'

The Maudree Král stopped tapping his claws and said, 'Bow.'

Miro hesitated. That was not the way one royal should talk to another. 'I have not come all this way to bow,' he said.

The fire shone in the Král's eyes. 'Then you must have come all this way to die.' He signalled to a big brute in a mask; a skret that was a head taller than the rest. The skret lumbered forward, carrying an axe in either hand. Miro took a step back and held up his arms.

'I'll do it,' he cried. 'I'll bow!'

The Maudree Král called his beast to heel and the audience jeered, enjoying the show. Miro hated them. He hated them all. When his uncle found out how he'd been treated . . . He glared at the skret king and bowed.

'Tell me, *human* –' the Maudree Král said the word like it was a dirty one – 'what are you doing in my mountain?'

'I've come to ask for your help.'

'And why would I help you?'

'It's not for me,' said Miro. 'It's for my friends.'

The Maudree Král made a great show of looking around. 'What friends?'

Miro trembled with rage. Or was it something else? Another drop of blood ran along his chin and this time it fell to the ground. He felt dizzy.

'They came here from another world,' said Miro. 'They came through a door in a tree, but they can't find the door and—'

'The Unseen Door is not for your kind. It cannot be opened by humans.'

'My friends . . .' Miro's voice trailed off and he swayed on his feet. He had to lie down. He didn't feel good. 'My uncle will pay for my safe return. Whatever you want, you can have it.'

'Is that so?' said the Král, smiling with triangular teeth. 'Anything I want?'

'Yes . . . anything.' More blood ran down Miro's cheek and the edges of the world went fuzzy.

'How about the Sertze Hora? I want the heart of the mountain.'

'We don't have your stupid heart! My uncle's a good man.'

'Your uncle is a thief and a traitor.'

Miro took a few steps forward. Then a few steps back. The heat was too much. The last thing he saw before he hit the floor was a wall of fire.

CHAPTER 70

'I wish I could have said goodbye to the boy,' said King Drakomor, lighting the library torches.

'What good would that have done?' said Anneshka.

'I just hadn't expected it to happen so quickly.'

'You did say to send him away . . .'

Drakomor ran his finger along the spines of the library books. 'And what about the lesni poacher?' Have the guards had any luck hunting her down?'

'I haven't heard anything,' said Anneshka.

The king picked up a shiny black book from the bottom shelf. He started turning the pages one by one. 'I hate moths,' he said, wrinkling his nose at a frilly-winged specimen that was pressed flat and sewn into the page.

'I'm not asking you to like them,' said Anneshka. 'I'm asking you to use them. No human will make the journey and we need to deliver our wedding invite to the Maudree Král.'

Drakomor continued to turn the book's pages. 'What are they like, the people Miro's staying with?' he asked.

'I don't know,' said Anneshka, keeping her eyes trained on the book. 'They're your family, not mine.'

'I don't have any family.'

'Your family by marriage. The boy has gone to stay with his mother's relatives, far beyond the mountains. Don't worry, I arranged an escort.'

'I see . . . In that case, I hope they make the crossing in time. The first snows can't be far off.'

'Aha!' Anneshka held down the page. Her sharp nail pointed at the wonky title: *Moths as Messengers*. 'Here – it tells you how to summon a moth,' she said. 'When did you do it last?'

'Never,' said Drakomor. 'It was always my brother's job, but it didn't look that hard.'

Drakomor and Anneshka read the instructions, then walked out to the library's balcony. They were high up, level with the top of the cathedral. Yaroslav's skyline gleamed in the moonlight with rows of tiled roofs, filigree steeples and sharp towers.

The king cleared his throat. 'Fly with courage and speed and the will of the stars. We have a message and it needs to go far.'

Nothing happened. Anneshka shivered.

'Perhaps you should say it again?' she suggested. 'Perhaps the moths didn't hear.'

'They heard.'

Two skret were scaling the cathedral, crawling along a flying buttress. 'Look,' whispered Anneshka, pointing at the misshapen silhouettes. She could have sworn they were looking back at her. 'Can they see us?' she asked, a little breathless.

'I doubt it,' said Drakomor. 'And they certainly can't get to us.'

'But they're trying, aren't they? They know the Sertze Hora is here.'

Drakomor didn't respond.

'The sooner they're dealt with, the better,' said Anneshka. She took a sharp breath. 'What's that?'

A shape fluttered towards the open window. Anneshka held out her hand and the black moth flew in a circle before landing on her palm. 'It worked!' she cried. 'What now?'

'Now we tell it our message,' said Drakomor.

CHAPTER 71

I t was late when Imogen, Marie and Lofkinye stood at the foot of the lightning-struck tree. The trunk was split down the middle and the remaining branches were as pale and naked as bones, but the stars were out and they hung round the tree like ghostly leaves.

'Look at that,' said Imogen. 'Look at all those stars.'

'I've never seen so many,' said Marie.

'They're gathering,' said Lofkinye.

'Gathering for what?'

'Perhaps they want to see what happens to the little prince.'

Behind the dead tree, in the side of the mountain, there were two low caves hidden by bushes and protected from the worst of the elements. Lofkinye checked for vipers with a sword. No snakes appeared, but a large red centipede marched out, waving its feelers in outrage.

The weary travellers removed their packs and boots and pushed them into the smaller of the two hollows. They crawled into the other, stringing their soggy fur coats across the entrance to keep out the wind.

It was a far cry from the snug tree houses they had slept in before, but at least it was dry. Lofkinye lit a candle and they ate dinner: twice-baked bread and some berries they'd picked that morning. Imogen's fingers were soon stained purple by the juice.

'I've been thinking,' she said, wiping her fingers on her trousers. 'Why aren't lesni people allowed to hunt?'

'The Royal Guards say there aren't enough wild animals,' replied Lofkinye. 'And they're right, but that doesn't make it just. It's one rule for me and another for the město. And if I don't hunt I don't eat. That's why . . .' She sighed. 'Enough of this. I'm not in the mood for storytelling tonight.'

The girls and the huntress put dry animal skins on the ground and wrapped themselves in blankets. They lay close together with Marie wedged in the middle. She was asleep within minutes, despite the hard floor.

Imogen was exhausted, more exhausted than she'd ever been, but she couldn't drift off. She watched the candle burn and she thought about Miro. She wondered where he was and what had happened to draw blood.

She propped herself up on her elbows and watched Marie's breath rise and fall. Lofkinye was watching too. Her dark eyes shone bright as if they were gathering light from the candle.

'What are you thinking about?' asked Imogen.

'You really want to know? I'm thinking we shouldn't have let the little prince get so far behind.'

Imogen swallowed. That wasn't what she wanted to hear. 'He should have asked us to slow down,' she said.

'He shouldn't have had to ask,' said Lofkinye rather sharply. 'You never leave people behind in the mountains.'

The coats at the cave entrance flapped in the wind and, for a second, a star peeked in.

'He saved my life, you know,' said Lofkinye. 'They were going to have me executed. If he hadn't freed me from the Hladomorna Pits, I'd be dead by now.'

Imogen didn't know what to say. She supposed Miro had saved her life too – when she and Marie had first arrived in Yaroslav. She didn't want to say it out loud though. It would only make things worse.

'Perhaps I shouldn't have told him about his uncle,' said the huntress. 'Or at least, not like that. He's just a child after all. A child with no parents.'

'But he's not a baby . . . And you were only telling the truth.'

'The truth!' Lofkinye laughed. 'What good is that now? It's like they always say: only children, fools and drunks tell the truth.' Imogen had never heard anyone say that, but she sensed Lofkinye was not in the mood to be contradicted.

'If the skret have hurt him,' continued Lofkinye, shaking

her head, 'it will be our fault. We should have kept him close.'

Marie mumbled something in her sleep and turned over. Her wild hair hadn't been brushed in days. It was beginning to resemble a bird's nest at the back. Imogen pulled the blankets up round her sister's chin and lay down.

'Where do you think the skret will take Miro?' she asked.

'To their caves in Klenot Mountain,' said Lofkinye. 'If he's still alive, that is.'

'If he's still alive,' whispered Imogen.

She thought Lofkinye might have some words of comfort to make that feeling go away – that gnawing in the pit of her belly – but Lofkinye's talk just made the feeling worse and Imogen knew its name: guilt.

CHAPTER 72

The monster received the black moth in his mountain-top cave. 'Do you bring news for Zuby?'

The moth landed on the stone floor and began crawling in a zigzag pattern, opening and closing its wings as if doing a dance. 'You bring a crustacean,' said the skret, scratching his bald head. 'That doesn't make sense.'

The moth flew back to its starting point and began again. The skret got on to all fours so that his great circular eyes were just centimetres from the insect.

'Aha!' he cried. 'Invitation, not crustacean! You bring an invitation. Keep going. You have my full attention.'

The moth traced an elaborate pattern on the cave floor. Swirling shapes were followed by straight lines and a frantic opening and closing of wings.

'From the string to his threading . . . no . . . from the wing to his heading . . .' The skret sprang to his feet. 'I've got it!' he cried. 'You bring an invitation from the king to his wedding! Well, this *is* unusual. I must go and tell the Král right away.'

Chapter 73

Meanwhile, back in Yaroslav, preparations for the royal wedding were well under way. Every serving girl was to get a new dress. Rolls of cotton and silk were carried into the castle, followed by an army of serious-looking seamstresses.

The head cook was making the biggest feast the kingdom had ever seen. She worked day and night. She chopped long lines of green and purple vegetables and tended to pots with lids that danced and rattled on the steam. She hired people that could bake, people that could gut, people that could skin things and turn them on spits.

There would be carp soup, stuffed swans, candied fruit and heart-shaped cherry tarts. A giant sugar sculpture of the happy couple was on order from the baker's, with gold-leaf eyes and marzipan faces. It would be the triumph of the table.

The pantry was filled with bread and cheese. The buttery was crammed with wine and ale. The cellars overflowed with buckets of wriggling eels.

In the evenings, the head cook sat with the butler and steward. The point of these meetings was for the cook, who couldn't write, to dictate her letters. She'd darn her boys' clothes while the two men scrawled.

'Do me one for the butcher down Misha Street,' said the cook. 'I'll need twenty oxen and fifty piglets slaughtered.'

'Twenty ox and fifty piggies,' repeated the butler.

Snip went the cook's scissors on the thread.

'Make sure they're young ones,' she said. 'I don't want any big, tough porkers.'

'Must be sucklings ...'

Scribble scribble scribble. Stitch stitch stitch.

'And that huntsman.'

'Blazen?'

'Yes, write me one for him. We'll need him to catch pheasants, partridges, starlings and storks.'

The torchlight cast their shadows in awkward shapes. The cook pulled a length of thread, held up her scissors and, for a moment, they were like the three blind fates, not servants at all.

'Did you hear the rumour about old Yeedarsh?' said the steward.

'No. I don't listen to gossip,' said the cook, but she leaned in all the same.

'They say it wasn't the skret that killed him.'

'But he was cut into pieces,' said the cook. 'That's what skret do.'

'Apparently, Anneshka Mazanar got someone to do it. She wanted it to look like a skret attack, but it was a human that did the slicing and dicing.'

'What!' cried the cook. 'Our new queen, a murderess?'

'Yeedarsh never thought she was good enough for the king,' said the steward. 'Now the old man's bear has stopped eating. Perhaps it's a sign – a bad sign – for the wedding. Perhaps we should make something to tempt the beast.'

'You want me to cook for a bear?'

'Queen Anneshka has plans for the animal,' said the steward. 'She says no wedding is complete without a dancing bear.'

'In that case, it might be no bad thing if the bear goes hungry,' cut in the butler. 'The only bears that dance are starved or frightened . . . I reckon starved is kinder.'

'What do bears eat?' asked the cook.

'Slugs and snails and puppy dogs' tails,' said the butler.

The cook clipped him over the back of his head. 'I'm serious,' she said.

'Eels?' suggested the steward.

'She's not having my eels,' said the cook. 'Do you know how much I paid for them? The bear will just have to make do with what she's given.'

'All right,' said the butler, rubbing his head. 'You're the boss.'

'Too right I am.'

CHAPTER 74

When he woke, Miro's tongue felt more like a dead slug than a part of his body. Where was he? He needed a drink.

He sat up and found blankets on his legs: rough blankets that smelled of wee, but blankets all the same.

Why was he in a cave? And then he remembered. He'd spoken to the Maudree Král. He was inside Klenot Mountain and, if the bars in front of him were anything to go by, he wasn't in the luxury guest quarters.

There was a bowl of water on the floor. Miro tipped it into his mouth, glugging until there was none left. Then he realised that his face hurt – really hurt. He lifted a hand to his cheek. The blood around the cut was gloopy and mixed with some kind of balm.

He pulled the blankets round his body. The candles lighting the cave had about an hour of burn-time left. At least it wasn't like the Hladomorna Pits. They never gave out blankets there. By contrast, this skret prison was a paradise.

Miro couldn't help thinking about his uncle; he wondered if Drakomor knew where he was. If the wedding was close, and it couldn't be far off, Drakomor might be too busy to negotiate Miro's release.

Here was an ugly thought: what if his uncle didn't *want* him back? Miro was pretty sure Anneshka didn't want him around and, when they were married, his uncle would probably feel the same. They'd have children of their own. That was what happened after weddings. A perfect little boy and a perfect little girl. Drakomor wouldn't need someone else's leftover son. Miro's heart ached.

As the candles burned down, he wrapped the blankets tighter round his body. Soon he'd be in total darkness. He should have been used to it. He'd spent enough time up in his tower, awake all night and watching the candles die. But Miro had never liked the dark. He couldn't stop thinking about the friends who'd abandoned him and the uncle who didn't want him back. He'd never felt so alone.

The candles went out and Miro didn't know how long he'd been sitting in the dark when a light appeared behind the bars of his cell. All he knew was that the cut on his face hurt more than ever and he was hungry.

A skret approached, carrying a candle and a set of jangling keys. 'Where are you?' said the skret in a scratchy, metallic voice. Miro stayed very still, hardly daring to breathe.

The skret let itself into the cell. 'I know you're in here, human. There's no point hiding.'

Miro pulled the blanket over his head and lay low. The skret's back claws scraped on the cave floor. It was getting closer. 'There you are!' Miro's cover was torn away.

'Leave me alone,' he cried, lashing out.

'I've not come to hurt you,' said the skret, stepping back. It had long teeth that stuck out from the bottom of its mouth, like upside-down fangs.

'What do you want?' said Miro.

'I've come to stitch you back together.'

'Stitch me? I won't let you!'

'That cut on your face – it won't heal right without stitches.'

Miro touched the edge of the wound. 'Won't heal right? What do you mean?'

'It'll take too long – get infected. I gave you some salve, but it looks like you've rubbed most of it off.'

'I didn't know what it was.'

'That's the problem with you humans: you don't know much.'

The skret left the cell and returned a few minutes later with more candles, a bowl of water and some medical items. It looked funny carrying that stuff: the ugliest nurse in Yaroslav. Miro would have laughed if he hadn't been so afraid.

The cut on his cheek felt like it was on fire and he couldn't take his eyes off the skret's claws. Each one was as long as a human thumb. How was the skret going to give him stitches? Wasn't the monster more likely to gouge out his eyes?

'Why are you doing this?' said Miro.

'It's my job,' said the skret. 'I'm in charge of prisoners and moths. There used to be someone else for the prisoners, but they died so here I am. The moths are better company to be honest . . .'

'But why not just let me rot? That's what we do in the Hladomorna Pits.'

The skret snorted out of the slits it had for nostrils. 'That's not what I do.' It sat down at the table, picking up a cloth. 'Bring your face close to the candle.'

Miro looked at the monster with the upside-down fangs. He didn't want to obey, but he also didn't see why, if the skret were going to kill him, they would do it with a needle and thread. Surely there were easier ways. He knelt by the table and turned his cheek to the light.

The skret washed Miro's face, dipping the cloth into the water and dabbing it round the cut. Miro looked at the monster's teeth. They were more like tusks.

This was the first chance he'd had to study a skret up close. He could see every wart and hair on the monster's pale skin. He could see the circular eyes. He could even see the luminous green rings that appeared round the irises when they were turned to the light. That meant the skret had good night vision. Miro's old tutor had taught him that.

This skret was ugly, just like the others, but there was something about him. Something that made him harder to hate. *That is*, thought Miro, *assuming it is a* he. It was almost impossible to tell the sexes apart. Miro's old tutor had taught him that too.

After a few minutes, the bowl of water was red and Miro plucked up the courage to ask a question.

'Why are your teeth so different from the other skrets' teeth?'

'Why shouldn't they be? Is every human the same?'

'No . . . But the skret skulls, the ones in Yaroslav, they have little triangular teeth.'

The monster frowned. 'That's a nasty habit. Putting skulls on display.'

'It's supposed to scare you away,' said Miro.

'We're not so easily scared,' muttered the skret, wringing out the cloth.

'But your teeth are quite big, aren't they?'

'Yes. That's why they call me *Zuby*. It means *teeth*. Isn't there anything different about you?'

'Of course. I'm a prince.'

342

Miro saw his reflection in the skret's eyes. He was dirty and his clothes had turned to rags. He didn't look very royal.

'And what does it mean to be a prince?' asked Zuby.

'It means that one day I'll be king and everyone will have to do as I say. Even the lords and ladies. Even the Royal Guards. Even my friends ... if I have any friends.'

'Princes don't have friends?'

'I used to have some, but they left me behind.'

Zuby threaded the needle with astonishing ease, holding it between the sharp tips of his claws. 'Put your head back,' he said.

'Will it hurt?'

'Yes.'

Miro held on to the edge of the table. He closed his eyes so he wouldn't see those claws working so close to his face and then he felt the needle go in. He cried out. He couldn't help it. Zuby didn't say a word. The needle went in again. Miro gripped on to the table with all his might.

'It's too painful!'

'Hold still. I'm almost done.'

Finally, the skret pulled away. Miro fought back tears. That had hurt a lot more than he'd thought it would, but he didn't want to cry in front of Zuby. He went back to his blankets. 'Thank you,' he said.

When the skret was on the other side of the bars, he

turned and looked at his captive. 'There's something I want to know,' he said. 'Why don't you just give it back?'

'Give what back?' said Miro.

'The Sertze Hora.'

Miro threw up his hands in despair. 'Because we don't have your stupid mountain heart! Why does everyone keep going on about it?'

'Because we're dying.'

Miro hesitated. That wasn't the response he'd expected. 'Everyone dies ... eventually.'

'No, you don't understand. Even the skřítek. Even our little ones are dying because of the Žal.'

Miro pulled the blanket over his head and shut his eyes. 'I don't know why you're telling me this. I don't have your stone.'

'I've been releasing moths,' said Zuby in his scratchy voice, 'and they say you're lying. They say the mountain heart is in that big castle where you live – up in the tallest tower.'

'Nonsense,' said Miro from under the blanket.

'The Král keeps sending skret, but they can't get into the castle. It's too secure. Too many high walls and locks and guards.'

'My uncle will never let you in.'

'That is where you're wrong,' said the skret, and with that he walked away.

CHAPTER 75

I mogen didn't know what time it was when she finally
fell asleep, but, when she woke up, daylight was spilling
in round the edges of the cave entrance. She lay still for
a minute, watching her breath freeze and thinking about
what Lofkinye had said last night. *Please*, she thought,
*please let Miro be okay. I'll be nice to him, I promise. Please let
him be okay.*

Marie was still fast asleep and Lofkinye was gone.
Imogen crawled stiffly towards the coats, which were
frozen solid. 'This is not good,' she muttered, forcing her
way past.

Outside, a few birds sang a feeble dawn chorus. There
was the lightning-struck tree and there was Lofkinye,
sitting at the foot of it. She looked tired. Imogen wondered
if she'd been awake all night.

Imogen walked over, feeling every joint complain. Too
much walking. Too hard a floor. Too cold a night.

Lofkinye was rubbing something on the string of her
bow. 'What's that?' asked Imogen.

'Beeswax. Stops the string from fraying.'

'Oh right.' Imogen shivered. 'The coats have frozen.'

'Perfect,' said Lofkinye. 'We can shake off the ice. They'll be nice and dry.'

Imogen hadn't thought of that.

Lofkinye continued: 'Today I'm going to the skret caves at the top of Klenot Mountain. It should be doable if I keep a steady pace. You and your sister should stay here. I'll get you on the way back down.'

'But what are you going to do?'

'Rescue the little prince.'

'You can't do that alone.'

Lofkinye dealt Imogen her broadest of smiles. 'I've got a plan.'

Imogen hesitated. She felt bad saying the words out loud. 'Does the plan include asking the Maudree Král about the door in the tree?'

For a split second, Lofkinye looked confused. She'd clearly forgotten all about that.

'We don't have to,' said Imogen. 'We don't have to ask if it would mess up your plan. It's just that . . . once Miro has been rescued, I would really like to find the way home. Marie needs her mum.'

Lofkinye nodded. 'And you?'

'I suppose I need my mum too.'

'Okay,' said Lofkinye. 'I'll ask the Král about your door. But what are you going to do in the meantime?'

'I'm coming with you, of course,' said Imogen.

'And so am I,' said Marie, who had snuck up unheard.

CHAPTER 76

The path up Klenot Mountain was made of stone. Sometimes it was so narrow that Imogen, Marie and Lofkinye had to walk sideways, inching along with their bellies pressed against the cliff. At other times, it was as wide as the roads back home, leading the travellers across windswept plateaus.

The only things thriving were prickly shrubs. Their barbed stems pulled at Imogen's trousers if she wandered too close to the edge of the path. Their spiked leaves pushed through the ribs of a skeleton. Lofkinye paused by the dead thing. 'The last of the wildcats,' she sighed, and she shepherded the girls on.

Sometimes they walked in silence. Sometimes Marie hummed until Imogen made her stop. Sometimes they talked. Lofkinye told stories about her life in the forests. In return, Imogen and Marie told Lofkinye about their home. They told her about computers and cars and the things they learned at school.

'Incredible,' said Lofkinye, shaking her head in

amazement. 'If every child has a tutor, your world must be very wealthy.'

They talked about how Mum read them stories, surrounded by fairy lights, about how, every Friday, she let them choose what to eat and they could pick anything they wanted – anything at all.

Thinking about Mum gave Imogen a surge of new energy. Every step was a step closer to home.

The higher they climbed, the colder it grew. The sun was just beginning to slip down the sky when they came to the edge of a vast expanse of ice. It was so blue and pure that it seemed to glow.

'Wow,' said Marie. 'What's that?'

'Klenot Glacier. This is where the path ends,' said Lofkinye. 'We need to cross the ice.'

'Is it safe?'

'Sure. As long as you don't slip down a crevasse.'

'What's a crevasse?'

'A crack in the ice. We should tie ourselves together, just in case.'

Lofkinye used a rope to fasten herself to Imogen. Then she used another rope to tie Imogen to Marie. 'Take it very slowly,' she said. 'We're not really wearing the right boots.'

Imogen took her first steps with her arms spread wide.

She hadn't gone far when the rope tugged at her middle. She turned round to see that Marie hadn't moved. 'Come on, Marie,' she called. 'You need to keep up.'

Marie looked like she'd seen a ghost.

'What's wrong?' shouted Lofkinye.

'There are men in the glacier,' said Marie.

Imogen and Lofkinye shuffled back and followed Marie's finger. Sure enough, there were three bodies curled up, encased in the ice. Their skin and hair were perfectly preserved, as if they'd died only yesterday. Imogen reached for Marie's hand.

'Merchants,' said Lofkinye.

'How did they get there?' asked Marie in a small voice.

'They probably died of cold. Crossing too late in the year.'

'But how did they get into the ice?'

'The glacier is always moving,' said Lofkinye. 'It's too slow to see, but eventually it swallows things up.'

'So they'll be frozen like that ... forever?'

'Yes, I suppose they will.'

Marie looked at the stretch of ice ahead of her. Then she looked at her sister. 'I'm not sure about this, Imogen. It doesn't feel like a good idea.'

'But I don't have any others and Miro needs our help. He came all this way for us and now it's our turn to do the rescuing. *Your* turn to be the knight.'

Marie swallowed. 'Like the knight from your play?'

'Yes, if you like.'

'No more bit parts?'

'No,' said Imogen firmly. 'No more bit parts.' Marie put one foot on the glacier.

'All right,' said Lofkinye. 'Follow me.'

The three travellers shuffled and skidded along. Staying upright required concentration and a steady pace. Imogen slipped a few times, but she never went far – Lofkinye's rope saw to that.

Beneath Imogen's feet, ribbons of electric blue ran through the ice. Lofkinye navigated them round deep cracks and yawning holes that plunged into darkness. Imogen didn't like walking near those things. Who knew what lurked down there?

When they reached the other side of the glacier, Lofkinye untied the rope. The peak of Klenot Mountain loomed above them, its jagged rocks sticking out of the snow like a giant's crown.

'That is where the Maudree Král lives,' said Lofkinye, and she almost looked excited. 'You've never seen caves like it. Great high ceilings, walls that glisten with jewels and a roaring fire that burns all winter long.'

They scrambled over rocks, sometimes crawling on all fours. Imogen soon missed the stone path. It was colder in the shade of the mountain and, despite her mittens, the tips of her fingers began to go numb. She clenched and released her hands, trying to keep them warm.

Lofkinye stopped at an opening in the side of the mountain. 'This tunnel is the fastest way to the skret caves,' she said. The gap was lined with icicles that hung down like teeth. 'We're just in time. In a few weeks, these icicles will touch the floor and the tunnel will be off limits.' She ducked under the ice fangs and the girls followed.

Lofkinye lit a torch from her pack and Imogen saw that they were standing in a giant passageway with frozen walls. The cold was inescapable. Even in her furs, Imogen was chilled to the bone. More icicles hung from the ceiling, threatening and beautiful.

As they walked deeper into the mountain, Imogen could have sworn she heard the icicles sing. Each one struck a note like a glass when you run a wet finger round the rim. Imogen wondered if the skret could hear the song.

'Have you met this Maudree Král before?' she said.

'Years ago,' replied Lofkinye, 'before the Sertze Hora was stolen.'

'And what was he like?'

'Well, he didn't kill people, for a start. The Maudree Král I knew was fair and wise.'

'But the skret kill people in Yaroslav all the time.'

'I suppose he's changed . . . We'll just have to see how much.'

The tunnel twisted into the mountain and the girls followed Lofkinye between columns of ice that were packed together like the pipes of a church organ. Marie started humming again and Imogen knew the tune. It was an irritating jingle from a film about a young boy who kills a dragon. Imogen thought about telling Marie to stop, but this time she decided against it. Perhaps it helped Marie stay brave.

As the path rose up, the cold seemed to fade and so did the ice. Bit by bit, the tunnel walls revealed themselves. They were made from rock and, in some places, they were covered in feathers.

'What are those things?' said Imogen. 'They're beautiful!'

It was only when she walked right up close that she saw that they were moths with their wings folded back. Some of the wings carried patterns like eyes; others shimmered in the low light.

'Don't touch them,' said Lofkinye.

'Are they alive?' asked Marie.

'Yes. They're hibernating.'

So Yeedarsh was right, thought Imogen. *The skret are friends with the moths.* She hoped he'd been right about the shadow moth too. She hoped it had been sent for a reason.

353

After all, if the Král had sent the moth to fetch them, surely he could make it take them home.

The ice tunnel climbed higher. 'Not far to go now,' said Lofkinye. Ahead, there was an orange glow and Imogen felt the nerves stir in her belly. It was hard to make her legs keep walking. She was weary from days of hiking, but it wasn't just that. She was afraid.

Then she remembered her mum's words: *It will always be the three of us, Imogen. No matter what.*

Imogen narrowed her eyes and kept walking towards the light.

CHAPTER 77

The orange light grew brighter with every step that Imogen took.

She reached for her sword, but Lofkinye stopped her. 'No weapons. We don't want the skret thinking we've come for a fight.'

The tunnel opened out into a gigantic cave, with a high ceiling that reminded Imogen of a cathedral and an enormous fire that did not. The roar of the flames was so loud that the girls had to shout to be heard. 'What a big bonfire!' cried Marie.

'That's not the right word,' said Imogen.

'What?'

'I said that's not the right . . . oh, never mind.'

'This is the fire the skret keep all winter,' said Lofkinye. 'Feel that heat.' She removed her mittens and held out her hands.

Imogen did the same until the cold had been banished from her nose and fingers. She made a joke in her head about a warm welcome, but decided against saying it out loud. Instead, she said, 'Where are all the skret? Are we in the right place?'

Lofkinye put her finger to her lips and pointed. Something was moving on the other side of the fire.

The three intruders dashed behind a pillar just before the skret appeared. The monsters were carrying a carafe and they were engaged in a lively debate. Imogen couldn't hear what they were saying, but it was funny to see them so deep in discussion – unnatural – like watching a monkey do the tango. *I suppose*, thought Imogen, *even monsters can't be killing people all the time.*

The skret disappeared through a door in the cave wall and Imogen's heart skipped a beat. That door – it looked just like the door in the tree. It was the same shape. It had the same handle. It was even the same size, as if it had been made for a child . . . or a skret.

Imogen rushed towards it and pressed her ear against the wood. There was some commotion on the other side, but it was hard to tell exactly what. She looked at Marie and Lofkinye. They nodded and Imogen opened the door.

There was music and firelight and skret. Lots of skret. They were sitting at long tables, picking at the remains of animal carcasses. They were shouting and banging plates and pouring drink into their mouths. Imogen had never seen such appalling table manners, and the smell of boiled meat was overpowering.

At the head of the longest table was a skret with a crown

on its head and a human child by its side. The child had far-apart eyes, dark olive skin and a mop of brown hair. There was a deep cut on his cheek and he hadn't touched his food.

Marie yelled, 'Miro!' and every head turned.

Hundreds of circular eyes blinked at the new arrivals, like a shoal of meat-eating fish. Imogen moved closer to Lofkinye. Marie moved closer to Imogen. There was a terrible silence.

The skret wearing the crown was the first to speak: 'So you must be *the friends*. I'm afraid we haven't saved you any of our feast.'

'Your Highness, please forgive the intrusion,' said Lofkinye and she bowed so low that the hood of her coat swept the floor.

'Shpitza said you were coming.' The Maudree Král gestured towards a skret with spikes along his back. Imogen recognised him as the one they'd met in the forest.

'We've come to offer you a deal,' said Lofkinye.

The Král picked up a bone and stripped off the last of the flesh. 'You have nothing worth trading.'

'I do. I have something you'd give your hind claws for.' Lofkinye sounded confident. Imogen wondered what she was up to.

'Go on,' said the Král.

'Yes, spit it out,' hissed the skret called Shpitza.

'I can get you the Sertze Hora,' said Lofkinye.

A murmur ran along the tables. Every skret turned to its neighbour in disbelief. Miro put his head in his hands.

'Quiet,' said the Maudree Král, but the chatter only grew louder so the skret king climbed on to the table and stamped his feet. 'QUIET!' he shouted and the room fell silent.

'I already know that the Sertze Hora is locked up in Castle Yaroslav,' snarled the Král. 'So tell me, how would you get your paws on my mountain's heart?'

A twitch above Lofkinye's eyebrow gave her away. She *was* nervous. 'Oh, you don't need to worry about that,' she said, smoothing her forehead with her palm.

'But I do,' said the Král, and he began to walk along the table towards his uninvited guests. 'This isn't a decorative diamond.' He booted dishes out of his way. Trotters and ribs went flying. 'The Sertze Hora is a living thing: the mountain's beating heart. It puts leaves on the trees and clean water in the rivers. And, since you humans decided to rip the heart from the body, we've all been bleeding to death.'

He smashed over a goblet with his fist. 'A few days ago, I saw my sister's skřítek – a child not more than three years old. His skin is mottled with black spots and he complains of a pain in his chest. It won't be long before he's dead like the rest of them.'

The skret king had reached the end of the table. He looked down at Lofkinye. 'So don't tell me not to worry.'

Every skret and human waited for Lofkinye's response.

'I'm sorry,' she said. 'I'm sorry that it was stolen from you.' She spoke softly as though trying to calm a spooked horse.

'Perhaps it was you that did the stealing,' sneered the Král. 'Perhaps you sold it to the město.'

'Drakomor Krishnov did the stealing,' said Lofkinye. 'You know that's the truth.'

Miro gave a stifled snort.

'You humans are all traitors. You're all the same,' said the Král.

He crouched down, wrapping his claws round the edge of the table and poking his face out between his knees. It was, thought Imogen, a most unkingly pose. She tried to shield Marie.

'Suppose I did accept your offer,' said the Král, 'what would you want in return?'

'Three wishes,' said Lofkinye.

'Do I look like a fairy?'

The girls and Lofkinye all shook their heads.

'Spit it out,' said the Král and he rocked with impatience.

'One: I want that boy released.' Lofkinye counted the wishes on her fingers. 'Two: reveal your magic door. My friends here need to go back to their own world. Three:

you must allow the lesni to return to the forests. This is our home just as much as it's yours.'

The Král snarled, revealing two rows of perfectly triangular teeth. 'And the heart? When do I get that?'

'After I've returned the boy to his uncle.'

The skret king sprang down from the table. He landed on his feet just in front of Lofkinye. Her hand reached for her bow, but he caught her wrist in his claws. 'I see through you,' he said. 'You mean to do a trade with the human king. The boy for the heart. Isn't that right?'

'No! That's not it at all!'

The Král released Lofkinye and stomped over to the table. 'That's not it, that's not it at all . . .' he mimicked. When he turned round, he was holding something between his gold-tipped claws. 'If you can trade the boy, then so can I.' He was holding a wishbone.

A memory flashed into Imogen's head. After Sunday lunch, her mum always gave her a wishbone to pull with Marie. One wish each. Back then she'd wished for many things. Now she just wanted to be home.

'You could never get into the castle,' said Lofkinye. 'They'd never let you near the king. Let me do the trade for you.'

'You're wrong!' cried the Král, and he held the wishbone above his head. 'I've already got my wish! Did you not receive your invitation?'

Imogen was suddenly aware of a grey moth crawling along one of the half-eaten carcasses.

'Invitation to what?' said Lofkinye. She was beginning to sound desperate.

'To the royal wedding of course!' The Král snapped the wishbone in two. 'So, you see, I don't need you at all.'

He gestured to the skret. Lofkinye pulled out her bow. Imogen sprinted towards the moth. The skret went wild and suddenly it was all shrieking and claws. Imogen was caught in a powerful grip. She thrashed and reached out for Marie, but there was nothing she could do. The skret were too strong. Her pack was pulled away, her sword too. Before she knew what was happening, she was inside a sack.

CHAPTER 78

Andel's brief was clear. He was to create a weapon for the wedding.

If he finished it too late, the king would take his remaining eye. If it wasn't powerful enough to kill the Maudree Král, the king would take his eye. If it wasn't beautiful enough to impress the people . . . well, you get the idea.

He was given the room at the top of the second tallest tower as his workshop – high above all the people he loved. Imagine Andel's surprise when he found his old friend waiting there. It ticked along, as though no time had passed since they last met. Five hands drew circles round a familiar wooden face.

'My clock,' muttered Andel, rubbing his eye. 'I didn't think I'd see you again.'

The clock's hatch popped open and a wooden lizard crawled out to greet him. Andel recognised it at once. It was a dragon. The miniature beast unfurled its wings, opened its mouth and breathed fire.

Andel beamed. The clock truly was his greatest creation

– tuned to the rhythm of the stars. He wished his daughter was allowed to come up and see it.

A spark from the dragon's mouth dropped on to its claw. For a moment, it glowed orange and then the flames took hold. Andel tried to blow it out, but that only made things worse.

'Sakra!' he cried. The fire gobbled up the dragon in a matter of seconds.

The hatch snapped shut and Andel was left with a small pile of ashes and a brilliant idea. He'd build the king a mechanical dragon, as big as a barn, with a bellyful of fire.

He made the dragon one part at a time – starting with the head and working his way along the spine. Each piece had to be small enough to fit down the spiral staircase.

He was drawn into the process in spite of himself. He fussed over the smallest details and insisted on materials of the highest quality. Fossilised tusks were ordered for the teeth, rubies for the eyes. The scales were made from flameproof ceramic tiles cut into diamonds.

Seeing the dragon take shape in the square below, Andel's chest swelled with pride. It felt good to be working on such an ambitious project, even if it was for a man he despised.

The night before the royal wedding, as the sun set behind

Klenot Mountain, Andel finished the final piece of his monster. 'Just in time,' he said, handing the tip of the tail to a servant.

He walked to the nearest window and looked down. The dragon stood in the square, with the sun's last rays glinting off its ceramic scales. Andel would go and inspect it in the morning, before the wedding guests arrived. He needed to check that everything had been assembled correctly.

'A beautiful weapon for a beautiful revenge,' he muttered. 'The king won't see this coming . . .'

Chapter 79

Something hit Imogen's back. It was the floor.

A skret, with enormous tusk-teeth, peered into her sack. 'What have we got here?' he said.

'Get off me!' cried Imogen, pushing her way out. She sprang to her feet, holding up her fists.

'There's no need for that,' said the skret. 'You've already lost the fight. You're prisoners now.'

Imogen saw that she was in a small cave with two beds, two chairs, a table and a couple of candles. There were bars across the entrance. She lowered her fists.

Something wriggled inside another sack. The skret untied the end, pulled out Marie and set her on her feet.

'I didn't know humans came in red,' he said, and he touched her hair with the tips of his claws.

Marie shrank back, staring at the monster's giant teeth. 'Who are you?' she said.

'And what have you done with our friends?' demanded Imogen.

The skret scratched his bald head. 'My name is Zuby.'

'You can't keep us here,' said Imogen. 'We're little girls. It's against our human rights.'

'You are quite small,' agreed the skret and then, as if they weren't in the room, 'small for humans and ugly too. So ugly they're almost cute.'

'Us?' said Imogen, confused.

'Are you going to cut us up and drink our blood?' said Marie.

'Why would I do that?' said the skret.

'The Král says we're traitors.'

'Slicing and dicing isn't really my area ...'

'Okay,' said Imogen, 'then let us go.'

'That would make *me* a traitor.' Zuby smiled so that a tusk almost touched the tip of his squished-in nose.

'Brilliant,' said Imogen, flopping down on a bed.

The skret picked up the empty sacks and let himself out of the cave, locking the girls in behind him. When the scratch of his claws had faded away, Imogen and Marie walked to the front of their prison and pressed their faces against the bars. They could fit their arms and legs through, but the gaps were too narrow for their heads.

'I wonder where the others are,' said Marie.

'Miro didn't look very well,' said Imogen.

'Miro's just fine,' said a small voice.

The girls looked at each other. 'Miro?'

Imogen grabbed a candle. When she held it out between the bars, she saw a familiar face in the neighbouring cell. 'Miro!' she cried. The prince smiled and then winced, touching the cut on his cheek. There were bloody dots running along either side of the wound.

'I can reach you,' said Imogen. She pushed her arm between the bars, right up to the shoulder. Miro reached out too and their fingertips touched. Rough skin had grown over the cut on his thumb, where they'd made the pact all those nights ago.

'It's good to see you,' said Imogen.

'It's good to see you too,' said the prince.

'What happened to your face?'

'One of the skret cut me, but it's okay. Zuby stitched it up.'

'It looks like Halloween face paint.'

'Hallo-what?'

'Never mind.' Imogen retracted her arm. 'We thought you were right behind us,' she said. 'That night when you went missing. We thought you were just there.'

'I was ambushed,' said Miro.

'We didn't know ...'

Miro moved away from the bars, retreating out of the candlelight. 'It's all right,' he said. 'You're here now.'

'Fat lot of good it's done,' said Imogen to the darkness. 'We're supposed to be rescuing you.'

'You tried. That's what counts.'

'No, it's not! The point of rescuing people is to get them out of prison, not join them in it.'

'It's what counts for me.'

'From now on, we'll stick together,' said Imogen as if that cleared everything up. She looked at Marie, who was shaking her head.

'*Sorry*,' mouthed Marie.

'*Why?*' mouthed Imogen.

'You haven't said it,' whispered Marie. 'To him.'

Imogen looked back at the space where Miro had been. 'All the same,' she continued, 'we didn't mean to get so . . . far ahead.'

'It's fine,' said Miro. 'Really it is.'

Imogen made a face at Marie that said, *See, it's okay!*

Marie scowled.

Imogen threw up her hands and mouthed several words all at once, not very nice ones, then she turned back to Miro's cell. 'Miro?' she said.

'Uh-huh?'

'I'm sorry . . . I'm sorry we left you behind. It's not what friends do and it won't happen again. I promise.'

Miro's face appeared behind the bars of his cell. 'You

don't have to be sorry,' he said. 'You're already the best friends I've ever had.'

Imogen felt a sort of release in her chest where she hadn't even known it had been tight.

Miro's expression darkened. 'But, you know, we might not be able to stick together for much longer.'

'What do you mean?'

'The Maudree Král said he's going to swap me for the Sertze Hora.'

'He can't have been serious,' said Imogen. 'Can he?'

'I don't know. For one thing, I don't see how he got an invite to my uncle's wedding. Uncle hates the skret. For another thing, the Sertze Hora doesn't exist.'

'It does seem strange,' agreed Imogen.

The girls took the blankets and straw-stuffed pillows from their beds, and moved them to the corner of the cell that was closest to Miro.

'I asked them about your magic door,' said the prince. 'The Král called it an "Unseen Door".'

'Did he say how we could get back to it?' said Marie.

'I'm afraid not. He said it isn't meant for humans ...'

'Well, it worked for us,' said Imogen, curling up and putting an arm round her sister.

'This is all a bit of a disaster,' said the prince.

'There is one good thing,' said Marie. 'If the Král is

telling the truth – if he does do some kind of swap – you'll be back with your uncle in no time. You'll be home.'

'I just hope those men with the swords have gone,' said Imogen.

'What men with swords?' said Miro.

'The ones we flew away from on the velecours. Don't you remember?'

'Oh, them!' cried Miro. 'Don't worry about them. It's like I said, I've known them for years. I'll talk to Uncle when I'm back . . . see what he wanted.'

'Hmmm,' said Imogen.

They weren't safe here, surrounded by monsters, but she wasn't convinced that Miro would be any safer at the castle.

CHAPTER 80

Imogen was woken by a terrible noise. She grabbed hold of Marie, but the commotion wasn't coming from their cell. It was Miro. Something was happening to Miro.

Imogen threw off her blanket and pressed her face against the bars. She couldn't see what was going on, but skret were yelling and Miro was too. There was a bang and a rustle, followed by a slam. Then the noise stopped.

Imogen pushed her arm between the bars and reached towards the other cell.

'Miro!' she cried. 'Miro, put your hand out to mine!'

But Miro didn't reply. He was gone.

CHAPTER 81

Blazen Bilbetz slapped six dead pheasants and three dead storks on the table. The head cook took the fattest pheasant in her muscular hands, lifting it by the tips of its wings so that they folded open and the head flopped back.

'They'll do,' she said. Blazen grinned. It was the morning of the royal wedding and this was his final delivery.

'Just in time,' he laughed.

'Not really,' said the cook. 'They'll want hanging for a few days before they're ready, but you're lucky. This lot are for later.'

The cook left the kitchen and Blazen surveyed his surroundings. It was as organised as a barracks before battle. Vegetables waited in pots of salted water. Cuts of meat were marinating in various sauces.

The cook returned and handed Blazen his bag of gold. That soft chink – he loved the sound of money. 'Thank you,' he said, ducking on the way out so he didn't smack his head.

Blazen walked down two corridors before sneaking into

an empty chamber. He knew better than to sit and count the coins in front of the head cook, but he wanted to make sure that he hadn't been short-changed.

The room he walked into was small and plain, with a made-up bed, an old wardrobe and a bear. Blazen did a double take.

Yes. There was a bear in the corner of the room and it wasn't stuffed.

The two creatures blinked at each other. Hunter at bear. Bear at hunter. It had been years since they'd last met, but Blazen recognised her all the same. Medveditze. He had stumbled into Yeedarsh's old room.

The bear had deep cuts across her face and body. 'What have they done to you?' muttered Blazen. He dropped his gold and approached slowly, stepping over a bowl of old turnips. 'I can't see you wanting to eat *that* rubbish.'

The bear's shaggy head followed the hunter. When he was close enough, Blazen inspected the chain round her neck. 'But I don't understand,' he said. 'Old Yeedarsh never kept you in chains.'

Medveditze grumbled, looking at him with sorrowful eyes.

'Why don't they release you? What use does the queen have for a bear?'

Something caught Blazen's attention. Something red at the edge of his vision. He turned and saw an enormous scarlet waistcoat hanging on the side of the wardrobe. The waistcoat had gold edging and shiny brass buttons. Navy trousers hung behind it. Blazen turned them round. There was a hole in the bum – just big enough for a tail to poke through. The hunter shook his head.

'I'm sorry,' he said, turning back to Medveditze. 'The head cook said there was going to be a dancing bear at the wedding feast. I should have guessed she meant you.' He eyed the gash across the bear's snout. It looked fresh. 'Training not going well, then?'

Medveditze shifted her weight from one side to the other, making her chains clatter.

'I know what you're thinking,' said the giant. 'I'm a hunter. You're a bear. We're not the most natural of friends, but I'll let you in on a little secret . . . Not all of the things they say about me are true.'

Blazen sat at the end of Yeedarsh's bed and looked down at his belly. The buttons on his jacket were threatening to pop. He was deciding which not-true thing to say out loud. 'For example,' he said, 'I've never killed a bear.'

Medveditze snorted.

'I know, I know . . . They say I've killed hundreds. It's not so. I let the stories spread. They do my reputation no harm, but the truth is I've never killed anything bigger than a deer.'

The bear turned her golden eyes away as if she'd known this about him all along.

'I have an idea,' said the hunter, slapping his thighs. 'I'll do you a deal. A pact, if you will. I'll get you some food before the wedding – some proper food, that is, not turnips – on the condition that you keep my secret. I can't have anyone else knowing. They'll think I'm a fraud. They're like that, people.'

Medveditze made another grumbling sound and Blazen knew the pact was agreed.

'All right,' he said, walking over to the door and picking up his gold. 'How would you like some fish?'

CHAPTER 82

The skret called Zuby pushed a pair of spoons and two mugs between the bars of the girls' cell. 'Here you go, humans. Eat up.'

Imogen picked up a mug. There was brown liquid inside, with things bobbing on the surface that could have been dumplings or eyeballs.

'What is this stuff?' she said.

'Zelí Shtyavy,' said the skret, looking strangely proud.

'Where has Miro gone?' asked Marie.

'Who's Miro?' said the skret.

'The boy that was in the cave next to us.'

Zuby looked at the empty cell. 'Ah, the prince! The prince has gone to Yaroslav. They're taking him home.'

Imogen dropped her spoon. 'Taking him home? Really?'

'Yes, that's what the Maudree Král said. Eat your Shtyavy.'

'I'm not hungry.'

'There's nothing else,' said the skret, wagging a claw.

'Are they going to swap Miro for the Sertze Hora?' asked Marie.

'Yes,' said Zuby. 'King Drakomor gets his boy. The mountain gets its heart. There ought to be a song in that.'

Imogen wasn't sure what to say. Miro clearly loved his uncle very much, but she couldn't shake off the memory of the guards who'd chased them through the castle and the story of how Andel lost his eye. Surely, the king wouldn't hurt his own nephew? She wished Miro hadn't been taken on his own.

'And what about us?' said Marie. 'Do we get to go home too?'

Zuby's face fell. 'I don't know. I'm just in charge of prisoners and moths.'

Marie put a spoonful of the Shtyavy in her mouth and spat it out. 'Urgh!' she cried, wiping her tongue on the back of her hand.

'Hang on a minute,' said Imogen. 'You're in charge of prisoners and what?'

'Moths,' said Zuby.

'What kind of moths?'

'Oh, all kinds. The Žal has hit them hard. Sometimes I give them food, make sure they've got enough energy to hibernate, shelter the eggs, that sort of thing.'

'Do you have any Mezi Můra?' asked Imogen.

Zuby came closer, wrapping his claws round the bars. 'I did have one . . . they're very rare. Why do you ask, little human?'

Imogen's heart beat faster. 'Because that's how we got

here. We followed a moth through a door in a tree.'

'That's strange,' said Zuby. 'I didn't think the Mezi Můra would show the Unseen Door to little humans.'

'Right,' said Imogen. 'So you don't think it's strange that a moth has a magic door, but you do think it's strange that it showed the door to us?'

'Exactly,' said the skret. 'You can't find the Unseen Door without the silver moth. And, even if you did, you wouldn't be able to open it. The Mezi Můra are living keys.'

Finally, thought Imogen, *we're getting somewhere!* That explained why they hadn't been able to get back to the gardens. They needed the shadow moth.

She decided to try the Shtyavy to show willing. A pale dumpling bobbed near the surface. It touched her nose as she took a sip. The soup smelled like old farts and tasted like rotting vegetables, but Imogen forced herself to swallow. She couldn't force herself to smile.

'That's . . . different,' she said, trying not to pull a face. Marie looked horrified.

'I'm glad you like it,' said the skret. 'It's made with my finest fermented cabbage.'

Imogen tried to find out more about the moth. 'People in Yaroslav say the Mezi Můra are bad omens. Is that what you think too?'

'Stuff and nonsense,' said Zuby. 'The Mezi Můra are

loyal to us skret, but that doesn't mean they're bad for you humans. They're very clever creatures. They always have a plan . . . I just wish I understood what it was. That moth was supposed to help me retrieve the Sertze Hora. I've been releasing a different species of moth every night . . . But why would the Mezi Mŭra bring me two human pups?'

'Maybe it thought we could help,' said Marie.

Zuby scratched his head. Imogen hated the noise his claws made on his scalp. *Itch itch itch.*

'In a way, you already have,' he said. 'You brought us the little prince, didn't you? He came up the mountain because of you?'

'Yes, but—'

'So, without you, the Král wouldn't have anything to trade.' Zuby stepped away from the bars. 'The moths told us King Drakomor has the stone, but we didn't know how to get it back. Not until you brought us the prince.'

'Miro is our friend!' shouted Imogen, throwing down her mug. Soup slopped across the cave floor. 'We didn't bring him here to be used by the skret!'

'Perhaps you didn't realise at the time,' said Zuby, still backing away, 'but that's exactly what you did.'

Imogen pulled at the bars. 'Let us go!'

'I'm sorry,' said Zuby. 'Really I am. But I can't do that.'

CHAPTER 83

In a different cave, Zuby delivered another mug of Zelí Shtyavy to another prisoner. Lofkinye drank it politely – lumps and all.

'Thank you,' she said. 'How are the children?'

'The little humans are just fine,' said the skret, looking down at his clawed feet. 'Although the girl ones are a bit on the angry side and they won't eat their Shtyavy.'

'I bet the boy one won't either,' said Lofkinye, giving Zuby a knowing smile.

'The boy one is gone.'

'What?'

'King Drakomor gets his boy. The mountain gets its heart.'

Zuby didn't need to say any more. Lofkinye understood. She also understood that this was her chance. She could see it glinting in the gloom – the possibility of escape.

Zuby turned his back as if to leave. 'Wait,' said Lofkinye. 'There's something you don't know.'

'There are many things I don't know,' said the skret and

he started to walk away. He made a clicking noise that Lofkinye guessed was a laugh.

'No, there's something you don't know about the little prince. The king won't swap him. You won't get the Sertze Hora.'

Zuby looked over his shoulder. His bulbous eyes shone green in the low light. 'What are you talking about?'

'It's only a short story,' she said.

'Story?' said the skret. 'What kind of story?'

She beckoned him closer. 'A true one.'

So Lofkinye told Zuby about her escape from the castle, with the children in tow. She told him how they'd been chased by the Royal Guards – the king's own men – and how they'd only escaped with their lives because of the velecours.

Zuby gasped. 'The prince was chased by his uncle's own men? And they wanted to hurt him?'

'Yes,' said Lofkinye.

'Because he was with you?'

'No. Not because of me. They said the king wanted to see the prince. They were after the boy, but I could see that they meant him no good. I could see that they had an evil intent.'

'But why?'

Lofkinye confessed that she didn't know. 'It was all very strange,' she said. 'I suspect that the little prince is not as beloved as you might think.'

Zuby shook his bald head. 'You don't think the king wants him back?'

'I'm fairly sure the king wants him dead.'

'So he won't swap the prince for the Sertze Hora?'

'No.'

'And the prince will be no guarantee of safety for the Maudree Král.'

Lofkinye shrugged. 'If you ask me, the Král's royal wedding invitation has all the hallmarks of a royal trap.'

Zuby struck himself on the forehead. 'We have been fools!' he cried. 'Invitations that are death threats. Harming your own young. You humans are even stranger than I thought. The Král could be in terrible danger! The prince too!'

Lofkinye watched him from the corners of her eyes. 'What are you going to do?' she said.

'I don't know!' The gaoler paced up and down in front of the bars. 'I don't know what to do!'

'I do,' said Lofkinye. 'I know *exactly* what to do.'

PART 4

CHAPTER 84

Imogen, Marie and Lofkinye stood on a frozen lake at the summit of Klenot Mountain. The lake was surrounded by jagged rocks. They were higher than the birds. If there had been clouds, they would have been higher than them too. Yaroslav was little more than a dark stain at the bottom of the valley.

'The city doesn't look much from here,' said Lofkinye, shielding her eyes.

'It looks like the shadow of the sun,' said Imogen.

'It looks like a plug in a big bath,' said Marie, lowering the tone.

Zuby appeared in a gap between two rocks. He was tugging at a rope, straining with all his might. Lofkinye and the girls went to help. Together they dragged a boat on to the ice.

'This is how the Král travels to Yaroslav,' said Zuby when he'd got his breath back. 'It's not normally allowed, but I'm already going to be in trouble for setting you free and we don't have time for anything else.'

The only difference that Imogen could see, between this thing and a conventional rowing boat, was that the skret boat had long, sharp skates on its hull.

'Nothing beats a vodní-bruslash for downhill speed,' said Zuby. 'Not even your město horses. It flies on ice *and* in the water.'

'But how does the Král get back up the mountain?' said Marie.

'That's easy. We carry him in the vodní-bruslash.'

'Doesn't sound easy to me,' said Lofkinye, inspecting the boat. 'It looks pretty solid.'

'Well, it's easy for the Král,' said Zuby.

Inside the boat, Zuby had packed their fur coats. The girls put them on, buttoning them up to their chins. He'd also packed a hooded cloak for himself, to keep the sun off his skin.

'So,' said the skret, turning to Lofkinye, 'tell me your plan.'

'It's easy,' she said with a smile. 'We rescue the prince. You rescue the Král. We recapture the Sertze Hora and everyone lives happily ever after.'

'Happily ever after,' repeated the skret. 'I like the sound of that.'

They positioned the skating boat near the edge of the lake. Between two giant rocks, the ice morphed into a frozen stream that ran down the mountain like a racetrack.

For about one hundred metres, it was tilted at a stomach-churning angle – straight and fast. After that, it swerved to the right, disappearing behind a smooth curve of perfect snow.

Imogen stared at the frozen stream. She'd never been great with heights or speed. She wriggled her toes to stop herself feeling dizzy, a trick her mum had taught her.

Lofkinye jumped into the front of the boat and Zuby helped the girls in behind her. 'There are paddles tied down by your feet,' he said. 'We'll need those on the river. And there's the rein.' He pointed to a length of leather that was secured to the boat next to Lofkinye.

'Is this for steering?' she asked.

Zuby did his clicking laugh. 'Steering? You can't steer a vodní-bruslash. No, it's to hold on to!'

Lofkinye's face hardly moved, but Imogen could tell she was afraid. She passed the end of the rein back so Imogen and Marie could hold on too.

'Now,' said Zuby, 'is everyone ready?'

Lofkinye gave a faint nod. Imogen couldn't bring herself to speak.

'We're ready!' cried Marie, grinning with a confidence that Imogen hadn't seen in her before.

'Okay!' called the skret and he gave the boat a shove before hopping in at the back.

They were heavy. The shove didn't move them far. The front of the boat hung over the edge of the lake. For a moment, they were perfectly balanced and Imogen couldn't look. They were really going to do this. They were really going over that drop.

She grabbed Marie's hand and the boat lurched forward. Everyone screamed. The boat plummeted, smashing on to the frozen stream with force.

The skates sliced through the ice and they began to pick up speed. They swung round the first corner. Imogen gripped the rein hard. Smooth curves of sparkling snow rose up on either side, keeping the boat on course, forcing it down the narrow track.

They turned another corner and the passengers slid to the left. The boat went faster still and their surroundings became a blur. Marie squealed, but she was still grinning. She'd found her courage or lost her fear. Imogen wished she could do the same. She felt as if her head was being pulled away from her body and she didn't like it one bit.

She pressed herself down, so she was almost lying flat, and she tried to make her sister do the same, but Marie shrugged her off. Marie wanted to sit up. She wanted to see where they were going.

The boat hurtled on, juddering over what must have been choppy water before it was frozen solid. Imogen's

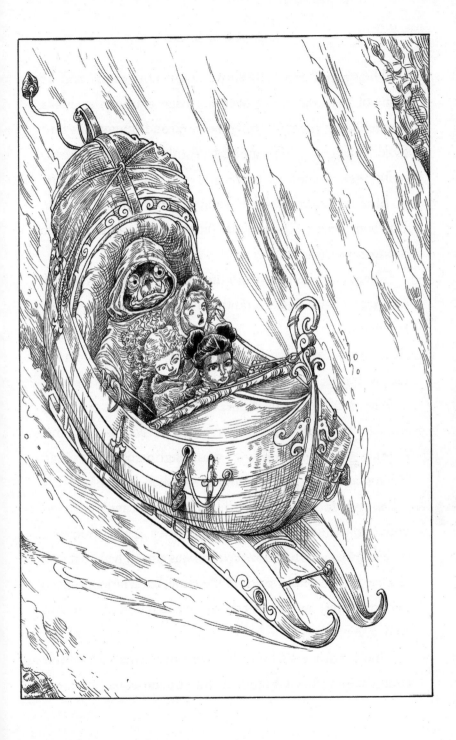

teeth chattered. She closed her eyes. This wasn't real. It was a fairground ride, like the one she'd been on with Mum last summer. Mum had promised that nothing bad would happen ... No one was promising that now.

Imogen peeped over the side of the skating boat just in time to see the blur of white snow turn to brown. The boat crashed into a rocky bank and she smacked her head on the side.

There was the forest. It was getting closer. Whizzing towards them faster than anything should whizz. Suddenly Imogen's bum left her seat. She was falling in slow motion, with the boat some way below. It landed in the river with a splash.

Back to double-speed. Water splattered into the boat. Imogen was almost thrown out, but Marie was still holding her hand and she scrambled back to her seat. 'Thank you,' she gasped, wiping water from her face.

Imogen looked around. They were no longer skating down the frozen stream. Instead, they drifted along a very not-frozen river. It carried them through the forests at a pace that would normally have been quite alarming, but compared to the ice-track it was a relief.

They barely needed the paddles – the water did all the hard work – Zuby only used them to correct their course when the riverbanks came too close.

'Is everyone all right?' called the skret in his scratchy voice.

'Yes!' said Marie. 'We're all okay and we're ready to do some rescuing.'

'Now that's what I like to hear.'

CHAPTER 85

Miro did not see how he travelled down Klenot Mountain, but he felt it all right. He was stuffed into a sack and carried until daylight shone through.

The skret dropped him into something with a damp floor; something that picked up speed fast and in a direction he could only describe as *downhill*.

The start of the journey was violent. Miro was thrown about as though he was a bunch of grapes being turned into wine. He'd have bruises on his bruises by the time this was over. Shouting didn't help. Wriggling just wasted his energy, so he adopted a foetal position and prayed that the journey would end soon.

Skret yelled in their crackle-hiss voices, but Miro couldn't make out the words.

There was a giant splash and he landed with a bump. After that, the bashing stopped. The jerky movements were replaced by a swaying motion.

Miro sat up. He noticed a little rip in the weave of

the sack and he worked at the tear until he could peep through the hole.

He was in some kind of boat. That much was clear. Trees bobbed up and down. He was floating on the river through the Kolsaney Forests and he knew where that river led: home!

In that moment, Miro didn't care that he was a prisoner. He didn't care that he was going to be swapped for a stone that didn't exist. He didn't even care that his uncle was getting married. Just wait until he told Drakomor what the skret had done, how they'd locked him up like a petty thief. His uncle wouldn't stand for it. His uncle would send them packing.

Miro played out the reunion in his head. He'd run to his uncle and his spare mother and they'd bend down to embrace him. They'd been worried sick. They'd been searching for him and they loved him so much. Miro's heart soared.

He would apologise for locking up a guard in the Hladomorna Pits and for running away. He'd explain that Imogen didn't mean to steal the wedding rings and he was sure that his uncle would understand, once he got to know her a bit better . . .

He'd tell his uncle that Imogen and Marie were his friends, his real friends, not just his friends because he was the prince. He'd say they were being held at the top of Klenot Mountain and his uncle would send the Royal Guards to rescue them and, the next day, they'd light a big fire and dance round it and eat all the leftovers from the wedding feast.

Miro looked through the hole in the sack. The trees had turned to meadows. The shadow of the city walls fell across him and the cathedral bells started to sound. It wasn't a single, repeated note, like the bells that rang at dawn and dusk. The cathedral bells chimed a joyful tune as if to say *the prince is coming home, the prince is coming home!*

The houses by the river got bigger and smarter. Miro recognised them all. He knew their painted facades and their family names as well as he knew his own boots. He wondered how many of those families would be attending his uncle's wedding.

The houses stopped moving and Miro was lifted up from the boat. He was shaken out of the sack as unceremoniously as he had been shoved in. Kneeling, he looked up at his captors.

They didn't look like skret at all. They were wearing cloaks with hoods that covered their bald heads. They wore masks too – no doubt they were designed to help them blend in, but it didn't work. The masks were parodies of human faces, with thin smiles that hid sharp teeth, and long slits that shielded bulbous eyes.

'What are you doing?' said Miro. 'Why are you dressed like that?' The masked monsters turned to each other, checking how they looked.

'It's protection,' hissed a skret.

'Worried you'll scare people if they see you for what you really are?' said Miro.

'The sun burns our skin. It's not natural to be out at this hour.'

One of the skret threw a mask and a cloak to Miro. He caught it and stood up. 'I don't need this.'

'Just put it on,' hissed the Maudree Král.

It was hard to see out of the mask's eye slits and the wood rubbed Miro's face, but that didn't matter. All of this would be over soon.

The skret walked in single file, with Miro in the middle. They were getting close to Castle Yaroslav. Behind his mask, Miro was all excitement and nerves.

The city was busy and people seemed to be in a celebratory mood. Flags hung out of windows and across narrow streets. The people of Yaroslav hadn't done that since Drakomor had been crowned.

A toddler was playing with a kitten, chattering in

a language only she understood. A group of women, dressed in their finest clothes, walked arm in arm, laughing. They all fell silent when the cloaked gargoyles walked by. Some people drew a cross over their chests. Others ran inside. The kitten's fur stood on end and it hissed.

The skret didn't respond to this less than warm reception. They were focused on one thing and one thing alone – getting to the castle.

Miro felt people's eyes on him and he wondered if they noticed that his feet, poking out from under his cloak, were booted instead of clawed. He wanted to pull off the mask, but he didn't dare disobey his captors. Not yet. Not until he could see his uncle.

They reached the city's main square and Miro thought he'd dissolve with nerves. Castle Yaroslav stood proud as ever. Next to the castle, the cathedral doors were open and the wedding guests were pouring in.

In the middle of the square, looking over the city with ruby-red eyes, was an enormous dragon. Miro stared in amazement. He'd never seen anything like it. And there, standing on the dragon as if they were riding the beast, were Miro's uncle and spare mother.

CHAPTER 86

Anneshka stood on the back of the mechanical dragon with Drakomor at her side. She waved graciously at the awestruck wedding guests, enjoying their reactions immensely. One old aristocrat was so alarmed that his wig almost fell off. Anneshka's own mother gasped and clung on to her husband, as if she was facing a real dragon. Anneshka wondered if her mother disapproved, before deciding that she didn't much care.

Ochi, the witch who'd read Anneshka's stars, arrived on her own. She'd been invited to stop her from cursing the wedding. She bowed before following the other guests into the cathedral.

'I only wish Miro could have been here,' said Drakomor. 'He would have loved having all these people about.'

'I'm sure he'd find it very dull,' said Anneshka. 'Children hate adult celebrations.'

She linked arms with the king, hoping they looked the part. Drakomor was dressed in a cream tunic dotted

with diamonds. Anneshka was wrapped in a white silk dress, with a frothy veil that covered her face.

Blazen Bilbetz was one of the last to arrive. He looked drunk, as usual, and was followed by his band of merry huntsmen. 'How I loathe that man,' muttered Anneshka, smiling down at him.

The last stragglers hurried past the dragon, their apologies drowned out by the cathedral bells. 'That's all of our human guests,' said Anneshka and she gave the king's arm an excited squeeze.

'I hope this works,' said Drakomor, gesturing at the lever at the top of the dragon's spine. All they had to do was pull that down and their weapon would spring into action.

'It will go like clockwork,' said Anneshka. 'Just like the one-eyed lesni said.'

A group of cloaked figures entered the square. Anneshka guessed there were twenty of them, no bigger than children, with their faces hidden behind masks. The cathedral bells stopped.

'So they did come,' murmured the king.

As the skret approached, Anneshka noticed that one of them was walking a little out of time with the others. They stopped just in front of the dragon. *The perfect position*, she thought.

The cloaked figures bowed. It was time for the ceremony to begin.

'That skret in the middle won't bow,' said Anneshka.

'Oh yes,' said the king. 'How odd.'

'We are honoured to be invited to your wedding,' said a skret near the front of the group. It had been years since Anneshka had heard a voice like it. The sound made her toes curl.

'We are honoured that you accepted,' replied the king.

Was it her imagination or was that skret, the one that didn't bow, struggling with the others? It was making her uneasy. This wasn't part of the plan.

'Shall I do it?' she whispered, impatient. Her petticoats rustled as she stepped closer to the lever that would bring the dragon to life.

The skret that wouldn't bow shouted something. It elbowed its neighbour in the chest and broke away from the group.

'What's going on down there?' said Drakomor. Some of the skret looked ready to pounce, but the tearaway was too fast. It pulled off its mask and pushed back its hood, revealing a dirty human face.

'On the count of three,' said Anneshka.

'That's Miroslav!' cried the king as the skret pounced on the boy.

'It can't be!' Anneshka lifted her veil to get a better look.

'It is!' exclaimed Drakomor. 'What's he doing here? I thought he'd been taken beyond the mountains!'

Anneshka put one hand on the lever and a gust of wind filled her dress. 'This is our chance,' she said.

Drakomor stared, horrified. 'You can't! Miroslav's down there!'

Anneshka stared back, fierce. 'Do not tell me what I can and cannot do.'

She forced the lever down. Drakomor seized her arm, but he was too late. The lever tugged on a pulley, which swung a weight, which rotated a cog, which sent more cogs spinning down the dragon's spine.

'What have you done?' cried the king. Something rumbled deep in the beast's belly. 'What have you done!'

CHAPTER 87

'Hush,' said Anneshka as the dragon creaked beneath her. 'I've made you a hero.'

'But the boy!'

'Get a grip, Drakomor. It's not as though he's yours.'

The rumbling in the dragon's belly coursed along its neck and then – in a blaze of orange – a giant fireball exploded from the beast's mouth and went flying across the square.

The skret scattered. A few of them were hit, but the prince was still standing. Anneshka gave a whoop of joy. Another rumble began somewhere beneath her feet.

Drakomor was trying to push the lever back up, to make the dragon stop, but it wouldn't budge.

For a king, he really is pathetic, thought Anneshka.

Another fireball burst out of the dragon's jaws and the whole thing swung round, throwing Anneshka off balance. The monster's tail ripped through houses. People were running from the cathedral, shrieking like frightened animals.

Now the beast was facing the castle.

'Was that supposed to happen?' said Anneshka, struggling to her feet.

'Certainly not,' said Drakomor. 'It's going to burn down my castle!'

'That clock-making cockroach has done it wrong!'

'We need to make it stop!' shouted the king. Again, he tried to unstick the lever, but it wouldn't move and fire poured out of the beast's jaws like lava from a volcano. Below, people were screaming.

'I'll kill him! I'll kill that one-eyed trickster!' Anneshka tore her veil out of her hair. She would do the killing with her own hands if she had to. She squinted at the figures running across the square. There were people all over the place, but she couldn't see Andel.

'I'm getting down,' said Drakomor. 'I need to find my nephew.'

'But this is supposed to be our moment!' wailed Anneshka. 'This is supposed to be when everyone sees us save Yaroslav from the skret!'

Drakomor began to climb down the ladder that hung from the dragon's side. 'Anneshka,' he cried, 'follow me! It's not safe up there!'

Anneshka was shouting and cursing in the most unladylike language. 'My darling, come quickly!' called the king.

'This isn't my destiny!' screamed Anneshka, tearing at her wedding dress. 'This isn't how it ends!'

Suddenly she felt the heat from the dragon through the soles of her shoes. That snapped her out of her rage. The beast was melting from the inside out. She ran to the ladder and started to hurry down it. Her dress billowed around her. Anneshka was near the bottom of the ladder when the metal between the dragon's scales turned fluorescent pink. The heat scorched her hands and she let go of the ladder, hitting the ground hard.

She looked up to see the skret heading towards the castle. The dragon's fire had taken hold in the West Wing. Even worse, Drakomor was sprinting after the monsters.

'Stop those skret!' he bellowed. 'They have Miroslav! They have my boy!'

CHAPTER 88

Miro knew there was no point in trying to fight the skret. He had learned from experience. He let them drag him towards the castle. Some of them were badly burnt, but they limped on, uncomplaining.

Wedding guests were shouting for their loved ones. The skret walked past them all, entering the castle through the main doorway. It was wide open. Any Royal Guards that had been stationed there for the wedding had already run away.

'Where are you taking me?' demanded Miro.

'To the tallest tower,' hissed the Maudree Král, throwing off his mask. 'To the heart of the mountain.'

'For the last time—' started Miro, but the Král covered the prince's mouth. The skret went quiet. They pulled back their masks and turned their eyes to the ceiling.

'Can you feel that?' said the Král. Miro couldn't feel anything, but the skret put their clawed hands to their chests. 'It's the Sertze Hora. It's here. Just like the moths said.'

'What shall we do with the human pup?' said the skret

with the spiked back, the one they called Shpitza. 'If we're not gonna swap him, we might as well slice him and dice him.'

'No,' said the Maudree Král. 'We'll keep him. At least until we have the heart. We might need a hostage.'

A pair of townsfolk rushed past the skret, hardly pausing to stare. Their arms were full of treasures from the king's collection. Miro wanted to stop them, to make them put it all back, but he wasn't in a position to do any such thing. The skret grabbed him by the collar and set off into the castle.

The closer they got to the East Wing, the fainter the sounds of fire became. The skret took torches from the walls to light their way.

As they passed by the feasting hall, there was a sound that made the skret break from a walk into a run. It was a sound that belonged to the forests and mountains: the sound of a roaring bear.

CHAPTER 89

By the time Imogen, Marie, Lofkinye and Zuby arrived in the square, clouds of smoke were choking the sun and the West Wing of Castle Yaroslav was burning as though it was made of dry twigs. The new arrivals stood, open-mouthed, shielding their eyes from the blaze.

The cathedral was on fire too. Imogen could see the hot glow through the stained-glass windows, turning the saints' faces a devilish red.

'What on earth happened?' said Lofkinye.

'You were right,' said Zuby. 'It *was* a trap.'

He nodded at a crumpled metal skeleton. It looked like it belonged to a dinosaur. The innards were molten and hundreds of ceramic scales were scattered across the square as if a massive snake had shed its skin.

'But who was the trap for?' said Lofkinye. 'Surely the king didn't mean for all this . . .'

A woman in a wedding dress was kneeling in the middle of the square. 'That must be Anneshka,' whispered Marie, 'the woman Miro's uncle is marrying.'

'I'll go and speak to her,' said Imogen. 'You wait here.'

As Imogen got closer, she saw that the woman's make-up was badly smudged. Her hands and parts of her face were scorched, but the woman didn't seem to care. She was muttering, 'I'll kill him, I'll kill him.' Her violet eyes were fixed on the fire.

'Excuse me,' said Imogen, 'but can you tell me what happened here?' The woman got to her feet and began walking towards the castle. Imogen caught hold of her dress. 'I'm looking for Prince Miroslav. Have you seen him?'

The woman turned and hissed in Imogen's face like a cat. Imogen was so shocked that she froze. The woman walked off, silk dress trailing.

'What did she say?' asked Marie, rushing to Imogen's side.

Imogen wiped spit from her face. 'I hate to say it, but Miro was right. I don't think his spare mother is a very nice person.'

She watched the bride stomp towards the castle. Everyone else was running in the opposite direction.

An old woman hobbled past with three tiaras on her head. Two boys dragged a stuffed wildcat by its teeth.

'Look!' said Marie. 'People are stealing the king's

collection! He'll be so angry when he finds out!'

'Never mind the king,' said Imogen. 'Where's Miro?'

Both girls looked at the castle. There was a terrible crash as the roof of the West Wing collapsed.

'I have a horrible feeling that he's somewhere in there,' said Marie.

Imogen swallowed.

'Hey, isn't that . . .?' A giant man strode by with a tangle of gold chains round his neck and diamonds the size of peaches in his hands. Sweat ran down his face and into his beard.

'Blazen!' shouted Imogen. The hunter looked over his shoulder. 'Blazen Bilbetz!' she cried. 'Over here!'

Blazen looked shame-faced. He'd been caught red-handed and he knew it. 'I don't have to answer to you—' he began.

'Have you seen Miro?' said Marie.

'Now you come to mention it, yes, I have. I saw him about five minutes ago, running into the castle with a load of hooded children.'

'Do you mean skret?'

'Could have been skret. Could have been children.'

'Blazen, that was the Maudree Král,' said Imogen. 'Did Miro look okay?'

'He looked like he'd rather not go in the castle, if you

know what I mean,' chuckled the giant. 'But I think he was all right.'

Something deep in the castle exploded and the flames shot higher. Imogen flinched. Blazen dropped a diamond.

'You have to help us,' said Marie. 'We need to rescue Miro.'

The giant looked perplexed. 'There's nothing we can do. It's too dangerous.'

He stooped to pick up his diamond and someone booted him in the behind. 'Oi!' he cried, turning to strike the offender. 'Oh. It's you.' He lowered his hand.

'Yes, it's me,' said Lofkinye. 'We're going in there.' She nodded at the castle. 'We're going to rescue the prince and the Sertze Hora . . . if we can.'

'The Sertze Hora's in *there*?' said the giant.

'Yes. Are you coming?'

Blazen looked at his diamonds.

'Surely *Blazen the Brave* wouldn't miss an opportunity like this?' said Lofkinye.

Blazen squirmed as if he was trying to wriggle out of his own skin. 'I'm not as young . . .'

'You've never been young. Not since I've known you. Still, we need all the help we can get . . . Don't make me tell them what *really* happened when you were chasing the Royal Stag.'

Blazen dropped the diamonds. 'Oh, all right,' he said. 'I'm in.'

CHAPTER 90

Blazen and Lofkinye entered the castle through the kitchens.

'I sent the girls to look in the South Wing,' said Lofkinye. 'It should be safer there. We'll have to search the rest of the castle – or what's left of it – before the fire takes hold.'

The dragon had hit the West Wing the worst, but it wasn't the only part of the castle on fire. When Blazen and Lofkinye saw flames, they found another route. When the smoke got too much, they crawled on the ground.

In one of the least smoky rooms, Blazen caught hold of Lofkinye's shoulder. 'Just one moment,' he said. 'Just let me catch my breath.'

'You're not out of breath.'

'You wouldn't really tell them . . .' blurted the giant.

There was a crackling sound in the room they'd just left. The fire was catching up.

'Wouldn't tell them what?' Lofkinye's eyes were streaming from the smoke. She wiped her cheeks on her wrists.

'That I didn't really kill the Royal Stag. That the story's not true. That I'm really, you know . . .'

'What, a fraud?' finished Lofkinye.

There was another roar, but this time it wasn't the roar of the fire.

'I forgot!' said Blazen, and he looked genuinely shocked. 'I forgot about her.'

'Who?'

'The bear!'

Blazen Bilbetz strode into the feasting hall and Lofkinye followed. It was baking hot. Flames dominated the far end of the room.

The table was set for the wedding feast and Lofkinye had never seen so much food. The crowning glory was a life-sized sugar sculpture of the happy couple, but it hadn't been made for these temperatures. The bride's face was sliding down her neck and the groom was flopped to the side, peeling away from his beloved as if he wasn't quite sure about her.

Lofkinye followed Blazen past the sugar sculpture, and there, dressed in navy trousers and a red waistcoat, was a huge bear.

The animal was straining to get free, but the chain round her neck was locked to a ring on the floor. The more she pulled, the more the chain tightened. There was a deep cut across her snout, and more cuts peeped out from underneath that ridiculous waistcoat.

The bear roared at the fire, showing her teeth and the whites of her eyes. The fire roared back.

Blazen grabbed a candlestick from the table and began smashing it against the ring on the floor. But the candlestick was soft and it gave way as he hammered, until soon it was little more than a lump of metal in the giant's hand.

'We don't have long!' shouted Lofkinye. The fire was only an arm's length from Blazen and the heat was intense.

'So help me!' he shouted back.

The hunter tossed the disfigured candlestick away and picked up a fire iron instead.

'It's no use!' said Lofkinye. 'If the bear can't break the chains, you won't be able to either.'

'Want a bet?' Blazen hammered at the lock with the fire iron, teeth gritted, face covered in sweat. A vein in his forehead looked like it might burst.

'This is madness,' muttered Lofkinye and she scanned the room. There must be an axe or something sharp, but no such luck. She looked back at the bear. The animal was grunting and smacking her paws on the ground.

'She's afraid,' said Blazen. 'The fire's too close.'

Something glinted around the bear's neck – dangling just above the waistcoat. If only Lofkinye could get close enough to see it properly. She approached the bear cautiously, without making eye contact. There was a key in among all that fur.

The bear snorted as Lofkinye leaned in. She talked to it in as calm a voice as she could muster, then she grabbed the key, snapping it free from its leather tie.

'Blazen, quick! Try this!'

The hunter shoved the key into the lock. It opened and Lofkinye pulled the heavy chains away from the animal's neck.

The bear in human clothing broke free. She smashed through the sugar sculpture, tore the door off its hinges and galloped away, without so much as a backward glance.

CHAPTER 91

Imogen and Marie searched the South Wing of the castle for the prince. The hall of statues was a furnace. The servants' quarters too.

They went to the staircase where they'd found Miro the last time he was missing. Marie stopped outside Miro's parents' bedroom, but Imogen marched straight in. It was quiet – peaceful even – as if the rest of the castle being on fire had nothing to do with this room.

'We're not allowed in there,' hissed Marie. 'And look, you've made footprints in the dust.'

'That hardly matters now,' said Imogen.

She picked up Miro's stuffed toy from the floor. 'I still think this cat looks odd.'

'It's not a cat,' said Marie. 'It's a lion, remember?'

Imogen wondered why Marie looked so sour. It wasn't *her* parents' room or *her* stuffed toy.

'Looks like a cat to me,' she said, dropping it back in the dust. 'Where should we go now? I'm all out of ideas.'

Marie took a few tentative steps into the room and

picked up the toy. 'There is one place we haven't looked yet,' she said. 'It's not in the South Wing, but I bet Lofkinye hasn't been there yet. Although it's actually pretty obvious . . .'

Now it was Imogen's turn to look sour. 'It's always obvious when you know.'

Marie brushed dust off the toy lion and tucked it into her pocket.

'Take your time,' said Imogen. 'This place is only burning to the ground.'

'We haven't looked in the second tallest tower,' said Marie.

The room at the top of the second tallest tower didn't look anything like the room Imogen remembered.

The heavy curtains were closed and a detailed drawing of a lizard had been left by the fireplace. Every surface was strewn with bits of machinery, strange tools and ceramic tiles. Miro's old clock was missing too. The room felt strangely quiet without its constant tick-tocking.

Imogen pushed back the curtains. Thick smoke obscured her view of the square. She tried another window. Smoke curled up like fingers, beckoning her out. She ran to a third window and threw back the drapes. From here, she could see the castle's tallest tower.

At first, she could only make out the tower's silhouette, but a gust of wind cleared a gap in the smoke and Imogen saw a face – a skret face – looking out of a window near the top of the tower.

'Marie!' she yelled and her sister rushed to her side. 'There's a skret at the top of the tallest tower.'

'But no one goes up there . . .'

'I swear I saw a skret!'

'It's okay, I believe you,' said Marie.

The castle groaned like a harpooned whale and Imogen thought she felt the floor tremble. 'We have to go,' she said.

'One minute,' said Marie. 'I'm thinking.'

'You can think while we run.'

'No. I'm thinking right now.'

Imogen was about to reply, but she bit her tongue.

Marie's face lit up. 'Of course!' she cried. 'I know how we can rescue Miro.'

'How?' said Imogen.

'The same way all knights do their rescuing – on horseback, of course!'

CHAPTER 92

Anneshka found Andel in a corridor near the castle gardens. He came hurtling round the corner, wearing a long cloak and clutching a pillowcase stuffed with something that wasn't a pillow.

'Your Highness,' he gasped, stopping dead.

'And where do you think you're going?' Anneshka sneered.

The man's eye darted from left to right, looking for an escape route.

'You did it on purpose, didn't you? That dragon was never designed to kill the Král.'

'You're burnt,' stammered Andel. 'I'm sorry. I never meant to hurt you. I just—'

'You just *what*?' snarled Anneshka. 'You just wanted to destroy the most important day of my life?' She took a step closer. 'I should have known better than to trust a lesni.'

Andel's face hardened. 'Yes,' he said. 'You should.'

That caught Anneshka off guard. 'So that's what this was? A lesni conspiracy?'

'The dragon is nothing to do with anyone else . . . It's *my* conspiracy, *my* revenge.'

Andel raised his chin. Was it her imagination or did the one-eyed idiot look proud?

'Revenge for what?' she demanded.

'King Drakomor stole the Sertze Hora. He forced me out of my home and then he took my eye when I wouldn't be his servant.' Andel was cradling the pillowcase like a baby.

So, thought Anneshka, *he's stealing the heart of the mountain.*

She smiled, feeling the burnt part of her lips crack. 'You're delusional. It was the skret that forced the lesni out of their homes.'

'The skret turned on us because of the king's theft!' cried Andel.

Anneshka took a torch from a bracket on the wall. 'So your revenge is to destroy the king's castle?'

'No. My revenge is to destroy the king's home.'

Anneshka lunged and grabbed Andel by the arm. She held the torch to his cloak. He twisted free and shoved her away, but he was too slow. His cloak had caught fire.

Andel dropped the pillowcase and tried to pull the cloak from his neck. Anneshka could see the panic on his face as the flames licked round his legs.

She picked up the pillowcase and ran away as quickly as her petticoats would allow. Behind her, Andel was crying for help, but she didn't slow down. She didn't look back. She dashed across the castle gardens, dodging between squawking velecours. One almost crashed into her, but it swerved at the last moment.

The Royal Guards must have fled because the garden gates were unprotected. Anneshka slipped out unseen. Still she didn't slow down. She didn't look back.

She ducked under skret bones that were strung up like bunting. She hurried down backstreets and crossed skull-studded bridges. She ran past blacksmiths and breweries and big fancy houses. She ran until she could run no more.

Then she looked back. Andel's revenge was complete. Half of the castle was engulfed in flames and it was only a matter of time before it spread to the rest of the building. The nearest houses were on fire too. If King Drakomor was still in the castle, it was unlikely he'd be coming out alive.

Anneshka hugged the pillowcase close to her chest and walked out through Yaroslav's smallest gate. On the other side of the wall there was a white pony tethered to a post. It was almost as if it had been put there for her.

Anneshka looked over her shoulder. There was no one about; they were all too busy gawping at the fire.

Her burnt hands throbbed as she untied the pony and

took the reins. The beast snorted, but it didn't resist, so Anneshka hitched up her dress and climbed into the saddle.

The pony carried her away from Yaroslav, across the fields, to the edge of the Kolsaney Forests. At the first line of trees, she brought her mount to a stop.

Anneshka peeped into the pillowcase, expecting to see the hot glow of the Sertze Hora. Instead, she saw wood. A clock face looked up at her with five motionless hands and an array of jewelled stars.

'What the—?' She almost dropped the bag.

But, she reasoned, if Andel had chosen this one thing to take, out of all the treasures in the king's collection . . . perhaps it was worth keeping.

Anneshka took one last look at Yaroslav. Black smoke billowed from its heart. She could just about make out the castle's tallest towers drifting in and out of the haze.

'Goodbye, láska,' she whispered.

And, with that, the woman who was fated to be queen rode into the forest.

CHAPTER 93

The skret half dragged, half carried Miro up the steps of the castle's tallest tower. They stopped outside the door to the topmost room and held him against the wall.

Miro had seen his uncle climbing down from the dragon. The beast looked like it was about to collapse. Miro hoped his uncle had made it. He closed his eyes and whispered a short prayer.

When he opened them, the skret with spikes along his spine was kneeling by the door, cursing. He had one claw hooked in the lock, but Miro knew it wouldn't open. His uncle had insisted that every lock in the castle be made skret-proof.

'What's wrong, Shpitza?' said the Král.

'It won't open.'

'Move out of the way,' said another skret. He tried his luck. There was a pause, a hiss. The skret thumped the door in frustration.

'I told you so,' said Shpitza.

'You're wasting your time,' said Miro. 'The Sertze Hora isn't up here.'

'We're not leaving until that door opens,' said the Král.

'But the fire,' said Miro. 'If it catches the bottom of the tower, this whole thing will go up like a matchstick.'

Shpitza looked out of the window. 'The human has a point,' he said, turning to the Král with concern.

'I don't care if it's spreading,' spat the Král. 'I don't care if we all burn to death. No one leaves until we've got that door open.'

Each of the monsters tried their luck. They banged and they scratched and they clawed at the lock. The Král got angrier each time they failed.

A droplet of sweat rolled down Miro's neck. It was too warm up here and he could feel a strange vibration in his chest. The fire must be close. The skret that was pinning him against the wall was sweating too. Miro wondered which would kill them first: the smoke or the flames or the collapse of the tower.

The last skret knelt by the door. He scraped at the lock with his claws, but they were too big to fit in the keyhole. When the skret turned to the Král, he looked frightened. Miro didn't know that skret were capable of being scared.

'I said no one leaves,' hissed the Král.

'I'll do it,' said Miro.

The Král looked at the boy. 'Break into your own tower?'

'Let go of me and I'll do it,' said Miro. 'I'll pick the lock.'

The skret hooted and jeered.

'And where exactly did you learn to pick locks?' asked the Král.

'Going places you shouldn't is one of the best games you can play on your own . . . I'll need a pair of cloak pins.'

Miro was released and handed the pins. He bent them into shape and began his work. A few minutes later, the door clicked open. Even hotter air whooshed out. The skret pushed past and Miro followed.

The room at the top of the tallest tower was circular, just like his own. The only furniture was a pedestal covered by a cloth. Thick smoke pressed up against the windows, but where was that heat coming from? There was no fire in here . . .

A tiny vibration went from Miro's fingertips up his arms and down to his chest. It pulsed, reverberating round his ribcage like a trapped bird.

The skret gathered by the pedestal, clicking with excitement. The Král reached out with his gold-tipped claws and, in what seemed like slow motion, he removed the cloth.

Miro knew what he was looking at the moment he saw it. The Sertze Hora announced itself in deep red and a vibration that went straight to the heart. Invisible strings seemed to reel him in, drawing him closer to the thing that didn't exist, that couldn't exist, that he was looking right into.

Colours swirled like the glass in an exquisite marble. But, unlike a marble, these colours moved. It was as though the stone was full of tiny explosions – miniature worlds making and remaking themselves. It was beautiful.

Miro lifted his hand to touch the stone, but a skret pounced on him from behind. 'Doesn't belong to you,' said Shpitza, digging in his claws.

'Doesn't belong to you either, skret,' said a man's voice.

King Drakomor stood at the doorway, a shield in one hand and a sword in the other. He looked like a hero from tales of old.

'Uncle!' gasped Miro, wriggling to get free.

'Don't try to stop us,' said the Maudree Král.

'Give me the boy. He doesn't belong to you,' said the king.

'He doesn't belong to you either,' cooed the Král. 'He belongs to the man that you sentenced to death.'

King Drakomor looked away and Miro saw that the skin on the left side of his face had peeled off. The burn extended down his neck.

'Not now,' said Drakomor. 'This isn't the time . . .'

The Král clicked his tongue and shook his head. He turned to Miro. 'Why is your uncle so afraid of the truth? Perhaps he doesn't want you to know that it was *his* actions that led to the death of your parents. *His* thieving. *His* greed.'

The Král's words seemed to stab at Miro's uncle like knives. He cowered by the door.

'My parents died in a hunting accident,' said Miro, with a wobble in his voice.

'No,' said the Král. 'Your parents died because your uncle betrayed us. He was invited to our caves as a guest. He was treated with the utmost respect. And he used that trust to steal our most precious possession. He has brought the mountain to its knees!'

'Miroslav!' cried the king, but Miro's eyes were fixed on the Král.

'Killing your parents was not my choice,' continued the Král. 'I would really rather . . . but a mountain's heart for a brother's blood.' Now he looked directly at Drakomor. 'Your family had to pay.'

'Get out of my castle.' Miro hardly recognised his uncle's voice.

'You can only have one,' said the Král. 'The boy or the stone. Which will it be?'

A boom from somewhere below sent sparks flying up past the windows. The king dropped the sword and reached out his hand. 'Give me the boy.' Another boom and the tower shuddered.

Something struck Miro on the back of the head. A searing pain. The world went black.

When Miro came round, the pedestal was empty. The skret were gone and there was a heap by the door: his uncle. Miro scrambled to Drakomor's side and tried to roll him over. He was too heavy. A dead weight.

'Wake up!' cried Miro, shaking his uncle's shoulder. Drakomor didn't stir. 'Wake up and I promise I'll be good, I'll never run away again, I'll be nice to my spare mother . . . just wake up . . . please.'

Miro threw his uncle's arm over his shoulder and tried to lift him. 'We need to get out of here,' he sobbed, collapsing to the floor. 'We need to leave!' The tower swayed and Miro howled with fear.

He took his uncle's arm again, but this time he curled up under it. The room started filling with smoke.

CHAPTER 94

Miro scrunched up his eyes. He imagined he could hear familiar voices. He imagined he could hear Marie – far away – as if she was talking to him through a wall. 'I'm sorry,' he muttered. 'I'm sorry I couldn't help you get home.'

The make-believe Marie yelled, 'The window!'

Miro opened his eyes. That was a strange thing for an imagined voice to say.

'Over here! Hurry up!'

Marie's face was at the window – pink and surrounded by a blaze of hair. For a confused second, Miro thought the smoke came from her curls.

How did she get to be there, hovering at the top of the tallest tower? Was he dead? Had Marie turned into an angel?

Marie shouted something. Miro scrambled to his feet and threw the window open.

Now he understood. She was flying on a velecour, tugging at a ribbon that was tied round its beak. The bird flapped wildly, but Marie steered it with the ribbon, keeping it close to the tower.

'It's really you!' gasped Miro, smoke getting into his eyes and throat.

'Of course,' said Marie. 'Who else? Listen, Miro, this tower's about to go. You need to climb on behind me. Lofkinye says one velecour will take our weight.'

Miro looked at the bird. Then he looked over his shoulder. 'I can't leave without my uncle.'

Marie's face fell. 'He's in there?'

'Yes, but he's not moving.'

'Is he breathing?'

'I don't know.'

Marie pressed her lips together. 'Okay. We can rescue him too, but it's not going to be easy.'

She pulled the ribbon-reins in the other direction and the velecour swerved away from the tower. Her shape became a silhouette in the smoke, then a smudge, then she disappeared altogether.

Miro felt like he waited for hours. Moths flew up and down in the smog, looking for a way into the tower. When Marie returned, she was flanked by three other shapes. Imogen, Lofkinye and Blazen had a velecour each. Blazen's velecour was huge – the biggest Miro had ever seen – but it still looked like it was struggling with his great weight. 'I brought back-up,' cried Marie, beaming.

Blazen steered his bird towards the tower. It resisted mightily, but, with a little help from Lofkinye and an extra tug on the reins, he managed to get the velecour's back level with the open window. Blazen handed Lofkinye the ribbon-reins.

'Step back,' he boomed. Miro did as he was told. Blazen rolled into the room at the top of the tallest tower. He grabbed Miro by the scruff of the neck as though he weighed no more than a puppy.

'My uncle,' cried Miro. 'We can't go without my uncle!' Blazen held the prince out of the window, legs dangling, and then he let go. Miro screamed, but he only fell a metre or so. He landed on the back of Marie's bird.

'Hold on,' she called. 'We're getting out of here.'

The velecour swooped up and away from the tower. Miro looked back. Blazen was standing at the window with the king's limp body slung over his shoulder. More smoke blew up, obscuring Miro's view. The hazy outline of the tower swayed to the right, like a ship casting off, then it slipped out of the sky altogether. Miro moved his lips, but no words came out. There was a sound like an earthquake. The tower had hit the ground.

Marie slipped the ribbon-reins off the velecour's beak and, suddenly, they were flying like an arrow – straight and fast and away from the castle.

CHAPTER 95

A lesni woman sat at the foot of a fountain. She wore green and her hair was tied in two tidy knots. The fountain was dry and children were perched all over it, swinging their legs in anticipation.

There were adults too. They kept their distance, but they were listening all right. A man smoked a pipe while leaning out of a window. An old woman scrubbed her doorstep, even though it was already clean. A pair of youths loitered nearby – not quite men, not quite boys, not quite sure whether they were invited to join in.

'Have I got a story for you,' said the woman by the fountain, smoothing out the creases from her skirt.

'Is it a true story?' asked a skinny child.

'A true story? Now why would you want one of those?'

'Tell us the truth! Tell us the truth!'

'Well, that's no problem,' said the woman. 'There's a bit of truth in every story.'

And so she began her tale. She started with two

sisters. They were a long way from home and as poor as peasants when they met a prince and a huntress.

The audience listened with open mouths as the children escaped on velecours. They cheered as the huntress talked her way out of skret prison and when the giant freed the bear. They jeered at the evil queen with her fire-breathing dragon and they gasped at the discovery of the king's betrayal.

'Did King Drakomor really steal the heart of the mountain?' asked a little girl.

'Who said anything about King Drakomor?' replied the woman.

'Isn't he the king in the story?'

'What do you think?'

'I think he is,' said the girl. 'I think he took the stone and that's why the skret got angry. That's why they kicked us out of the forests.'

'And that's why he's not king any more!' shouted one of the youths. The children nodded in agreement, looking at the storyteller to see if she agreed.

The woman pulled a coin out of her pocket. She flipped it in the air and slapped it down on the back of her hand. 'King Drakomor is gone,' she said. 'His castle's in ruins. His body too. Perhaps he finally got what he deserved.' She uncovered the coin and the children crowded closer to see which way it had landed.

'Heads,' squeaked the girl. 'It's the king's head!'

'Off with his head!' shouted the youth.

'But what if it wasn't him that did it?' asked a boy with missing teeth.

'Then his would be a very sad story indeed,' said the woman. 'But I'll let you in on a secret . . . The night when the stone first went missing, I saw Drakomor fleeing from Klenot Mountain. He stole the Sertze Hora. Of that you can be sure.'

The woman handed the boy the coin. He took it and ran, disappearing down an impossibly narrow alley. The other children began to disperse too.

The woman pulled her shawl tighter round her shoulders. Even in the city, winter was beginning to bite.

At the edge of the square, there was one figure that didn't leave. He wore a velvet jacket and a fur-lined cap. His lower legs were wrapped in bandages and, as the woman walked by, she noticed that he only had one eye.

'That was quite the story,' said the man. 'You ought to be careful. Tall tales like that can bring kingdoms to their knees.'

The woman hesitated. 'Have we met?'

'We have now.' He held out his hand. 'My name's Andel. What's yours?'

'Lofkinye Lolo,' she replied.

CHAPTER 96

News of King Drakomor's death spread quickly. He'd perished, along with his precious collection. Blazen Bilbetz had been attempting to rescue him when the tower gave way with them both still inside.

Some people were pleased Drakomor was dead and some people were sad. There were bonfires and feasts and readings of prayers. Jan, the Chief of the Royal Guards, said that if the king hadn't died he would have killed him anyway. You can't steal the heart of the mountain and expect to live happily ever after. You just can't.

Everyone agreed that Blazen had died a hero's death. Oh, the songs they would sing! Oh, the tales they would tell! There was even talk of putting up a new statue of the giant.

The head cook said she'd spotted the king's almost-wife, that Anneshka woman, riding off into the sunset like they do in old legends. The cook doubted that Anneshka had made it across the mountains alive. Not at this time of year. Not in that dress.

There were rumours going around that she'd killed

Yeedarsh and Petr. There were even reports that she'd tried to murder the prince. But she was from a good family and so pretty too ... Surely stories like that couldn't be true?

The disappearance of the skret was less controversial. No one missed their night-time raids. That first evening, when parts of the castle were still on fire and others glowed red, the bells of Yaroslav sounded at dusk. The people shut up their windows and bolted their doors. They waited in silence, but no skret arrived. Not a single one. And so it had been every night since.

The skret bones that had once decorated every building in the city began to disappear. They were removed from bakehouses and churches and shops. They were taken down from street corners. People weren't interested in warding off monsters any more.

Soon, all that was left to remind the good people of Yaroslav of the bad times they'd known were the ruins of the castle. Towers turned to rubble. Treasures turned to dust.

One of the strangest things found among the ruins were the singed bodies of hundreds of moths. They were everywhere – drawn to the flames or the heart of the mountain. Either way, the město weren't too sad about a load of dead insects.

At night, the castle's ruins were thought to be haunted. Some said they'd seen the ghost of Blazen the Brave. Others said they'd seen the king's spirit. He shuffled round the square, tapping on doors and peeping between shutters. No one was sure what he sought. Did he look for his love or for the young prince? Did he seek the Sertze Hora, even after death?

'But we all know,' said the head cook, as she tucked her boys in for the night, 'that there are no ghosts – except ghosts of the mind.' The boys pulled the bedsheets up to their eyeballs.

'How do you get ghosts in your mind?' asked the youngest.

'Pear brandy,' said their mother, blowing out the last candle. 'That's how.'

CHAPTER 97

While life in Yaroslav was going back to normal, there was one boy for whom things would never be normal again.

Miro was alone in Lofkinye's tree house. She'd said he could stay for as long as he liked and her home spanned four trees so there was plenty of space.

It had gone midday, but the prince was still curled up in bed. He'd been exhausted since the fire. It was as if the shock of his uncle's death and the truth about the Sertze Hora had dealt him a physical blow. His legs felt heavy. His arms were weak. He was still coming to terms with the truth.

When Miro first woke, his mind would be a blank. He'd lie there with his eyes closed until he remembered that the Sertze Hora was real. Then he'd remember that his uncle had stolen it. His uncle had lied. His uncle was the real reason his parents were dead. It was the same every day. He wasn't just grieving for Drakomor. He was grieving for his parents all over again.

Miro would hug his knees close and let misery consume him.

But then he'd remember the other things. He'd remember that his uncle had come to his rescue. His uncle had loved him. He'd loved him more than the most precious stone in the kingdom. That was when the real healing began.

Miro sat up, banging his head on a branch above the bed. 'Ow!' he cried, rubbing the sore bit. There were branches throughout Lofkinye's home. Some were used as hangers. Others were beams that supported the roof. A few, like this one, were just accidents waiting to happen.

He swung his legs out of bed and the cold came to greet him, wrapping itself round his exposed ankles. There were no servants to light fires here.

The prince looked around the bedroom. Most of the objects were unfamiliar, fragments of Lofkinye's life, but there was one face that he knew well. A toy lion with buttons for eyes sat on a rocking chair, in the corner of the room. Miro was too old for toys, but the lion seemed to be smiling at him all the same. He gave it a little smile back.

A few weeks ago, if someone had told Miro he'd be homeless, he would have laughed. Now he wasn't just homeless, he was dependent on the very people he used to despise. The lying lesni. That's what he'd called them. The thought made his face burn with shame.

There were voices in the forest below. The prince went out to the balcony and lowered a ladder to the ground.

Marie was the first to climb up. She stuck out her tongue. It was stained pink. Imogen was next.

'Look what we found,' she said, kneeling on the balcony. She untied a square of fabric to reveal a pile of rosehips. They shone like pink and orange jewels.

'It's like Lofkinye told us,' said Imogen. 'If you give them a squeeze, the yummy stuff shoots out.' She demonstrated, squeezing a rosehip into her mouth.

'Can I have a go?' said Miro. Imogen let him take a handful and the three friends sat on the floor to devour their find. When there were no rosehips left, they looked out over the forest. Many of the trees had shed their leaves and the mountains were turning white.

'I can't believe we went all the way up there,' said Marie, pointing to Klenot Mountain. 'I wouldn't have thought we could do it.'

'Let's not tell Mum,' said Imogen. 'She'll make us go on walks all the time.'

Both sisters laughed, but Miro could tell it wasn't heartfelt. Lofkinye was letting the girls stay with her too, but, as Imogen looked away, Miro wondered if she was thinking about her real home.

'I'm sorry that we didn't find the door in the tree,' he

said. There was a pause. He felt a little bolder. 'What are you going to do now?'

'I don't know,' said Imogen, frowning.

'We don't even know how long we've been gone,' said Marie.

'You could always stay,' ventured Miro, not quite daring to look at either sister.

'We can't stay forever,' said Imogen, without missing a beat. 'We need to get back to our mum.'

A flock of birds flew past the balcony and into the trees, tweeting as they went. 'Do you think the birds are here because the Sertze Hora has been returned?' said Marie.

'I don't know,' said Imogen. 'I don't know how quickly the Žal will end. I just hope those birds weren't looking for rosehips . . .'

CHAPTER 98

Later that afternoon, Lofkinye walked out of Yaroslav's West Gate with a spring in her step. She crossed a field, lined with fat cauliflowers, and made her way towards the Kolsaney Forests. A gang of goats stared as she strode through their meadow. She shook her head, amused. Why did goats always look like they were up to no good?

Before long, Lofkinye was walking between trees. The dried leaves, crunching beneath her feet, seemed to announce her arrival. The bare branches, waving in the wind, welcomed her home.

She felt a thrill as she remembered: from now on, every day would be like this. She lived in the forests. There would be no more fighting with the skret. No more město rules. She could hunt as many rabbits as the famous Blazen Bilbetz . . .

Lofkinye slowed. Poor old Blazen. She could still picture his face when the tower trembled – when he realised it was too late . . . In many ways the man had been a coward, but he'd lived up to his stories in the end.

Lofkinye stopped by the trees that held up her house. She could hear the children laughing and she wondered if they were hungry. Tonight, she'd cook something she hadn't made for a while. Tonight, they'd feast on rabbit stew.

CHAPTER 99

The children made dumplings to go with Lofkinye's stew. Miro made the dough, Marie rolled it into a sausage, and Imogen boiled and sliced it up. She couldn't help thinking that she had the most difficult job.

'I didn't know lesni ate dumplings,' said Miro, leaning over the pot so the steam wafted up past his face.

'What did you think we ate?' said Lofkinye, raising an eyebrow. 'Old leaves?'

'I don't actually know what I thought . . .'

Miro glanced at the girls. He looked self-conscious. Imogen tried to look like she wasn't listening.

'Lofkinye, I'm sorry,' he murmured. 'I'm sorry for the things that I said about the lesni. I was wrong. You're not liars at all.'

'Well, some of us are,' said Lofkinye, 'but then so are some město.'

Imogen thought of King Drakomor and the terrible lies he had told. Perhaps Miro was thinking the same because his face turned scarlet.

'Yes,' said the prince. 'Some město lie . . . Do you think you can forgive me?'

Lofkinye stopped stirring her pot and bent down so her face was level with Miro's. 'You've said some bad things, little prince. You didn't question what you were told about people who are different to you. You didn't see us as people at all . . . and for that I accept your apology. But never forget that you've done good things too.'

'I have?'

'Of course! You risked a lot to help your friends and who knows what would have happened if you hadn't picked that lock for the Král. The Sertze Hora would have been destroyed and then we'd all be in trouble – lesni, město and skret. You've been very heroic . . . in your own strange way.'

'But I didn't believe you,' said Miro. 'I didn't even think the Sertze Hora was real.'

'Even heroes get it wrong sometimes.'

'You really think so?'

Lofkinye frowned. 'I'm not going to say it again.'

Imogen, Marie and the huntress sat down to eat while Miro trotted upstairs to fetch extra socks. The evenings were getting colder.

'I still can't believe that Drakomor lied for so long,' said Marie, glancing at the stairs to check that Miro wasn't coming back down.

'I'm not sure I can forgive him,' said Imogen, 'even though he's dead.' She took a mouthful of the stew. It was a bit like her mum's chicken casserole, but not quite as good. Nothing was as good as Mum's chicken casserole.

'I'm not sure I can forgive the king either,' said Lofkinye, spearing a dumpling. 'But there's no point in holding on to the past. You can't go back.'

Imogen froze with her spoon halfway to her mouth. What if Lofkinye was right? What if she couldn't go back?

There's no point in holding on to the past . . . Imogen repeated the sentence in her head.

When she'd first arrived in Yaroslav, she'd been so angry that Mum had a new boyfriend.

There's no point in holding on . . .

Now she'd put up with one hundred Marks to see Mum. She wanted to tell her that it was all okay, that her casserole was the best, that she didn't care if Mum had a boyfriend, so long as Imogen had *her*.

'There's no point,' muttered Imogen, putting down the spoon. The thought had robbed her of her appetite.

'What did you say?' asked Marie. Her cheeks were stuffed, hamster-style.

'We can't find the door without my moth,' said Imogen. 'That's what Zuby said . . . So what happens if it never comes back?'

Marie frowned. 'The moth brought us here to help the skret,' she said. 'So surely, now the skret have the heart, the moth will take us home.'

Both girls looked at Lofkinye. 'I don't know,' said the huntress, shaking her head. 'You'd have to ask your moth.'

CHAPTER 100

A few nights later, Imogen was woken up by a faint tickling on her arm. It was just a moth. She brushed it away and rolled over.

Hang on a minute. It wasn't just any old moth – it was her moth! Her moth with its fleecy body and extravagant antennae. Her moth with its lovely grey wings. Imogen sat up in bed.

The shadow moth settled on Marie's cheek. It twirled its antennae as if saying *hello*.

'Hi,' whispered Imogen. 'Sorry about that. It has . . . it's been a while.'

The moth flew towards the bedroom window, which was very slightly ajar, and Imogen knew what to do. She picked up the candle that was burning low, next to the bed, and pushed her covers off.

Her boots were by the door. As she tiptoed towards them, a floorboard squeaked. Marie didn't wake. Imogen hesitated. In the old days, she would have gone without so much as a backward glance. These days, things were different.

The moth was fluttering about on the other side of the window. 'Yes, I'm coming,' said Imogen. 'Just give me a minute.'

She shut the window. Lofkinye didn't like it when she let out warm air. Then she crept back to the bed and shook Marie by the shoulder. 'What is it?' murmured Marie, with her eyes still closed.

'We're going outside,' said Imogen.

'What for? It's the middle of the night.'

'For an adventure.'

Marie's eyes snapped open. Imogen pointed out of the window at the moth. 'What about Miro?' whispered Marie.

'Go and wake him,' said Imogen.

The three children pulled on their fur coats and laced up their boots. They lowered the ladder and climbed down from the tree house. When Imogen reached the ground, she removed three fresh candles from her pocket and lit them, handing Marie and Miro one each.

They set off into the night, following the moth through the forest.

'How do you know it's the same moth that you saw before?' said Miro.

'I just do,' said Imogen. 'We're friends.'

'Where will it take us?' said Marie.

'I don't know. That's why it's an adventure.'

After they'd been walking for a few minutes, Imogen spotted another moth flitting about between the trees. This one was pale grey, almost white. It greeted her moth with a circular dance and then they flew on together. The children followed. The last leaves fell from the trees, as silent as feathers.

The next moth they saw was a shimmer of gold. It glittered like a secret in the velvet night. 'That's my favourite,' said Marie. 'That's *my* moth.'

Imogen noticed that the ground beneath her feet was ever so slightly tilted. They were walking uphill. Two more moths joined the parade. From one angle, their wings blended into the night. From another angle, they were blue. As they flew, they seemed to flicker on and off and on and off.

Soon Imogen's moth was leading a long trail of followers. Their wings formed a fluttering canopy above the children's heads. Marie stretched up, but she couldn't quite reach. Miro walked with an open mouth. 'I've never seen so many,' he said. 'I wonder what it means.'

The trees grew closer together and the children stopped walking. They were surrounded by hundreds of moths. The moths hung on to branches like leaves. They flew in whirling circles round the children's heads. They weren't interested in the candlelight at all.

Imogen's moth settled on a tree trunk and she gasped. 'Marie! Look at that!'

The sisters walked up to the enormous tree. Miro waited a little way back. The shadow moth crawled across the rough bark and the girls watched. Soon it wasn't crawling on bark any more, but smooth, polished wood. Imogen ran her finger across this new texture. She knew what it was. She said it out loud. 'There's a door in this tree.'

'Is it the same one?' called Miro.

'I guess there's only one way to find out,' said Imogen.

The grey moth crawled down to the keyhole, folded back its wings and wriggled through. Imogen tried the door. It clicked open. 'As easy as that,' she laughed.

On the other side of the door there was a garden. It looked overgrown, but it was nowhere near as wild as the forest. 'I know that place,' said Marie. 'It's Mrs Haberdash's gardens.'

Imogen looked at Miro. A scab had grown over the cut on his cheek. His face was pale and serious. Imogen felt awkward.

'So,' said Miro, 'I suppose this is goodbye.'

'But what about Lofkinye?' said Marie. 'Shouldn't we say goodbye to her too?'

'We can't,' said Imogen. 'We'll never find our way back to the door.'

'Imogen's right,' said Miro. 'This is your chance to go home – you should take it. I'll tell Lofkinye what happened.'

Imogen started biting her nails. She hated goodbyes. She wanted this over. 'Right,' she said. 'Thanks for having us.' She blew out her candle and held out her hand.

Marie rolled her eyes. 'That's not a proper goodbye.' She dropped her candle and launched herself at Miro, giving him a hug that almost knocked him off his feet.

Imogen stamped out the candle's flame.

'We don't want to leave you behind,' said Marie, still hugging Miro. 'You're a good friend – the best of friends. Why don't you come with us? I'm sure Mum would love you.'

'Yes,' said Imogen. 'That's a great idea.'

Now it was Miro's turn to look awkward. 'Th-thanks,' he stammered. 'I don't know what to say.'

'Say yes,' said Marie and she threw up her hands, making the moths on a nearby tree take off.

'But I can't,' said Miro.

'Why not?'

'I've got responsibilities.'

'What do you mean?' said Imogen.

'Now my uncle is ... gone, technically speaking, I'm king.'

'Oh right ...' Imogen trailed off.

'Everything's a bit confused in Yaroslav right now, but sooner or later I'll have to go back to the city.'

The girls processed this information in silence.

'I hope your mother isn't too angry with you,' said Miro, 'for running away, I mean.'

Imogen wanted to say that they didn't run away, but she decided against it. 'Thanks,' she said. 'I hope so too.'

'Oh! I almost forgot,' said Marie. She unbuttoned her coat and reached into an inside pocket. 'There's something I want to give Miro.'

In the middle of her palm there was a small stone. It had a beautiful silvery shine.

Imogen recognised it as if from a dream. 'Is that –' she searched for the right memory – 'is that from my rock collection?'

'Yes,' said Marie sheepishly.

'You kept it all this time?'

'I thought it would be a nice present,' said Marie, visibly shrinking.

But Imogen didn't explode. She didn't even get angry. She smiled at her sister. 'I think that's a brilliant idea.'

Marie put the fool's gold into Miro's hand and closed his fingers round it. 'Thank you,' he said with a solemn face. 'Now I'll always remember.'

Imogen took one final look at the forest and the moth-cloaked trees. She took one final look at the boy who was king. His fingers, wrapped round the candle, were still clustered with rings. His ears still poked out. His eyes were still far apart. Imogen would miss him enormously.

She waved. The boy waved back. Then she pushed the door open and stepped through.

The girls stood in the Haberdash Gardens. It was summer and it had been raining.

'Do you remember the way to the tea rooms?' said Imogen.

'I think so,' said Marie. 'Follow me.'

PART 5

Chapter 101

The bear soon lost her human clothes. First they turned to rags and then they were no more.

It felt good to be back among the trees. It felt good to roam. To put her paws on moss instead of cobbles. To hide in caves.

It felt good to find an interesting smell and to track it for hours. It felt good to be all beast. There were many things she remembered.

But, most of all, it felt good to be home.

CHAPTER 102

The girls soon lost their fur coats. Imogen shook her arms free from the sleeves as she walked through the Haberdash Gardens. The coat fell to the ground.

All around, water dripped from leaves and vines. It was light, but Imogen had no idea what time it was and, once again, her moth had disappeared.

The fallen tree still lay across the river. Marie climbed on and helped Imogen up behind her. Together, they edged along the trunk and hopped down on the other side of the water.

Here it smelled like summer. Flowers were in bloom and bumblebees hummed their wordless tunes. The birds were louder and more numerous than Imogen had ever thought possible.

And there was the gate. It was wrapped in plastic tape that said **POLICE LINE DO NOT CROSS**. The rusted lock was still on the floor where Imogen had dropped it. She pushed the gate open and crawled under the police tape.

The car park was empty. The girls ran to the tea rooms

and Imogen threw the door open. 'Mrs Haberdash!' she called. There was no answer. 'Mrs Haberdash, we're back!'

She peered round the room. There were no cakes on the counter and it smelled kind of musty. 'How long have we been gone?' whispered Marie. 'Do you think . . . could she . . . is Mrs Haberdash . . .'

'Dead?' finished Imogen.

A yapping sound made both girls jump. Along the corridor, behind the counter, came the scampering of feet and a series of high-pitched barks. Mrs Haberdash's dogs came racing into view. They jumped up and licked the girls' hands.

Behind the dogs came the electric whirr of a mobility scooter. 'Children!' cried the old woman as if it was the most beautiful word in the world. 'There are children in my tea rooms!'

Mrs Haberdash was wearing a big cotton nightie and her grey spiral hair hung loose round her face. She looked different without all her finery. 'There are children . . .' Her bottom lip trembled. Imogen rushed forward and threw her arms round Mrs Haberdash's shoulders. The old woman felt small and frail; her bones seemed as light as a bird's.

'We thought you were gone,' sobbed Mrs Haberdash. 'We thought you'd never come back.'

When the hugging was over, Mrs Haberdash whizzed over to her phone. It was the old-fashioned kind, with wires. She dialled a number off by heart. 'Cathy,' she said, her voice high and wobbly. 'Cathy, I've got the children.'

Imogen and Marie waited for their mum by the window. A dog climbed on to the chair next to Imogen and she stroked its head nervously, wondering what her mum would say. Would she be angry? Would they be in trouble? Mrs Haberdash fussed around them, asking where they'd been and whether they were all right and could she get them a cup of tea?

A car pulled up, tyres crunching over the gravel. 'Whose car is that?' said Marie. It had one of those roofs – the type that came off – and there was a man in the driving seat. The dogs ran outside, barking.

The man stepped out of the car. It was Mark. A woman got out of the passenger seat. It was Mum.

'Your parents are here,' said Mrs Haberdash. The next moment, Mum was in the tea rooms. She bent down and opened her arms. Imogen and Marie ran to her.

'My girls!' she cried. 'You're alive! You're home!'

Imogen buried her face in Mum's shoulder. She was crying, but she didn't know why. She wasn't sad. The tears ran down her face, into Mum's T-shirt. She couldn't see Mum's face, but she knew she was crying too. She was crying in big sobs that made her body shake. Imogen held on to her tightly.

'You're alive! You're home!' Mum repeated the words between sobs.

Mark stood by the door. Not quite in. Not quite out. Not quite sure what to do with his hands. '*Always the three of us,*' mouthed Imogen.

Eventually, Mum started breathing more normally. She released her grip on Imogen and Marie. 'What happened?' she said, looking at her girls' faces. 'Did someone hurt you?'

'No one hurt us,' said Marie. 'We've been having an adventure!'

'W-what do you mean?' said Mum. She really did look bad. She looked like she'd been awake for centuries.

'Imogen found a door in a tree and we went through it and it took us to another world and—'

'Who told you to say that?' snapped Mum.

'No one.' Marie looked crestfallen.

'Never mind,' said Mum, softening. 'The police will get to the bottom of it. All that matters now is you're back. You're home!'

'She's telling the truth,' said Imogen. 'We did go through a door in a tree.'

Mum stroked Imogen's cheek. 'My poor darlings. What on earth have they filled your heads with?'

'They could be in shock,' said Mark.

'Yes,' said Mum. 'That's probably it.'

She looked at Imogen's star-embroidered tunic. 'What *are* you wearing?'

'The prince gave them to us,' said Marie.

Mum glanced over her shoulder at Mark. When she looked back, she was frowning. 'Well, isn't that nice of him? I'd like to hear more about this prince. Perhaps tomorrow, when you've had a good sleep, you can tell me and the inspector all about him.'

CHAPTER 103

The police searched the Haberdash Gardens. They couldn't find anything out of the ordinary, apart from a pair of manky fur coats. They couldn't find a door in a tree. And they certainly couldn't find any trace of the kidnapper whom the newspapers were calling 'the prince'.

Meanwhile, Imogen and Marie settled back into life at home. It had been the beginning of the summer holidays when Grandma first took them to the tea rooms. Now the holidays were almost over. School would be starting in less than a week.

Imogen lay in her bed, content. She was full of ice cream. Mum had taken them to the cinema and let them eat whatever they wanted. Grandma had come too and now she was talking to Mum in the kitchen. Imogen snuggled down under her duvet. It was nice knowing that the house was full of people she loved.

Tomorrow she would put on a new play. It was a story about a knight and a sea slug, who were always trying to kill each other. Imogen would be the knight and Marie would be the monster, but the play wouldn't end like the others.

The sea slug would be winning – it would be about to kill the hero – when suddenly it would reveal that it didn't really like eating knights. Their armour was too crunchy and the sea slug had a sweet tooth. Then the knight would reveal that she was a brilliant baker and she would promise to make the monster a cake. They would both live happily ever after. Imogen couldn't wait to see the look of surprise on Grandma's face.

The night was warm so Mum had left the window by Imogen's bed open. A gust of wind blew the curtains apart. Imogen sat up and found herself peeping outside. The garden was dark. She looked up at the sky. There was no moon, but the stars were out in force. 'Goodnight, Miro,' she whispered.

One of the youngest stars winked back.

CHAPTER 104

Zuby stood alone on the side of the mountain. Across one shoulder he carried a long pole with a sack tied to the end. Within that sack was everything he owned.

There was a faint flutter in the darkness and Zuby looked up. 'Hello,' he said in his crackle-hiss voice.

A pearly grey moth landed on his hand and made a series of movements with its wings, meaning *where are you going?*

Zuby wasn't surprised. After all, the Mezi Mǔra had updated him on the whereabouts and well-being of the little humans. It was only fair for Zuby to share his plans with the moth.

'I'm going beyond the mountains,' said the skret.

The insect ran up his arm in a zigzag pattern.

'Not ... pear ...?'

The moth retraced its steps.

'Ah – not fair! That's where you're wrong. The punishment for releasing prisoners without the Král's permission is death by slicing and dicing. The Král is very kind to send me away.'

Zuby sucked in the cold air between his great tusk-teeth and gazed down at the forests. Then he looked back at his winged companion.

'I have a question for you,' he said. 'I want to know why you showed those human pups the Unseen Door. They brought us the prince – that much I understand. Without him, we'd still be living with the Žal. But was that your plan all along? How did you know what would happen?'

The moth flew to a rock, one of the few places that wasn't covered in snow, and began its dance. The skret watched intently.

'You didn't know the gut would fatten. You cannot feed the jaguars.' Zuby scratched his head. 'Well, that doesn't answer my question.'

The moth did its dance once more, moving across the rock in an elaborate pattern. 'You didn't know what would happen. You cannot read the stars.'

Zuby let go of the pole, exasperated. 'If you didn't know what would happen, why did you let those humans through the door?'

The moth flapped in Zuby's face as if it was exasperated too.

'All right,' rasped the skret. 'But why them? I liked

them very much, but they were runty, half-grown things. They should have been at home with their parents, not traipsing around in the snow.'

The moth danced in circles on the rock, waving its antennae and stamping its tiny feet. Zuby leaned in. 'You were searching for someone to save us . . . and the girl, she looked like a hero.'

The moth turned clockwise, indicating *yes*.

The skret scratched his head. 'All right, if you say so. I suppose they were brave . . . I suppose they did help things to click into place . . . but we all did our bit, didn't we? Even old Zuby.'

He picked up the pole and slung it across his shoulder, turning away from the mountain he called home. 'I wonder if I'll ever see those little humans again.'

The stars did not reply.

EPILOGUE

Anneshka was supposed to be sitting on a throne in Castle Yaroslav, not on the back of a pony in the Kolsaney Forests. Yet here she was, riding deeper into the woods. She dug her heels into the pony's sides, urging it on.

In the half-light of dusk, the forests were made of abstract shapes. No matter which way Anneshka turned, there was a never-ending pattern of vertical lines. The trees were repeating themselves.

If I was queen, she thought, *I'd have them all chopped down.*

Even here, miles away from Yaroslav, the air smelled faintly of smoke. Anneshka wondered if the castle was still on fire. She wondered who people would blame for the accident with the dragon.

It was no secret that Andel had built the beast. It was no secret that she and Drakomor had made him do it. But she thought it likely that the king was dead and soon all the things she'd done would come tumbling

474

out . . . It was best to be far beyond the mountains when that happened.

The further she travelled from the city, the more the trees seemed to lean in, closing their twig-fingers over her head. Branches caught on her wedding dress. Cursing, she tore herself free. Despite the cold, her hands still felt like they were burning. The skin was turning to blisters.

When it was too dark to continue, Anneshka slid off the pony and tied it to a branch, securing the pillowcase to the saddle. She collapsed at the foot of a tree. Her petticoats had lost their shape and her silk skirts were in tatters. She looked like a wilted lily with giant droopy petals.

When the darkness was complete, Anneshka's mind started to drift. The trunk against her back was her only anchor. Without it, she could be anywhere. She could be floating in a starless sky or down at the bottom of a well. She could be a speck of dust or a grain of sand. She felt smaller than she'd ever felt before. Anneshka didn't like feeling small.

Something blinked in the blackness and she turned, but she couldn't see what it was. 'There are no more wolves in the forests,' she whispered, trying to reassure herself.

Eyes watched her from above. She glanced up and they disappeared. Then Anneshka saw it. Straight ahead. Gleaming in the darkness. An eyeball the size of an apple.

She struggled to her feet. 'Whoever you are, I have nothing of value.' Another eye appeared above the first. The pupil was slit like a snake's.

'You can have the pony,' she stammered, 'and the clock.' Several more eyes blinked themselves into being. There were two to her left and three to her right. Some were high above her head. Others were down among the bracken.

'Please!' cried Anneshka, her voice catching in her throat. 'Whatever you've heard about me, it's not true!'

A hooded figure, carrying a lantern, emerged from the shadows. In the yellow light, Anneshka saw that the floating eyeballs weren't floating at all. They were embedded in the bark of the trees.

'Out so late, child?' said the stranger in a woman's voice. She pushed back her hood and Anneshka recognised her at once. The black hair plaited down her back. The eyes as dark as rosewood. The skin as pale as silver birch. It was Ochi the forest witch.

'You!' gasped Anneshka. 'You said I'd be queen. You said it was written in the stars.'

'And so it was,' said the witch. She untied the pony and it nuzzled her as if they were old friends.

'Well, what happened?' said Anneshka, not bothering to hide her bitterness. 'Did the stars change their minds?'

'The stars do not change anything much,' said Ochi. 'But your story's not over. Why don't you come and warm yourself by my fire?'

The witch began to walk away, swinging her lantern back and forth.

'Besides,' she said, her voice disappearing into the forest, 'the stars said you'd rule. They did not say *where*.'

The pony followed the witch. After a moment's hesitation, so did Anneshka.

The trees watched her leave.

Thank you to . . .

Mum and Dad for a childhood full of stories. Thank you for the birthday pantomimes, for 'the classics' on cassette, for queuing at ASDA at midnight. Thank you for giving me the confidence to write.

Joe for upping my downs, for the walks and the wonder. For the good coffee, the terrible jokes and the brilliant ideas. Without you, this book would be little more than a squiggle in the sand. *Miluji tě.*

Bonnie and Mini, my first and last readers. Thank you for your support, for the art and the plays and the never-ending games. Thank you for the strawberries. I hope you're not too traumatised.

Josef and Edita for the writing retreat. I have so many happy memories of visiting you and working on this book.

Nick Lake, my editor, for that initial encouraging message and for being my fairy godfather ever since. Thank you for making this book better.

Claire Wilson, my agent, for your wisdom and kindness. You're all the best bits of a grown-up rolled into one.

Chris Riddell for the out-of-this-world illustrations.

Samantha Stewart, Lowri Ribbons, David McDougall, Elorine Grant, Deborah Wilton, Nicole Linhardt-Rich, Alex Cowan, Jo-Anna Parkinson, Sally Wilks, Jane Tait and Mary O'Riordan at HarperCollins Children's Books. Miriam Tobin at Rogers, Coleridge & White.

Inclusive Minds for connecting me with their Inclusion Ambassador network, especially Lois Brookes-Jones.

Lucy Holloway, Emily Kerr, Aisha Bushby, Damian Le Bas, Georgie Strachan and Sebastian Umrigar for your thoughtful and thought-provoking feedback.

The writers of WOW, who have taught me so much. Mr Craig, for another kind of teaching.

The friends who've encouraged me along the way, including Stuart Whyte, Charles Leveroni, Anna Rawcliffe, Joe Nicholson, Alyssa Hulme, Helen Bowen Ashwin, Kirsty Egan and Suze Goldsmith.

Denis Pavlov and Eva Maillebiau, for your early reviews.

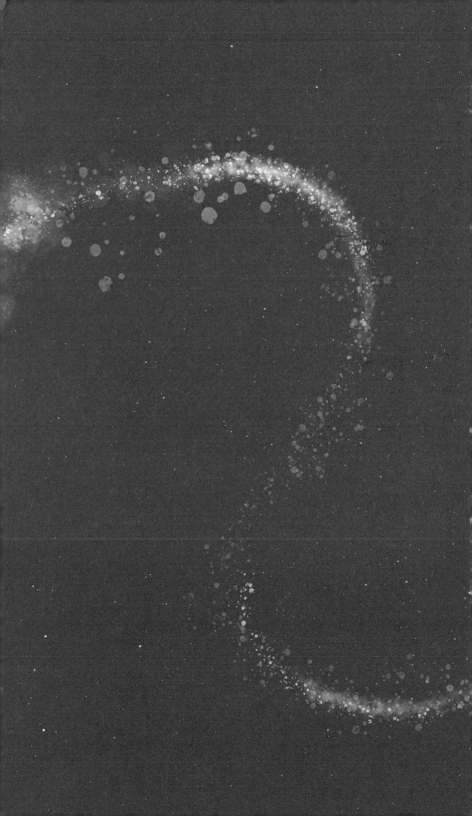